About the Author

Naomi P. Lane was born in England and raised in British Columbia, Canada. She is a retired special education / French Immersion teacher of thirty years. Happily married with two grown children and one very spoiled rescue cat, she lives next to a beautiful, forested provincial park. Currently working on her second novel, which is a humorous look at the perils of midlife, Naomi enjoys collaborating on social media with other authors. On the average day, you will find her reading, writing, listening to world music, walking in the forest, swimming in the lake, doing yoga or playing guitar.

D1665126

The Ordinary Life of Nadia Lewis

Naomi P. Lane

The Ordinary Life of Nadia Lewis

Olympia Publishers
London

www.olympiapublishers.com
OLYMPIA PAPERBACK EDITION

A CIP catalogue record for this title is
available from the British Library.

ISBN: 978-1-78830-901-1

First Published in 2021

Olympia Publishers
Tallis House
2 Tallis Street
London
EC4Y 0AB

Printed in Great Britain

Dedication

To lifelong friends;
the ones who knew you before children,
after they've gone,
and who forgive the blur in between.

Chapter One
Childhood

Nadia and Susan met the summer before grade three, in 1970. Susan's family had just moved into the house kitty-corner to Nadia's house, so they were new neighbours. Their parents had chatted in the road at the summer block party and had invited Nadia over for a playdate. They had hit it off immediately playing Barbies, riding bikes and running through sprinklers in the back yard. The two girls were thrilled to find out in September they would be in the same class.

Nadia had light-brown, curly, shoulder-length hair, green eyes and freckles on her nose that made her look innocent. She was strapping and athletic and played soccer and softball. She had a broad face and a big smile that invited the world in. She had no fear of entering a room full of strangers because she could easily talk to anyone.

Susan had straight, dark hair and big, brown, doe eyes. She was petite, thin and a bit clumsy. She was not interested in joining any sports team. She preferred pottery classes, piano lessons and Brownies. However, they shared a silly sense of humour that was all their own.

They first became collaborators in the grade three class when a boy named Billy Parsons started harassing another really sweet kid named Robert Thorp. Nadia and Susan both liked Robert Thorp because they had been paired up with him to build an Amazon rainforest project together and they admired his talent at drawing. He had created all the giant parrots, sloths and ocelots that they had wanted for their display. Billy Parsons was a nasty piece of work. His clothes were always dirty, and he smelled bad.

One day at recess, Billy was trying to push Robert off the giant, cement world map playground where they played tag. If you were on the ocean you were fair game, but once you got to any continent you were safe. Even though there were four other boys in the game, they dared not stand up to Billy. Nadia and Susan strode right up close to Billy's face and confronted him.

"Leave Robert alone or my big sister will beat you up. She's in grade eight and has enormous boobs so you don't want to mess with her!" Nadia warned.

"Yah, you big bully, leave him alone or I'll tell Miss Kennedy that you were cheating on your spelling test because you're too stupid to spell the word cat!" Susan backed her up.

Billy was more surprised than scared, but he moved on to his next victim and left Robert in peace. Somehow this exchange cemented the girls' bond and they realised that together, they were invincible. Little Robert just looked on in amazement at these two marvelous girls and was eternally grateful that they were in his class.

Every day, the girls raced home to watch their favourite game show, Beat the Clock, on television. They would drink milk and eat chocolate chip cookies and yell at the TV contestants to move it faster to get through the obstacle course, so they could guess which letter the big money was stashed behind. They jumped off the couch every time anybody won the huge sum of $500! What could they buy for that kind of money? Enough beads to make a million friendship bracelets, they figured, or enough candy to fill up an entire bathtub! The possibilities were endless.

In the summer, they played 'kick the can' every night with all the other kids on Westbrook Street. They would squish their whole bodies between the giant cedar hedgerow along the Johnson's front yard and their hair would hold the lovely scent of the oily cedar boughs for days. To run up and rescue everyone caught, by kicking the pop can, was the greatest feeling ever. They would hang off the bank at the back of the Davis' yard by the tendrils of the white-flowered morning glory vines that grew wild down to the back alley and then hoist themselves back up when the coast was clear. One by one, mothers would call their names down the street when it started getting dark and they would reluctantly go in, covered in dirt and brambles.

In the daytime, it was all sprinklers and bike rides and grape popsicles doled out by the ice cream man, who was friendly and harmless. All the children roamed freely from house to house down the street and every door was open to every child. You could get a band-aid, a cold drink, a snack or use the bathroom just by appearing at the front door. Everybody knew that old Mrs Martin had the best home-baked cookies and her front porch always smelled strongly of the honeysuckle vine as you sat there devouring one with a glass of milk. You could drop your bike on anyone's front lawn or go into their yard to retrieve a ball without fear of reprisal. The neighbours all knew each other and were kind and generous.

In grade four, they did a family tree project in class and became fascinated with their ancestry. Nadia learned that Lewis was not her father's real last name; he had changed it after leaving Nazi Germany as a teenager right before the war. His real last name was Leventhal and he was Jewish. She began to ask him questions about what this meant. He explained that she was not Jewish because the lineage has to be maternal. She thought this was all very weird, but tried to explain it to her class, nonetheless. She learned about the Holocaust and the great burden that her father was carrying around with him, since his parents had both been killed in the war. She was still too young to really internalise the depth of this, but she understood it more in a factual way.

Susan's last name was Harper, which she said was very boring. She was the descendant of medieval harp makers or players, who were apparently highly regarded in Old English life. She drew a fancy, golden harp and a castle and brought a fake sword to share with the class and said she would be invited to play for royalty and Knights of the Round Table and such. She found the whole thing embarrassing, even though all the boys thought it was cool because they wanted to be a knight in a castle.

When they were ten, they loved to sit on a bench at the mall and people watch. They would make up names for each person who passed by and then invent the complete story of their lives. The prissy-looking lady became Pamela Pruitt from Sioux Falls, church choir director, who was having a secret affair with the rich widower next door. The weird-looking hippy guy became Ruben Kemp from Salt Spring Island, marijuana farmer with three wives and ten children. They would sit there for hours, sipping Orange Julius and giggling under their breath.

They were the only two girls their age on their whole street, other than Gillian Sharp. All the other neighbours had boys. Nadia and Susan decided that all of these boys were such disgusting rejects that there must have been some leak in the water lines around their neighbourhood ten years earlier, that only affected the male genome. They imagined these boys hatching out of eggs in some primordial ooze under old Mr Decker's balcony.

When they started writing books together, this became one of their first stories. Together they filled notepads with elaborate outlines of drawings and prose. Their relatives didn't escape lightly either. Their mothers received entirely new upbringings that explained all their current flaws. Nadia's mother was born miniature inside a toadstool and later grew large because of all the fertiliser on the lawn. That's why she loved gardening so much. Susan's mother grew out of bacteria inside the hair dryer hood at the local beauty salon. That's why she was always looking in the mirror and fixing her hair. The kids in their class all had interesting back-stories that explained their idiosyncrasies in some dark and twisted way. There was always a serious tone when they were writing, which ended in hilarity and uncontrollable giggling. One time, Nadia fell over laughing so hard that she put a hole in Susan's bedroom wall, which understandably annoyed her parents a great deal.

In their early teens, they loved re-enacting Monty Python skits and tape recording their voices, telling stupid jokes and making up talk-show interviews with famous people. Susan became Barbara Walters interviewing Nadia as Farrah Fawcett, asking her how she had let herself go, to become so fat right after the famous, orange swimsuit poster.

Nadia escaped to Susan's house whenever she could because she thought her own parents were old and boring.

They were an older European couple who had children later in life. They would never show affection to each other or go out anywhere. Her dad frequently came home from work angry at her mother for no reason whatsoever. He would criticise her for a messy house or a meal he didn't like and then disappear into his study to smoke cigars and watch the news. He was not a happy man.

Susan's parents were very strait-laced but extremely nice. They had both grown up on farms in Alberta and knew the value of a hard day's work. Nadia liked staying for dinner because Susan's mother always baked yummy desserts. They always drank milk and it was Susan's job to pour it. Afterwards, the girls would go down in the basement and listen to 45 rpm records on Susan's portable, pink, box turntable. They would dance to the Beach Boys and swoon over Teen Beat magazine pictures of David Cassidy, Donny Osmond and Bobby Sherman.

As they got older, their records got bigger and they started collecting the best albums. They loved Led Zeppelin and Rush, the Doobie Brothers and David Bowie. The agreed on which bands were too sappy and boring to consider. They would lie on the basement floor for hours listening to music and learning all the lyrics by heart. When they went to the park, they would always bring their AM, pocket, transistor radio and keep the dial turned to the only decent rock station in the city.

They had a typical middle-class suburban upbringing near Vancouver, Canada. Nadia had a much older sister named Rosanne, who was already running around with boys having sex and experimenting with drugs. Her parents were constantly trying to rescue her from precarious situations. When Rosanne was eighteen, she ran off with this much older truck driver to

Alberta and he gave her these powerful drugs. She called Nadia in tears, freaking out from some truck stop in Princeton. Nadia had to lie to her parents and tell them she was camping with a boyfriend from high school. She went to the bus depot and paid for her return ticket out of her birthday money to get her home again.

Susan had a little brother named Peter, who was as stupid and annoying as any other little brother. He mostly played with the boy next door and stayed out of their hair. Occasionally, he was useful as a soccer goalie or a taste-tester for one of their cooking experiments.

Nadia and Susan were able to grow up in their own carefree world of imagination and laughter. Other people sometimes interfered with their daily existence, but they could usually ignore or work around them. It wasn't until high school that their different interests started pulling them into different social groups. Nadia was heavily into sports and Susan was drawn to the artsy, theatre crowd, but somehow, they managed to reconnect on a regular basis, even if it was just to ride the same bus home together. They would always catch up or check in to see how the other was doing.

Things got rocky between them in grade nine, when Nadia started hanging out with a girl named Kelly from her soccer team. They spent all their time together and Susan felt pushed aside. Nadia knew that Susan felt jealous and resented Kelly for stealing all her best friend's time and attention, so Nadia tried to make amends by inviting them both to her birthday dinner with her family at a fancy restaurant. Nadia pointedly remarked on how both Kelly and Susan were huge fans of scary movies, so they would have something to bond over. It worked, up to a point, until Susan realised that Nadia was planning a camping trip with Kelly and her older cousin as the chaperone. Then she got quiet and looked rejected.

The following day Nadia spoke to Kelly about this.

"Can't we invite Susan to come along? She's actually hilarious once you get to know her."

"I don't know Nadia. She got pretty quiet when we were talking about it."

"She's just upset because I've been spending all my time with you. Can't we throw her a bone to make her feel better?"

"Okay, I will ask my cousin Jenny if there's room in her car with all our gear."

It turned out there was enough room, so Susan was invited and reluctantly agreed. The four of them headed out to Golden Ears Provincial Park for the long weekend. They set up one huge tent and their propane stove and a tarp in case it rained, but it was supposed to stay sunny and warm. Kelly's cousin Jenny was twenty-five and already working full-time as a dental assistant. She surprised the sixteen-year-olds by bringing a twenty-four pack of beer for them to share. The girls were very impressed with how cool she was.

"Is it okay if I smoke?" Susan had stashed her pack of cigarettes just in case the cousin turned out to be very strait-laced.

"Sure, no problem. I don't care, as long as it doesn't get back to Kelly's parents."

"Wow, you're awesome." Susan liked this cool chaperone.

After setting up camp, they walked down to the lake for a swim. They lay out in the sun working on their tans and swapping stories about all the different cliques at high school.

"So which girls on your soccer team are already dating

someone?" Susan asked.

Kelly gave the full report. "Well Marion Dumont is going out with Fraser George. Jocelyne Tibault is going out with Tyler Mackenzie. Jennifer Markum is going out with Graham Piggot. That's the only three I know who are in serious relationships."

"What about you Kelly? Who do you like?"

"I'm not going to tell you guys. What if you can't keep a secret?"

"Come on Kelly. I already know who it is. If you don't tell Susan, then I will."

"All right, all right... it's Jonathan Verlaine. He is so hot, but I doubt he even notices me in science class. I am just praying that he gets moved to be my lab partner soon."

"Yah, he's pretty cute," Susan had to agree, "but doesn't he smoke a lot of pot?"

"Who cares," Kelly brushed it off, but shot Nadia a sideways look of complicity.

Susan noticed this and pushed to know more.

"Have you two tried it already?"

Nadia didn't know if it was cool to talk about this in front of her cousin Jenny. Jenny picked up on their hesitation to disclose and said, "It's okay, I smoke pot too. I won't tell your parents."

Nadia relaxed and confessed to Susan, "Yah, my sister let me try some last month when my parents went away to Seattle. It was really fun, and I laughed my stupid head off for about an hour."

Kelly chimed in, "I tried it at the last soccer party. Our goalie, Linda, brought some joints that her big brother gave her. It was awesome."

Susan felt left behind by Nadia and her friend. "Well I want to try it now," she said, "so Nadia, why don't you ask your sister to give you another joint for us sometime."

"I'm way ahead of you girl," Nadia pulled out a secret stash from her bag.

"Holy shit, that's awesome!" Kelly got excited. She looked at her cousin. "Is it okay if we light up now?"

"Well we shouldn't smoke it right here out in the open. Let's swim, dry off and then we can go back to our campsite and smoke it and make supper."

Nadia jumped into the lake first and reported that the water was perfect, so they all floated around for a while. When three teenage boys came down to the beach with a frisbee and started to chuck it around, the girls huddled together in the water to assess the situation.

"They're cute. I like the one with the curly, black hair," Nadia called dibs.

"Yah, I like the one with the green shorts," Kelly chose second.

Susan was left with the nerdy one. "No fair, he looks like a geek," she complained.

"Well you don't have to marry him or anything," Kelly wasn't very sympathetic. "Let's go ask if we can play frisbee with them."

They joined in with the boys, as their chaperone looked on, smiling to herself from their blanket and reading her magazine. Their names were Josh, Paul and Derek and they lived across the river in Langley; all three went to the same high school. They loved heavy metal music and riding dirt bikes. It turned out that they had brought beer as well, so they agreed to come over to the girls' campsite after dinner and party with them. The girls were very excited.

They grilled smokie hot dogs and talked really fast in anticipation of what might happen.

"I wonder if they each have their own pup tent to sleep in," Kelly said.

"Why, are you going to sleep with one of them?" Susan teased.

"If you do, you'd better hope they brought a condom," Nadia warned, "otherwise there may be another little Kelly running around here soon."

"Yah, like you wouldn't Nadia? I'm guessing if that guy Josh invited you back to his tent, you'd be there in a flash."

"What do you think I am, a total slut?" Nadia laughed.

"Well if the shoe fits," Kelly teased.

Cousin Jenny had the sense to keep out of this conversation. She knew that the guys' camp was close enough that she could go and rescue them if one of the guys turned out to be a rapist or serial killer, and she felt positive she could beat the crap out of any one of them.

After they ate, the guys came over and Nadia sparked up the joint that she brought. They each had a few tokes, which was more than enough to get these novices high. Jenny wisely abstained, in case she had to babysit anybody who got paranoid and started freaking out.

They had a wonderful evening, talking and laughing around the fire pit. They eventually moved closer to each other and paired off in the manner predicted. Jenny said she was going to bed and disappeared into the tent. The couples started making out and went back to the guy's individual tents. After much heavy petting, only Susan retreated back to the girls' tent. Both Nadia and Kelly spent the night.

In the morning, they dragged their hung-over butts back to their own camp, where Susan and Jenny were already cooking bacon.

"Well, top of the morning to you. Aren't you two a sight for sore eyes?" Jenny remarked.

Susan wanted a full report. She was dying to know if Nadia had lost her virginity overnight.

"Um... maybe," Nadia hesitated. "Let's just say I might have trouble walking today." She was smiling ear to ear.

"I knew it, you little slut!" Susan couldn't contain herself. "So how was it?"

"Um, it was nice I guess." She didn't sound overly enthusiastic.

"Wow, what an endorsement." Susan couldn't help sounding jealous.

Kelly came clean." I passed out after he took my bra off. I don't even remember whether I touched his dick or not."

"How romantic!" They were killing themselves laughing now.

"What happened to you Susan?" Nadia asked.

"I'm not losing my virginity to that guy," she said proudly, "I know I can do a lot better than him!"

"Okay Miss Perfect, save yourself for Mr Right then, but don't wait too long. You don't want to graduate high school with your flower intact," Kelly said.

Susan took offence. "So what if I do? That's my business and I don't give a shit what you or anyone else thinks about it!"

"Okay, okay, I'm sorry. Take a chill pill," Kelly sort of apologised.

"The bacon is ready girls." Thank God Jenny changed the subject.

After they sat down to eat breakfast, they were somewhat relieved to find out that the guys were leaving. They had plans to go dirt-biking further out on a nearby logging road and stay out there for the rest of the weekend. They politely exchanged phone numbers, knowing full well that they would never see each other again.

The girls had fun for the rest of the weekend, and Susan and Kelly actually got along quite well. Nadia finally managed to bridge the gap between her two closest friends, now she didn't have to choose sides or feel awkward about them running into each other at school. She could spend time with each of them separately and Susan wouldn't get upset anymore, which was a huge relief.

Two years later, on their high-school graduation day, Nadia and Susan were both single so they decided to go as each other's dates. They had lots of friends to sit with, so it didn't really seem like a big deal. They got totally done up in long, fancy dresses, but Nadia wasn't comfortable in heels, so she just wore flats. Susan's mother curled her hair into a bob and Nadia wore her hair up in a tight ponytail with two loose long curls down the sides of her face. They were meeting Kelly later on at the dance, after the awards banquet.

Nadia won a thousand-dollar athletics scholarship towards university for her leadership on the soccer and volleyball teams. She was surprised and thrilled. Her teammates whistled and cheered as she walked up to receive it. Susan won a plaque and a $200 gift card from the drama club for her work behind the scenes on the school production of West Side Story. Nadia could hear the whole drama table chanting "Susan," repeatedly as she walked up to the stage.

The DJ for the dance played great classic rock and disco songs. A few boys asked them to dance, but nobody they had a crush on. It was just a fun evening with friends. They spotted Kelly across the gym and yelled at her to come to dance with them. Kelly pulled them into the crowded, sweaty bathroom to take a hit off a flask of vodka she had stashed in her nylons. They thought this was very ingenious.

"I need to tell you guys some big news," Kelly confided between swigs.

"What's up girl?" Nadia asked.

"I'm moving to Germany."

"What the hell?"

"Yah, my grandmother is German and I'm going to live with her in Cologne to go to university."

"Holy crap, this is major. Well I'm happy for you, but I'm obviously sad to see you go," Nadia said.

Susan didn't say anything.

They hugged and went back to dancing to a Cyndi Lauper song in the gym. Nadia leaned into Susan to get her real thoughts.

"So, are you happy that she's leaving?"

"Well, to be honest, I can't say that I'm all broken up about it," Susan admitted.

"Yah, I know. You two never really saw eye to eye." Nadia knew she had created a friendship triangle that just didn't work.

"Well, I guess you've got me all to yourself again now, right?" Nadia teased sarcastically.

"Lucky me," Susan said sardonically, and gave her a big cheesy grin.

"You love me, and you can't help yourself," she grabbed Susan and kissed her on the cheek and they both laughed and went back to dancing.

After graduation, Nadia had plans to start university right away in the fall, but Susan wanted to take some time off to work and save up money to travel and eventually move out. She got a job waitressing at a local burger restaurant and began to stash away her tips. They were both eighteen and the future held endless possibilities.

Chapter Two
Whistler

In 1980, Nadia had just started at Simon Fraser University, which sits on top of a mountain overlooking downtown Vancouver. The crisp fall air made everything seem so alive and she loved every moment of being there. She could drink coffee and talk for hours with someone she just met in Spanish class or listen over lunch to some impassioned protestor decry the development of an old-growth forest. At eighteen, she truly believed she could do anything.

After several months of waitressing, Susan was not as enamoured with life at the moment. She was bored and looking for a change, but she had no interest in going back to school. She was still petite and skinny and had cut her black hair short and it curled under her jaw line like a 1920s flapper girl. With her big, brown eyes and long lashes, it was a complete look. She had large breasts that the guys loved to ogle but somehow, she had still remained a virgin due to a feisty standoffishness that made her unapproachable. Even though she had been Nadia's sidekick all through high school, she was about to come into her own.

When Nadia arrived home one afternoon, her mom told her to call Susan right away because she had some big news.

"What's your big news?" Nadia asked impatiently.

"I quit my waitressing job and I'm moving up to

Whistler."

"Wow, that's so ballsy! Are your parents okay with that?"

"Not really, but I'm doing it anyways. A waitress who quit last year has already moved up there and she's looking for another roommate. She lives with a guy and the rent's only $250 a month each. I'm leaving this weekend to start applying for jobs before the ski season starts."

"That's so exciting! I can come up there on weekends and ski and party with you. There will be so many hot guys up there. You will finally pop your cherry."

"Stop pressuring me. Like that's my highest priority. You need to get a life."

"Okay, okay I'm sorry. Touchy subject obviously. No seriously, I'm proud of you for leaving the nest. It will be so awesome for you to get some breathing room away from your parents."

"Yah, no kidding. If I have to watch my mother dust one more damn knick-knack, I think I'll shoot myself."

Nadia laughed. "Yah, she might be the most uptight person I know, but she sure can pull off a pink polyester pantsuit."

"So, can you help me pack up my life or what? Get over here."

Nadia hung up the receiver. She suddenly felt jealous of her best friend's courage to leave home. She saw four years of university ahead of her as a daunting amount of time. She had decided to become a French Immersion teacher because she knew they were in high demand. At least she had the basement to herself now that her older sister had moved out. Her parents gave her the freedom to do pretty much what she wanted anyhow. They believed in fostering her independence.

Besides, they had been through so much drama with her older sister Rosanne that she could basically light herself on fire and they wouldn't even blink.

Soon after Susan moved to Whistler, Nadia had a free weekend, so she caught the Greyhound bus from downtown Vancouver and took the two-hour ride up the winding Sea-to-Sky highway. The ski season was about to start, and the village was buzzing with attractive, young twenty-somethings who had just been hired and were settling into their new service jobs and buying season passes. They all looked like they were straight out of a Tommy Hilfiger ad, except with hiking boots instead of deck shoes.

Nadia gave Susan a big hug and slid beside her into the back seat of her roommate Mark's old, beat-up Toyota to head to her new place in Alta Vista. It was a modern three-bedroom condo with a fireplace and a small deck out back. Their furniture was a dilapidated, old couch, a few brightly covered bean-bag chairs and a white dinette set; but they had everything they needed in terms of dishes and cutlery. Luckily for Susan, Mark had a stereo, so they plunked in a Roxy Music cassette and began cooking spaghetti.

"Thanks for picking me up Mark," said Nadia.

"No probs, I just got off work anyhow."

"Where do you work?" she asked.

"In the village ski rental shop," he replied.

"Susan, have you found a job yet?" Nadia asked reluctantly, not wishing to pressure her friend.

"Yah, I have my first shift tomorrow at the bakery. Luckily for me I don't have enough experience to do the early baking shift, so I start at nine o'clock and just serve and work cash. It only pays minimum wage to start, but that's okay."

"That's great," Nadia was enthusiastic, "but how will you get to work?"

"Well if Mark's not working, there's a shuttle every half hour or I can just hitchhike. Everybody does it up here," Susan explained.

"Where's your other roommate? I'd like to meet her," Nadia inquired.

"Tracy works at Moguls night club, so she doesn't get home until late. I'm hoping she can get me on there soon because the tips are awesome." She sounded hopeful.

They cracked a cold beer and dished up the spaghetti. Nadia was impressed with how comfortable Susan seemed in her new home. She seemed to have a newfound, self-assurance and even looked prettier and more alive. Her cheeks were pink from all the fresh mountain air and she was obviously happier.

Later that night, as they settled into her double bed side by side, Nadia shared her thoughts.

"You seem really happy here and Mark is really nice. I'm so jealous that you made the big move and I'm still stuck at home."

"Thanks, yah I do feel really happy right now. Everything is falling into place. I'm glad you came up here. Tomorrow night we can go to a party with Mark at his buddy's place in Alpine."

"I think Mark likes you. Watch out or you might screw up the roommate agreement if you sleep with him," Nadia teased.

Susan was quick to shut her down. "Don't worry, I'm not that stupid."

It turns out she was that stupid though, because two weeks later Nadia's prediction came true and Susan and Mark were already a couple. Nadia was happy that her friend had finally lost her virginity, but worried that it might ruin her living situation, which it eventually did. Susan had to move again in January to get away from Mark, who was moping around miserably after she broke up with him.

On a brighter note, Susan had moved in with a hilarious, older guy from Ontario named David, who had a truck and could drive them around. David was fairly short and heavy-set, with bushy, brown hair that seemed to grow straight up so it looked like a helmet. He was always smiling and had an insanely positive outlook on life. He had a geology degree and worked for the municipality's public works yard down at the junction, so he made good money. He would treat them to beers at Dooley's pub and always had weed. Neither Nadia nor Susan, had ever considered him as boyfriend material because they weren't physically attracted to him. He was just the nicest, most easy-going person they had ever met. David became the guy whose social connections would form the nucleus of Nadia and Susan's lives for many years to come; it was the beginning of everything.

When Nadia arrived at Susan's new place on Friday night, she asked what the plans were for the weekend.

"Well, I have to work tomorrow early shift at the bakery, so you might as well ski until noon and then I can meet you at the Bighorn for lunch afterwards. David is off at one and he has invited us to his friend Alex's house for dinner. Then a guy from my work is having a party in Alta Vista."

"Sounds great. I brought you some bagels, cream cheese and beer so let's eat. I'm starving!"

They cranked up the UB40, made some food, smoked a joint and chilled for the rest of the night. David told an amazing story of crashing a motorcycle into a ditch in

Newfoundland and lying there, overnight, half-dead until someone came walking a dog and found him. Susan complained about stupid customers at work and Nadia longed for the end of term at university so she could work full time for the summer and save up for a ski pass. All the problems of the world seemed minor because life was so good. There was fresh powder, food, beer, weed and friends and that's all that mattered.

The next day after skiing and lunch, the three of them rode with David to his friend Alex's place near Alta Lake. It was a small A-frame cabin with a balcony out front and a neat, wood pile to stoke the cute, black wood-burning stove. Alex lived with a roommate and worked at one of the restaurants in the village.

Susan took an immediate shine to Alex, which was fairly obvious to Nadia. He was striking in appearance, having black hair contrasting with very light blue eyes and a wide face and nose. It turned out his mother was from the Algonquin First Nation in Ontario. Susan and Alex were in the kitchen talking and cutting up veggies and already standing way too close together within the first hour. Nadia wondered if Susan would make it out of here tonight or end up skipping the party all together to stay with Alex. She was happy for her friend but didn't want to end up crashing at her place without her there.

As it turned out, Alex went to the party with them after dinner too. It was packed and there were already several naked people in the hot tub doing shots of peach Schnapps. The reggae was loud, and a group of people were playing the Dating Game with some young stud asking three blindfolded girls ultra-personal questions on kitchen stools, to everyone's great amusement. Alex came over to Susan and put his arm around her.

"There's a punchbowl on the coffee table with several hits of acid dissolved in it. Do you want to partake?"

Susan looked at Nadia nervously. Neither of them had ever done acid before. "What's it like?" she asked him honestly.

"It's like you just feel uninhibited, talkative and energised."

"Well, what do you think Nadia?" Susan asked nervously.

"We could just take a couple of sips and then wait and see."

"Okay I'm in if you are, but you guys have to promise to take care of me if I get freaked out."

"We promise. Let's just stick close together for the rest of the night."

They ended up sitting in someone's bedroom just talking for hours about everything under the sun and completely lost track of time. Nadia started sharing all her big sister's most personal details, like how she had recently followed a much older, black guy to Alberta to live with him in a shitty little apartment while he worked on a gas rig. She got a job slinging beer in a local strip club. Nadia was worried about her now because they were using drugs regularly, like the little purple bennies she showed her to stay 'up' at work into the wee hours of the morning. Nadia realised how much she missed her and suddenly felt sad and went quiet.

Susan picked up the slack and started blathering about life at the bakery and how an older German woman had come in to buy coffee and had made a pass at her. She told her she was beautiful and invited her back to the best hotel in the village for a hot tub. Susan had politely declined. It was the first time she had ever been hit on by a woman. She asked Nadia if she would ever 'go that way'.

"Maybe if she was hot and I was horny, why not? You never know. Maybe it would be more fun playing for the other team." Nadia was high and open to anything. Another random ginger-haired girl in the room joined in the conversation.

"I slept with my roommate in college and it was awesome. She knew exactly where my clitoris was, unlike most guys."

"Woah!" Susan and Nadia were shocked by her candour.

"You're awesome!" Nadia declared.

Some blond guy sitting on the floor got offended. "We know where your clitoris is," he complained, "but maybe we just don't care that much."

"Asshole!" Susan shot back. "Well you should care if you want a girlfriend to stick around for more than five minutes."

That shut him up. Susan gave him her warmest smile to soften the blow and he gave her a forced, cheesy, fake smile in return.

"What do you think about aliens?" the ginger suddenly asked.

"Oh, they're out there," Nadia did not hesitate. "We must be the stupidest life forms in the universe. There's no other explanation for life on this planet."

Susan fell off the bed laughing. "You're totally right girl! We are stupid! I bet they're watching us right now and collecting data. Then they will pick us up and move us like farm animals to some colony planet and start milking us." She was hysterical now.

The conversation got steadily dumber the later it got. David finally found them at two in the morning and said it was time to go. Alex crashed in Susan's bed and Nadia slept on the floor beside them because they were too high to have sex anyhow. They didn't realise that after this party, Alex would become a permanent fixture in Susan's life, thus changing the course of history.

Chapter Three
Vancouver

The following year Susan and Alex had moved in together at Creekside near the gondola, in the days just before Blackcomb ski resort was built. Susan was slinging beer at the Chairlift pub and Alex still worked as a waiter at one of the fancier restaurants in the village, so his tips were great. They shared their place with two other people and life was good.

Nadia came up more in the summer that year, when university was finished. They skinny dipped at Lost Lake or Alta Lake on Susan's days off or drove up to Meager Creek hot springs for overnight campouts or went fruit picking in the small adjacent town of Pemberton. David would come over often for meals or they would go for a hike or a bike ride together. Whistler was quieter in the summer, but that suited them just fine, as ski season was usually really hectic with so many tourists.

As Susan and Nadia approached their mid-twenties, the nagging reality of life after Whistler started to seep into their minds. One hot August afternoon, they discussed what the future might look like over a cold beer.

"When are we going to become contributing members of society and get like, real jobs?" Nadia asked Susan one day. "I am graduating next year you know."

"My mom keeps telling me to come back home and sell

condos with her," replied Susan. "That sounds like some sort of fresh hell to me."

"Well you can't sling beer forever. Your elbow is already killing you from carrying those heavy trays. I'm thinking of taking my fifth year to become a teacher."

"Jesus, more school? Well, if I'm honest I will probably talk to my friend Sarah in Vancouver. She said she could get me on at her work selling photocopiers. The pay is pretty good, and you get to drive around the city so it's not as boring as being stuck in an office all day," Susan decided.

"What does Alex think about leaving Whistler? Would he go with you?" asked Nadia.

"We have talked about it. He wants to go into a two-year college programme to become a surveyor so he can work with David on geology sites. He said he would get a student loan to pay the rent."

"So, is it settled then? Are you moving back to Vancouver in September?"

"Sure," agreed Susan, "why not move to the city? Sounds good to me."

"But not before we take a little trip to Europe, just you and me girl," Nadia coaxed.

"I can't afford that! I've only saved enough money for one month's damage deposit and maybe half a month's rent with Alex," Susan protested.

"Well I thought he was getting a big student loan, so problem solved right? Besides, our neighbour Jill is a travel agent, remember? She can get us a sweet deal and I have some money my grandma left me that I've put aside for this. I was just waiting for the right time to tell you," Nadia was stoked.

Susan looked at Alex longingly. "Would you be okay if

we took a little trip later this summer before you start your program in the city?"

"For sure, no problem." Alex was a total sweetheart. "I want to go home to Ontario for my mom's birthday at the end of this month anyhow."

"You're the best boyfriend ever," Susan was getting excited. "Okay Nadia, call Jill and let's get this thing booked before I come to my senses."

A few weeks later, Nadia and Susan were strolling down Las Ramblas in Barcelona eating ice cream in the hot sun and checking out all the hot Latin guys.

"This place is dangerous girl," Susan laughed, "let's go to a club tonight."

"For sure." Nadia was already getting a freckled tan after one day. "There's supposed to be a great spot right down by the water called La Bella Noche. We can wear those new strappy sun dresses we bought today. We can go back to the hostel and braid our hair in little corn-rows so we won't be so hot dancing."

The night was crystal clear, but the air was humid and smelled of bougainvillea and cigarettes. After eating tapas of meatballs, calamari and patatas fritas and drinking several glasses of sangria, they strolled the boardwalk listening to every language pass by.

The line-up for the club wasn't too long because it was a weeknight. There were jugglers, musicians and body painters passing the hat while they waited. The girl with the mural of the Sagrada Familia tattooed on her back was most impressive. Susan and Nadia gathered whatever coins they had left to contribute.

Once inside, the thumping rhythms and sweaty dancing

were intoxicating. They grabbed a beer and stood by the back bar to get some space to talk for a few minutes. A very good-looking, older Spanish guy approached them and yelled over the noise.

"Can we buy you beautiful ladies a drink?"

They noticed his equally handsome friend standing by the bar holding four shots adeptly between his widely spread fingers. Nadia and Susan looked at each other and leaned in.

"Why not?" Nadia was keen to get the real Spanish experience.

"Well, they're a little too old for us don't you think?"

"Experience is everything girl. You only live once right?"

Susan relented and they introduced themselves to Alejandro and Joaquin. Nadia suspected they were married and had taken off their wedding rings, but she didn't really care. She would be gone in a week anyhow and it wasn't her problem. They threw back the ouzo shots and danced the night away, getting physically closer the later it got. At two in the morning, they all went back to Alejandro's apartment and made out like cats in heat. Nadia thought Joaquin was the sexiest man she had ever been with. He knew exactly what to do with his tongue and his body was gorgeous. They were on the living room couch trying not to make too much noise. Susan and Alejandro were in the bedroom and Nadia could hear her friend moaning with pleasure. Afterwards, they all passed out like drunken fools and awoke to a harsh sun that made their heads hurt. Alejandro made them all coffee and said he had to get to work so they were ushered out quite suddenly.

After they exchanged numbers, Susan and Nadia went on their way feeling blissfully tired and deeply satisfied with their authentic Spanish evening. They strolled down the avenue, having no real idea where they were. Eventually they stumbled upon the Passeig de Gracia metro and found their way back to the hostel. Nadia promised never to tell Alex about their escapade, and they went to find some breakfast at a little cafe. They dunked chocolate pastries into strong cafe con leches and felt like life was marvelous. They agreed to see them twice more before they left Barcelona and tried not to get too attached to these wonderful, sexy men who they knew they would never see again. It turned out they were in their early thirties and not yet married, which was surprising, given their obvious attributes. They were hot, employed and charming. What were these Spanish women thinking? Oh well, their loss is our gain, thought Nadia and Susan.

When they got back to Vancouver, Nadia went back to her parents' house to do her teaching practicum year, but she escaped to the city to be with her friends as often as possible. After teaching all week, she would hang out with David and go to bars, parties and street festivals. Susan and Alex had moved into a small apartment close by, off Hastings near Nanaimo Street, by the Pacific National Exhibition fairgrounds. Nadia would either crash on Susan and Alex's couch for the weekend or at David's rental house nearby, where there was lots of space. Sunday would inevitably come around and she would have to roll back to reality and catch the bus home to suburbia to face drafting lesson plans, designing craft projects for thirty kids and marking spelling tests again.

Alex began his surveyor programme at college and Susan sold photocopiers to offices around Vancouver. They were happy and felt like adults for the first time in their lives. The concept of marriage started coming up as a regular topic of conversation, but they both agreed it was too soon for that.

It was Halloween 1987 and the geologists were throwing a huge bash. Flyers had been sent around the Commercial Drive neighbourhood, depicting missiles flying into naked baby dolls with Fidel Castro sporting a giant Salvador Dali moustache riding on a donkey and waving an American flag. This was the flavour of hilarious insanity they were striving for. It was a costume affair of course and there were bare chested nuns and guys dressed as the Village People. David and his new geologist roommate got a keg and decorated the house with streamers and balloons and many broken naked dolls.

Nadia found her mom's old full-length dress from the 1940s and made herself up as some sort of Princess Gwendolyn. She phoned Susan and found out that she would be coming as Edith Prickly from SCTV, complete with cat glasses and leopard skin dress.

"That's hilarious! You really pull off that look," exclaimed Nadia, when she arrived at the party house.

"I want you to meet David's new roommate, Sam," said Susan.

"Hi there. Nice dress!" He leered at Nadia as if she were a fresh piece of meat. He was obviously already half-cut and had no inhibitions whatsoever.

"Fuck off," retorted Nadia, putting him in his place. She pulled Susan away from him and into the next room. She leaned into her friend to give her honest assessment, "What a douchebag!"

They danced until midnight and had a wonderful time. The artist from next door ended up spray painting David's old Buick outside and several party-goers stuck macaroni all over it.

Someone brought out a bag of mushrooms and many people grabbed a pinch. Susan and Nadia had done them before up in Whistler and had a good time, so they joined in. This proved to be a mistake because they ended up having a bad trip and lying on the bed upstairs together, crying and hugging each other. Alex found them and rescued them and took them home to bed. He gave up his half of the bed for Nadia and slept on the couch, like the sweetheart that he was.

It wouldn't be until New Year's Day, at the polar bear swim on English Bay, that Nadia would run into Sam again but this time he was sober. After the freezing cold swim, they went back to someone's house who had a sauna and Nadia realised that this Sam, when wrapped in just a towel and talking about his worldwide travels, was much more attractive and interesting than she had originally given him credit for. He asked her out for dinner the following night and Nadia was excited.

The next evening, Nadia met Sam at the Nanaimo Skytrain station. Sam pulled up and she hopped onto the front bench seat of his blue pick-up truck, and he drove the ten blocks to a Korean barbeque. She thought he looked really cute with his tousled, brown curly locks getting long over his big, brown eyes. He had the wiry, muscular body of someone who worked physically for a living.

When they arrived at the restaurant the hostess led Sam and Nadia to a red, vinyl booth with a circular, black, iron barbeque inserted in the centre. Sliding into the comfortable benches, Nadia immediately noticed his long eyelashes and had to stop herself from staring. She felt slightly overdressed in a skirt, since he had on jeans and a black t-shirt with a picture of Iggy Pop grinning on the front.

"Wow, I have never been to a Korean restaurant before," Nadia began.

"It's great because the food is prepared fresh in front of you and it's piping hot," Sam explained.

After ordering beef with assorted vegetables and fat noodles, they sipped their Korean beer and got to know each other.

"So, tell me more about your travels. You mentioned something on New Year's about going around the world before you turn thirty?" Nadia inquired.

"Yup, I've been to five continents already, but not Asia or Australia yet."

"Holy shit, how old are you again?" she was impressed.

"Twenty-three."

"Jesus, how did you do all that already?

"Well, it helps that I helped skipper a sailboat from England to Africa and then from Miami to Argentina. The owner of the boat is a family friend."

Nadia became more and more impressed with this guy's accomplishments, but she didn't want to appear over-enthused. Besides, she had also travelled quite a bit in her young life.

"I've been to Europe three times and to Haiti on a university trip," she explained. "Most of my relatives are in England, Holland and Germany."

"That's cool." Sam gave her props.

Nadia watched the waitress bring plates of chopped cabbage, beansprouts, shredded beef, ginger, kimchee, noodles and various sauces that looked a little scary. She deftly lit the barbeque centrepiece and swept each ingredient onto the platform one by one to a delightful sizzling effect. After two minutes of stirring, she served them each a plate, pointing out the soya sauce, fish sauce and hot chili sauce.

"So, what about your job?" She was curious whether he had two nickels to rub together.

"I was working for two years as a geology surveyor for a big mining company downtown. Then the office politics got really weird, so I quit. Now I am working for a smaller geology company, the one where David works. That's how we met. It's a way better work environment. It's only my first year there, but it's going really well."

Nadia was impressed again. How could he have figured all this out at twenty-three?

"Well, I've got one more practicum term and then I will be a bona fide French Immersion teacher. I can't wait to make my own money and stop living off student loans."

"That's awesome. So, you like working with kids then?"

"It has its moments, that's for sure. Last term, a boy I was working with pissed in another boy's rubber boot." They both laughed.

After eating and chatting easily for an hour, they left and went back to Sam's place for a beer. They slept together and so began their relationship.

Nadia would take the Skytrain into the city as often as she could to spend the weekend with Sam. Usually David was home too and Susan and Alex would join them at some point to hang out at the two geologists' house. They would listen to music, smoke, drink beer and unwind together after a long week of working or studying. Sometimes they would go out to Joe's cafe on Commercial Drive to shoot pool, go dancing at a bar or catch a concert at the Commodore Ballroom. They all got along famously and kept teasing David that he should get more serious about finding a girlfriend, but he seemed happy hitting on women and bringing home the occasional one-night stands. He loved his dog, a big rottweiler named Rufus, and his independence.

Nadia even brought Sam home to the suburbs to meet her parents for dinner. They liked him immediately because he was gregarious and hard working. They could see that their daughter was smitten and trusted her judgement. Nadia also met his family gradually. His brother John and his mom Brenda both lived in the city, but his dad had died tragically in a boating accident some years before. This was a soft spot for Sam that she left alone, unless he brought it up. She could tell that there was a lot of emotion just under the surface around his father, both good and bad. From what she had heard, he had been far from the perfect dad.

University was going well, and she was starting her teaching year. The coursework load was quite heavy but she enjoyed it. She spent her evenings gathering materials and planning lessons to present in class the following day. Whether she was directing her classmates to sort buttons into groups of ten or mix paints into various colours, it would all be useful eventually when she got her own classroom. She visited a few local schools and decided she would like to teach the intermediate years, around age ten, because they were old enough to tie their own shoes but still young enough to be curious and open to learning. She was afraid to tackle the hormonal teen years.

Living at home was hard now, because she really wanted to be with Sam, but she knew what she had to do and the end goal was in sight. She couldn't shake a stick at the money and time she was saving by staying at home. Her mom would still cook and do her laundry and she was grateful for that. She realised how lucky she was to have a solid family because many students in her programme had to work at night to pay for rent and food. She still had a little of her grandma's inheritance left, just enough to finish the program if she was frugal.

Nadia had to admit to herself that she was falling in love with Sam. She had never felt this way about anyone before and it was kind of scary. They talked on the phone every night and she missed him like crazy during the week. For her birthday he bought her a necklace with two silver hearts, that she wore all the time now. They had started saying, "I love you," whenever they parted on Sunday nights to go back to their separate lives. Nadia was excited for the future.

Chapter Four
Babyland

Nadia was awakened by the sound of Susan's voice speaking into the answering machine.

"If you ever get out of bed, call me back because I have some big news."

Nadia dragged herself into the kitchen, poured herself a coffee, sat down at the table and dialed her best friend.

"What do you want, you uppity, old hag?"

"We're getting married and you're the maid of honour!"

"Wow! When is this happening?"

"July 24th at the Hungarian Cultural Centre, where my grandma is a member. We are renting the reception room there and you have to find a pale green dress because Alex is wearing a green tuxedo, just to be different."

"Are your parents going to pay for the booze and food?"

"Oh probably. We haven't got that far yet. But I won't be drinking anyhow because I'M PREGNANT!"

They were both screaming into the phone now in unison.

"How the hell did that happen?"

"The usual way. Penis in, sperm out, hello baby omelette."

"Well that's just fascinating. So, it's a shotgun wedding then? Fantastic. Your parents must be so proud."

"Oh please. They're not that old fashioned. Besides, I will

look awesome in the photos with my big belly."

"You take the cake girlfriend. Well I need to go take a shower so I can digest all this news, god damn it. How am I supposed to have a normal day after this? But seriously, that's very exciting. Go take some prenatal vitamins or something. I'll talk to you later."

Three months later, it was the day of the big event and Susan and Nadia were preening themselves with the help of various mothers and aunties, in the back rooms of the Hungarian Cultural Centre. Susan already had a sizeable bump showing, but she still looked gorgeous with a crown of tiny baby's breath in her hair and a white dress.

Nadia looked more nervous than Susan. She was afraid that Sam might drink too much and French kiss Susan's mother, like he did at the Easter dinner. Maybe he had a drinking problem? She couldn't focus on that now. As maid of honour, Susan needed her to be calm, cool and collected.

Sam's old high school girlfriend Lisa was coming as David's plus one. Nadia doubted there would be any chemistry between them: he was short, brunette and stocky; she was tall, blonde and sort of elegant. But who knew what made people click nowadays? She officially gave up after seeing Susan's Aunt Martha with this total weirdo of a husband. He was clearly no match for her quick wit and good looks. Opposites definitely seemed to attract, though she had no idea why.

When Susan came down the aisle, Nadia lost her cool and started tearing up. Here was her best friend in the whole world about to lose the freedom of her partying youth and become a wife and mother. It was too much to take in. How did they get here so fast? Susan flashed her a loving look and squeezed her hand, but remained stoic and dry-eyed throughout the short, secular service. Afterwards, there were many photos and some drinks and mingling before the formal dinner. They ate crab cakes and veal scaloppini with roast vegetables and chocolate mousse. Then the huge cake was cut and there were many toasts. Nadia had somehow managed to stave off having to speak, which she dreaded because she knew she would cry. It was the older generation who took the mic to embarrass Susan with stories about how cute and sweet she was as a child and how this Alex fellow seemed to make her happy.

Nadia was surprised at how David and Lisa were obviously hitting it off so well. They were leaning in and giggling about something at the groom's end of the head table. Nadia turned to Sam and said,

"Have you seen these two lovebirds at the other end of the table? Go figure?"

"Yah I know," Sam agreed, "David told me in the john that he thinks she's super-hot and is hoping to make a move on her later after a few more drinks."

"Wow, that's subtle," Nadia admired his forthrightness, "maybe the Ramada Inn will be hot and heavy tonight?"

"I hope so," said Sam, "maybe even I can get lucky?"

"If you play your cards right, who knows?" Nadia smiled and gave him a long, sweet kiss. She loved this guy, with his curly, tousled, brown hair and long eyelashes.

It was time for Susan to toss the bouquet. Nadia tried her best to elbow the other girls out of the way, but it was Lisa who got lucky and made the catch. They danced into the wee hours to a Rock-a-Billy band who were friends of David's from Whistler. Even the old folks busted a move and Susan's grandmother was adorable dancing with some ten-year-old cousin of hers from out of town. When Nadia was finally able to wrestle Susan away from her relatives for a few minutes, she asked her quite seriously,

"So how does it feel to be Mrs Alex Tretiak?"

"My feet are killing me, and I just want to go to take off this outfit and lie down!" Susan was feeling the weight of her pregnancy. "But I'm happy that everything turned out so well. It's such a relief after three months of planning."

"Sit down girl and let me rub your feet," Nadia offered. She went and dunked two table napkins into an ice bucket and wrapped them around Susan's feet on her lap.

"Oh my God, I love you." Susan flopped back into the chair. "I should have married you instead of that giant man-boy over there."

"Na, you did good," Nadia disagreed, "besides, he's way hotter than me."

"Yah he is pretty hot," Susan boasted, "and I think he will make a great daddy for whatever creature comes out of here," she said, rubbing her belly.

"Do you think it's a boy or a girl?" Nadia asked.

"I think it's a girl," Susan said without hesitation. "I just feel this feminine energy in there, don't ask me how. Mother's intuition I guess."

"Well either way, this kid will be awesome!" She hugged her friend and kissed her belly.

"Thanks Nadia, I mean for everything. You have been an amazing maid of honour all day and hopefully I can return the favour someday soon."

"Oh really? Do you know something that I don't know?" Nadia asked.

"Nope, I just think Sam looks pretty smitten at the

moment."

It turned out she was right because that night in bed at the hotel, Sam was too drunk to make love but just drunk enough to get all mushy and propose to her in his own haphazard way.

"I think we should do this too. Let's get married."

"Ask me in the morning when you're sober." Nadia was not giving in that easily.

"I want one of those rug-rats too!" Sam announced.

"Holy shit! Really? Since when?"

"Kids are awesome." Sam was full of surprises. "Besides, I want our kid to grow up knowing Alex and Susan's kid, don't you?"

"Well sure, but this is a lot to take in. Let's talk about it some more when you're sober."

"I love you so much." Sam passed out about ten seconds later.

"I love you too." Nadia kissed his forehead and lay awake for a while trying to process what had just happened. She didn't know if she was ready for any of this. She hadn't even finished her teaching practicum yet. Even though she would eventually get maternity benefits, could they even afford to have a kid? Did Sam drink too much to be a good husband or father? She couldn't get a clear perspective on that. He did enjoy a couple of beers every night after work, but who didn't? Especially with all the physical labour outside. It seemed like all young guys drank beer after work. So what? His job was going well and seemed stable. Susan would be thrilled if Nadia got pregnant. Then they could hang out and go for stroller walks and mom and tot classes at the Rec Centre together. It would be pretty awesome. Nadia finally dozed off with visions of dirty diapers dancing in her head.

To her amazement, the next morning Sam remembered their conversation from the night before and still wanted to marry her. He even got down on bended knee with a slice of bacon hanging out of his mouth to make her laugh. They agreed that it was a good idea and he took a piece of string from their slice of souvenir wedding cake and tied it around her ring finger. Nadia called Susan that afternoon to share the news.

"That's awesome, girl! I told you this would happen. Well you can use my wedding planner list to save yourself some time."

"One step at a time. We're not going to do anything until we have tried living together first," Nadia said, "besides, whenever we do decide to get married, we would probably just get hitched at city hall and then throw a wild party." Nadia hated any formality; besides, her family was so tiny she couldn't rustle up enough relatives to fill any venue.

"Hey Susan, Sam said he wants to have a kid!"

"Holy crap! Yay! Then our kids can be buddies growing up. That would be amazing!"

"Well, we'll see what happens." Nadia felt like she was in a dream state even saying this. How could she have gone from single and carefree one day to engaged and contemplating motherhood the next? Things were happening so fast and she didn't feel ready. She had nearly completed her teaching coursework and would hopefully be working full-time in September. She needed to slow things down a little, so she told Sam she would stay at her parents' place, at least until the university term was finished. Nadia was freaking out.

Meanwhile, David and Lisa started seeing each other and much to Nadia's amazement, they seemed really compatible.

David's wicked sense of humour offset Lisa's reserved elegance perfectly, so they balanced each other out. She had a six-year-old son when she was really young named Isaac, who David bonded with almost instantly as the fun guy who happened to be dating his mother.

Sam said he had never seen David like this before. The usually fiercely independent party boy had turned into a devoted stepdad to Lisa's son Isaac, virtually overnight. They had become super-buds and were hanging out together on bikes, skateboards and video games. David would even walk him to school in the morning and let Lisa sleep in. It was the most adorable thing ever.

One day David announced to Sam that he wanted to move in with Lisa. Sam was surprised this was happening so fast but he had to be supportive of his best bro. David didn't want to leave him in the lurch for the month's rent, and offered to help him find a new roommate, but Sam brushed him off.

"I already have somebody in mind," Sam said coyly, with a wink.

"Oh yah?" David was curious. "Would that be a woman with curly hair and green eyes by any chance?"

"Maybe," smiled Sam, thinking about Nadia.

"That's awesome bro," his buddy was excited. "Look at us, all shacked up and mature like. Who woulda thunk it?"

"Well we have to bite the bullet sometime, I guess," Sam reflected. "Besides, now that Alex and Susan are having a kid, maybe we should join them in the daddy game?"

"Woah slow your roll player! I have just become a step-dad to Isaac these past four months, and I have to admit I love it, but now you're moving too fast for me man."

"Okay, okay. Well let's just see what happens. Nadia and

I can help you move and I'm sure Alex and Susan will help too."

"Thanks man, you're the best. That would be awesome. How about Saturday the 30th?"

So, two weeks later, all six friends were loading David's belongings into his truck to move to Lisa's. Little Isaac was super excited to help out by carrying the small stuff. He was obviously so thrilled that his new super big bro was moving in, especially since his biological dad wasn't really around that much. Lisa was over the moon to have a loving, supportive man in her son's life. She had never experienced this kind of devotion before. David would do anything for her, he was such a sweetheart.

After the move, they all went for burgers and beers together and called it an early night.

The following day, Nadia's mom called her to come take a call from Sam.

"Hey there. You sound sleepy?"

"Yah I am. I stayed up past midnight rummaging around my mother's kitchen collecting powders for a science lesson on acid and alkali. What's happening?"

"Since David has moved out of the house and in with Lisa, I can't afford to pay the rent on my own, so I think you should move in with me now."

"Wow, okay I need a cup of coffee for this. I appreciate the invite, but I thought we were doing this after my practicum. I need to process this and talk to mom. Can I call you back in like, half an hour?"

"Sure, sure, no problem. But the rent here is $1200 and I know you're not working yet, but I thought maybe with your student loan you could afford to pay $400 a month. Does that sound reasonable?"

"I guess so. I'll have to crunch the numbers for next term's tuition and books and transit and food, so give me an hour to talk to the parents."

"Take all the time you need. No pressure, but it would be awesome to have you here every night."

"What about the daytime? Would that be awesome too? Or do you just want to sleep with me?" Nadia joked.

"Yah, of course, I love you every minute of every day. Just call me back when you're awake, woman."

Nadia dragged her sleepy self into the kitchen and poured herself a big coffee. Here mom was cutting vegetables at the counter. After exchanging good mornings, Nadia sat down at the table and made a list of all her expenses for the final term of her teaching practicum. The commute from Vancouver to the university would be a lot farther, but she only had to be up there one day a week. Her placement was in the suburb of Burnaby so she could manage that on the bus, but it would be so much easier if she had a car. After she got her head together, she decided to talk to her mom about all this.

"Mom, Sam has asked me to move in with him."

She suddenly stopped cutting up mushrooms and turned around.

"Wow, that's a big step. What do you think?"

"I think it would be awesome, but I'm worried about money, of course. My student loan will just about cover it until I start working in September but honestly, I'm not looking forward to catching the bus to Burnaby every morning for my practicum. Is there any way you and dad could loan me the money for a used car?"

"Well we probably don't have enough in the bank for that

right now, but we could co-sign a loan for you. Let me talk to him tonight and I'll let you know. It's a good thing I like Sam, or this wouldn't even be a conversation you know. Besides, I will miss having you around here every day. My baby is flying the coop."

"I know mom. I will miss you too. I really appreciate you even considering it. I do love Sam. He proposed to me right after Susan's wedding."

"What? Why didn't you tell us?"

"Well he was kind of drunk so I made him do it again to be sure, but I think we might be heading to city hall at some point soon."

"Well we can do better than that. At least let us pay for a family dinner at some sort of nice restaurant. We at least want to be witnesses if you decide to go the casual route."

"Of course, Mom. I wasn't planning on eloping without telling you."

They hugged for a long minute and both got a little teary. Nadia was so grateful for her mother's support. She always knew she would be okay because her parents always had her back. She felt lucky that they mostly treated her like an adult and generally trusted her decision making.

A month later, Nadia had purchased an old, brown Toyota Tercel with the help of her parents. It ran well, but it looked like a piece of shit. She had moved in with Sam and they began setting up their life together, but not in the geologist's house. After much discussion, they decided the old place was too big and expensive for two people, so they rented a smaller Vancouver special off Knight street, complete with orange shag carpeting.

The next morning, Lisa came over to help Nadia unpack.

They had grown quite close these past few months. Even though she was Sam's old high-school girlfriend, Nadia couldn't help liking her. They shared a sharp wit and sarcastic view of the world. She brought over some croissants to have with their coffee, and they put some Lisa Loeb on the stereo and sat down at the kitchen table.

"So how are you feeling about everything since you moved in with David?" Nadia asked.

"Honestly, I am so happy. I have never seen my son so excited about anything. He just loves David to death."

"That is so wonderful. What's not to love? David is such a great guy and you went through the ringer with your last marriage. You deserve this."

"Thanks Nadia. You know what? You're right! I do deserve this, god damn it. I'm a nice person. I have worked hard to be a good, single mom. Maybe it's just my turn to get a little love and respect. Why not?"

"You're damn right girl! You're awesome and so am I and we should be worshipped like the goddesses we are!" They both had a good chuckle at that.

They spent the morning moving some furniture around and unpacking Nadia's stuff while dancing around and singing to some great tunes.

Nadia decorated the space with her own touches. She hung some colourful batiks she had bought at the Honduran market on Commercial drive. She collected dried flowers and ferns and made a corner piece in a blue glass vase from the thrift shop. She hung photos of herself and Sam and their friends from various fun outings. She loved the feeling of having their own place to start fresh. It was her first time nesting away from her parents and she suddenly felt all grown up.

They took a break for lunch and Lisa made sandwiches. While they were eating, she surprised Nadia with some big news.

"My period is four days late."

"Is that unusual for you?" Nadia asked.

"Yah, I am usually like clockwork. Maybe it's psychological, but I think my boobs are kind of sore too."

"Jesus girl, have you mentioned this to David yet?"

"No, I don't want to alarm him unnecessarily before I know it's really something. He just moved in for Christ's sake."

"Okay well why don't we go get a pee test right now and put your mind at ease?"

"I'm not sure I'm ready for the truth yet." Lisa sounded scared.

"I will be here to lean on," Nadia coaxed her. "You really need to find out, one way or another."

Lisa acquiesced, so Nadia drove to the drugstore. Then she stood outside the bathroom door. After waiting the required three minutes, she could hear Lisa swearing.

"Shit, shit, shit, shit."

She came out and showed Nadia the positive lines on the pee stick. Nadia gave her a long hug.

"So, what are you thinking?"

"Well I guess that depends on David's reaction. I would love for Isaac to have a sibling, but I have no idea if David is ready for such a big upheaval. I know that having an abortion would be a lot tougher for me this time around."

Nadia knew she was referring to the time when Sam had got Lisa pregnant at the end of high school. Neither of them was anywhere near ready for a kid at that point. He had taken off to Africa and left her to get the abortion alone. Nadia had not been impressed with this story when Lisa first told her, but she had never confronted Sam about it. She was deliberately avoiding an ugly conversation.

"Well I'm here for you girl, whatever you decide. Call me after you talk to David and if you need someone to go to the clinic with you, I'm there. I will drive you and stay with you after, if you have sedation."

"Thanks Nadia. You're the best. I'll let you know what happens either way. But please don't tell Sam or Susan or Alex until we figure this out okay?"

"I promise. This is between you and David right now. I get how you need some privacy to sort this out. It's a huge deal."

They finished hanging up Nadia's photos and placing her plants in the windows. Nadia thanked Lisa and hugged her new friend as she left for the day. That night she had a hard time keeping the news to herself. She wondered what she would do in the same situation. Lisa had a good job working nights in the hospital laundry. It was unionised and she would get maternity benefits for sure, so money wasn't the issue. She also had a reliable partner now, so that was a huge bonus. Nadia wondered how David would react to becoming a father. He was such a natural with Isaac and really, let's face it, they weren't getting any younger. These were the prime, baby-making years. Nadia had always resented having older parents who never wanted to do fun things like camping or going on rides at the fair. She knew that David would be the most fun dad ever, so why not take the plunge?

Two days later, she got the call she had been waiting for

from Lisa.

They were going to have a baby! Nadia was overjoyed for them. David was going to tell Alex and Sam at work that day. Nadia was dying to call Susan, but figured it was Lisa's news to share. Half an hour after she hung up with Lisa, she got a call from Susan.

"Isn't it amazing?" Susan sounded so excited. "My little one is going to have a playmate!"

"I know, it's fantastic news. Lisa was freaking out at first, but now it's all good."

"So, when are you going to join the party?" Susan teased her.

"Well I haven't even settled into a full-time job yet. Give me a second to catch up to you bitches. I don't want to live in the poorhouse."

"Well life happens when you least expect it." Susan was not letting this go.

"Okay friend, whatever you say. I wonder if David and Lisa will get married?"

It turned out they had no intention of marrying. They both felt it was an unnecessary piece of paper, Lisa because of her previous troubles in that department and David because he was a bit of an anarchist at heart.

Nadia had just started her teaching practicum and it was going well. She loved her sponsor teacher Marion, and the grade six class was really sweet, except for one boy who was challenging. After a long chat with Marion, she found some tricks to bring him on side and felt quite proud of herself. They were now bonding over his favourite video game and rock collection. The work was tiring, for sure, but rewarding. She couldn't wait to get hired in the fall and start earning a real pay cheque to pay off her loans.

When the time came for Susan to give birth, Nadia was invited to come into the delivery room, along with Alex and Susan's mom. Nadia was psyched about it and spent much of the day rubbing Susan's lower back and reassuring Alex that everything was fine. Nadia loved the whole experience, even when Susan was moaning in pain, she felt it was a calling to cheer on her friend and enthusiastically tell her what a great job she was doing. After ten hours, Susan pushed out a slime-coated baby girl who had all her required parts and was deemed healthy. After the nurses cleaned her up, she was actually really cute. They all took turns holding her and cooing with admiration. Nadia felt closer to Susan than ever before. Susan and Alex named their daughter Raina.

Six months later, Lisa had a baby girl called Malory and David's heart exploded. They moved into a bigger apartment before the birth, but they were still in East Vancouver. Isaac became a doting big brother who loved to coo over his baby sister and giggle at her funny, poop faces and smelly diapers. The new family settled into their new routine and life seemed wonderful for them.

During the summer break of 1990, Nadia and Sam were married in a casual, outdoor wedding. They had borrowed a friend's cabin in the sticks outside of Revelstoke B.C. and all their friends camped out for the weekend. The ceremony was officiated by a local Justice of the Peace, who rode up on a horse. There was a beer keg in a clawfoot bathtub, a live band, a pig roast, tiki torches and tents pitched everywhere. Everyone said it was the best wedding ever.

In September, Nadia got a full-time position teaching grade four and life with Sam was good. They were finally able to pay their bills comfortably and her commute to work was easy. She loved her classroom and the staff seemed really welcoming and supportive of her as the newbie. Sam enjoyed making dinner, so Nadia would mark her spelling tests and plan for the next day while he cooked. Their life fell into an easy rhythm and they were lucky enough to have weekends off together at this early stage in their careers.

Susan had finished her maternity leave and went back to selling photocopiers. Her mom was babysitting two days a week and she had a neighbour for the other days. Baby Raina was thriving as she started to crawl and then walk. Alex loved his daughter to bits and couldn't wait for her to be old enough to play t-ball and all the other sports he loved. Alex was a natural jock, so he wanted to coach her teams and imagined her as a natural athlete like himself, although that remained to be seen.

Sam kept begging Nadia because he couldn't wait to become a dad. Once Nadia agreed to have a baby, she got pregnant quite quickly. The first few months were a bit rough and Nadia had to pull over on the drive to work a couple of times to barf into a plastic bag, drink ginger ale, eat soda crackers and then keep going. Then came the triple H's: heartburn, haemorrhoids and heat of summer. Sam would rub ice chips on the back of her neck and bring her Dairy Queen blackberry milkshakes to ease the discomfort of getting bigger. They bought a plastic kiddie pool so she could sit in cold water out on the deck like a sack of hot potatoes.

The next fall, baby Stella was born. She was cheerful and smiley from the start and Nadia had a year off from teaching. For now, Susan was only working part-time selling photocopiers. She would come over often and they hung out together on the back porch in Babyland, drinking coffee and talking, with two playpens between them. Alex had finished his surveyor's course and got hired at David and Sam's geology firm, so all three couples had enough money to pay the bills now, which was a big relief.

Occasionally, the three moms would all get sitters or Grandmas to take the babies and they would go out drinking and dancing to feel relevant again, if just for one night. Even the hangover the next day was a welcome diversion from their day to day routine. They had sewn their wild oats for almost a decade, but still felt prematurely old and wondered how they had reached adulthood so fast.

Chapter Five
Nadia and Sam

The first year of baby Stella's life was wonderful. Nadia had never experienced such joy as watching Sam interact with their daughter. Whenever he made her laugh by dancing around the kitchen with cooking pots on his head, she felt like her heart would explode. Stella looked like him a lot and he clearly adored her. The first thing he would do when he got home from work was to cuddle and coo with her and then throw her up in the air and catch her over and over, as she giggled wildly with joy. He even took part in all the feeding and changing routines willingly. Nadia thought he was a great dad.

On the weekends they would walk down Commercial Drive with Stella in the stroller and usually grab a nice, greasy bacon and egg breakfast at their local, cheap cafe. Stella would mash hash browns between her fingers happily and watch the other customers intently. Then they would go home and put Stella down for her nap and sometimes make love before falling into a contented, deep sleep themselves. Then in the evenings, they would get together with Susan and Alex or Lisa and David and order in Chinese food, drink a few beers and watch a movie while the kids played on the floor. It was a happy time for all of them in Babyland.

Suddenly, things started to change. Sam's curly, brown hair and big, brown eyes couldn't make up for the fact that he was becoming sullen and withdrawn. Nadia was getting understandably worried. She had never seen him like this. Some days he couldn't even get out of bed and he had to call in sick several times over the course of a month. He would curl up in the foetal position for days in bed and not eat or talk to her. Nadia was desperate so she called Sam's brother, John. She explained about his mood and behaviour and started crying on the phone. John sympathised, and told her he had seen this, many times, throughout Sam's life and that he was prone to these bouts of depression.

"Well why has he never sought treatment then?" she asked.

"He did get counselling from our mom's friend, Ruben over the years and he tried naturopathic remedies, but mom doesn't believe in medication to solve these issues."

"Well that's the stupidest thing I've ever heard!" Nadia couldn't help blurting this out, she was so frustrated. "He obviously needs medication. He's a total mess! He can't even get out of bed, never mind going to work."

"Okay Nadia, calm down."

"Calm down? Are you kidding me? You don't have to live with him in a relationship like this. Can't you help me get him to a doctor?"

"Well, it will be challenging, but I can try." John said he would be over in an hour.

After a long discussion behind the closed bedroom door, John emerged with Sam and he was actually dressed. John gave Nadia a private thumbs up and the two of them left without saying a word.

When they returned two hours later, Sam went straight into the bedroom, got back into bed and shut the door. John sat down with Nadia at the kitchen table.

"Well, the doctor talked him into doing a trial of meds and I got him to take his first pill. He needs to take one every morning for two weeks and then he has a follow-up appointment. Here's the details. It's an antidepressant, but it could take up to three weeks to be fully effective."

"Thank you so much John. You have no idea how much I appreciate this. You're a life-saver."

"You're welcome, but just don't tell my mom about this. Like I said, she doesn't approve of meds."

"What's with all the secrets in this family?" Nadia complained. "How is anyone supposed to support each other with half-truths and denial?"

"Well, she's sixty-three years old. She's not going to change her opinion just because you say so. Maybe if Sam sees a real improvement and feels better, then he can convince her himself why it's important to take the drugs."

"God, I hope so. I find her attitude to be so retrograde. Next thing I know she'll be telling me not to take birth control either."

"Okay Nadia, now you're just being silly. She's not that bad. She just believes in more holistic treatment, that's all."

"Yah, and it's hippy-dippy bullshit. If modern science has given us better ways of coping, why not embrace them? Sam needs all the help he can get."

John agreed with her and they hugged it out. He left her to make Sam some chicken noodle soup, which he had apparently requested, and things gradually turned around. The medication worked quite quickly, and Sam was able to return to work the following week, much to Nadia's relief. He apologised to her for being such a pain in the ass and they had a long talk about how his mother's attitudes had done him a serious disservice over the course of many years. He even agreed to go for counselling to try and stay the course. Their relationship stabilised and they got back to their 'happy place' over the next few months.

Then, when Stella was a year old, there came a phone call one morning that changed Nadia's perspective.

"Is Sam there?" a female voice asked.

"No, I'm sorry, he's at work. Can I take a message?"

"Yah, tell him it's Crystal and I'm in town for a few days and would love to get together."

When Sam got home that evening, Nadia asked,

"Who is this Crystal that wants to get together with you?"

"Um, that's an old girlfriend from three years ago."

Nadia felt a wave of jealousy come over her.

"Great. What does she want with you now then? Doesn't she know you're married with a kid now?"

"Yah, I'm sure Lisa told her that. They keep in touch."

"So, was this Crystal also part of your high school crowd?"

"Um, nope. She's fifty. "

"Fifty! What the fuck? Are you sleeping with grannies now?"

"Don't be so judgmental. She's an awesome lady. You would really like her."

"God, do you have mommy issues or something?" Nadia couldn't stop herself. She heard her own voice and hated that she sounded like a shrew.

"Okay, can we drop this now?" Sam implored.

"Are you going to see her?"

"Well how about if I invite her over for dinner and then

you can see that she's not evil."

As it turned out, she wasn't evil, she was really nice and actually very beautiful, which didn't help Nadia feel less jealous. They had shared a period in Sam's life when he was breaking away from his parents' craziness and finding himself and she had been his port in the storm. She was moving back to the city, which made Nadia uneasy. They were a little too close for her liking.

As it turned out, she had good reason to worry because Sam began making secret rendezvous to her place after work to 'talk'. Nadia found out from his credit card statement that he had been in North Vancouver at restaurants on several evenings. She confronted him one night when he came home late.

"So, were you having dinner with Crystal again? Why are you keeping secrets from me?"

"We are just catching up. You don't need to get all crazy about it. There's nothing going on."

Nadia felt so insecure that she phoned Lisa and walked over to her place for coffee the next day. Lisa had been such a supportive friend and confidante lately. Hopefully she knew about his relationship with Crystal and could clarify what was really going on. Nadia explained what was troubling her, as Stella and Malory played on the carpet.

"This Crystal thing is driving me insane. I think he's having an affair. He tells me it's just a friendship, but I can't handle it."

Lisa reassured her. "They have been friends for years and I promise you Crystal would not sleep with him when he's married to you and has a kid. She raised her own kid on her own and has too much respect for us single moms to do that.

She is just a good ear for him, because she knows all the shit he's been through with his parents."

"Okay if you say so, but I'm finding it hard to trust him. Also, he's been drinking a lot more lately and that worries me too."

"Sam has suffered from bouts of depression since he was a kid. The drinking is his coping mechanism."

"Well that's a lousy coping mechanism, especially when he's already taking antidepressants. Booze makes you more depressed and it's a dangerous mix. Should I say something to him about my jealousy issues or leave it alone?"

"I would show him that you trust him with Crystal. Bring her in closer, like maybe if you call her up and get together with her yourself, this will all blow over."

Nadia took Lisa's advice and met with Crystal for coffee. After a few minutes of friendly chat, she couldn't help herself.

"Are you and Sam having an affair?" she blurted out.

"Oh my God. Is that what you think? No, no, my dear. I would never do that to you. That ship has sailed. Sam and I are just good friends."

Nadia apologised for being so insecure. She felt like an idiot. Crystal was really sweet and put her at ease and they went on to become good friends. Her sixth sense had been wrong, but not too far wrong. The secrecy and coming home late was a true indicator that something was up. Sam was having an affair, just not with Crystal. What was worse was that Crystal knew this and wasn't letting on. She was his confidante in all the lies.

Nadia started finding little clues that something was amiss, like the credit card receipts that had various outings and gifts that she knew nothing about. She also found long strands of dark hair on the passenger seat in his truck that were not hers and she thought she could smell perfume in there. There was a work trip out of town that Nadia was dying to ask David or Alex to give her details on, but she hesitated to involve them in their best friend's marital drama. She figured that they would be bound to uphold the guy code of silence, so she didn't go there. She sheepishly asked Susan and Lisa if they had heard anything untoward about the three husbands' work trip, but they had nothing negative to tell her. Nadia felt a ball of fear and distrust building in the pit of her stomach.

Their marriage started to unravel fairly quickly from that point. To make matters worse, Sam got laid off from work during a slow-down in business because he was the last guy hired. After a rough Christmas dinner with Nadia's family, Sam took to bed for a week with a serious bout of depression. He wouldn't talk, eat or play with Stella.

Finally, after a week in bed, Sam got up and made himself a cup of coffee. He sat down at the kitchen table and blurted it out.

"I have been sleeping with another woman for the past six months."

Nadia kicked the baby chair across the room and put a hole in the wall. Sam quietly got up and packed a bag.

When Sam resurfaced after running away, Nadia decided that she and Stella would move out of the house into an apartment. This was a stupid decision because she was young and naive and didn't fully understand her legal rights. She ended up losing her half of the house because Sam negotiated a lousy deal to sell it quickly below the value of their mortgage.

Moving day was the most depressing scene ever. She

made the mistake of letting Sam and his work friend Dan help with the move because he had a truck that was free of charge. She felt so much anger and bitterness every time Sam carried some of their joint belongings into her new space that she just wanted to punch him in the head. Thank God little Stella was at her mother's house for the weekend. There was little conversation after it was done; he unceremoniously left, and she sat on the floor in the middle of all the boxes and bawled her eyes out. It was one of her lowest moments ever.

After falling asleep on the sofa for an hour, she woke up, looked around at the mess of boxes and called Susan.

"Hi there. It has been a really rough day, but it's done. I'm in the apartment."

"Oh my god girl, I'm so sorry. You knew this was going to be hard right?"

"I should never have let Sam help me. It was a huge mistake."

"Yah, I was wondering how that was going to work. Can I come over now and help you unpack?"

"That would be amazing. I can't even face where to start right now. It's so overwhelming."

"I'll be there in half an hour. Do you want food?"

"Just bring me a large coffee with double cream and sugar please and something sweet."

"You got it girl. I'll stop at Starbucks on the way."

"God, I love you right now. See you soon."

They started with Stella's room and made it look as much like her old room as possible, with the exception of substituting a small bookcase for her old shelves. They displayed all her favourite stuffies, figurines and toys and made up her bed. Then they moved to the kitchen for the essentials of daily life. They made up Nadia's bed and moved the living room furniture into place. Finally, Susan hooked up the TV and by midnight it was livable.

Susan crashed on the couch and went to find them take-out breakfast sandwiches the next morning. They finished setting up the bathroom with all Stella's tub toys and made her a nice, little craft table outside on the patio. They hung a few pictures on the wall to make it look like a home and by noon, Susan had to leave so that Alex could go to baseball. Nadia thanked her about a thousand times, and they hugged good-bye.

When Nadia's mom dropped Stella off at the new apartment, she was very excited to see her new home, but confused. At three years old, she couldn't quite grasp the concept of moving. She kept asking, "Where's Daddy going to sleep?" This forced Nadia to put on a brave face and tell her that he was going to be staying at the old house, but she could still see him whenever she wanted, which she knew was a lie. Nadia already guessed that his selfishness would mean that she could only see him on his terms. Thankfully Stella was distracted enough by all the cute new spaces in the apartment, to forget about Daddy for a little while and she played while Nadia had tea with her mom.

"Thank you so much for keeping her for two days mom. I couldn't have done this without you."

"Of course, honey. She was a delight, but I am a little tired, to be honest. I'm not used to the energy level of a little one anymore."

"I know. She's busy all the time."

"How did it go with Sam?"

"It was awful mom. It was silent treatment other than telling him and his friend where to put things and then he got the hell out. It was all I could do not to scream at him."

"Well I don't blame you, after all the cheating and lies. He's not winning any father of the year award any time soon. So how did you get so much set up in a day Nadia? You must be exhausted."

"Oh, Susan was here overnight mom. She did so much work. I could never have done it without her."

"That girl is an angel. We should do something nice for her. Let me get her a thank you gift. What would she like?"

"Wow, that would be awesome. I know she's had her eye on a pair of boots at the Fox and Fluevog store in Gastown, so maybe a gift card?"

"Okay, consider it done. I will mail it to her and sign both our names. Is that okay?"

"Of course. Thank you so much mom. She will love that."

"It's the least I can do. She has been such an amazing friend to you over the years."

"That's an understatement. I would be lost without her… and without you of course. I'm really lucky to have you and dad as a back-up. I can't imagine how women with kids go through divorce without any support system. It must be so brutal."

"You're right Nadia. I had a friend at work who had immigrated from El Salvador and when her marriage ended, she was very alone. I tried to rally some of the staff to help her out. It was a bad time."

"That is so nice mom. You're a bloody saint."

"Well I wouldn't go that far Nadia. I just try to notice when people around me are struggling. Just having someone to talk to is half the battle."

"I love you mom. Thanks again for watching Stella all weekend."

They hugged good-bye and Josephine left. Nadia got dinner ready and let Stella eat on her small table while watching Barney the Dinosaur. Then she gave her a bath and read her a favourite story in her new bedroom. Stella organised her favourite stuffies around her on the bed, as she read and when Nadia finished, she asked:

"Why is daddy sleeping in the old house?"

"Well my love, mommy and daddy can't live together anymore, so we have two houses now."

"Why?"

"Well, your daddy and I decided it is better if we live apart now."

"Don't you love him anymore?"

"Well, I guess I will always love him because he is your daddy, but I will love him in a different way now, that's all. It will be more like I love my close friends, like Susan. Does that make sense?"

"I guess so, but I still love daddy too."

"Of course you do sweetheart, and I love you!" She kissed her and gave her a big squeeze. Then thankfully she fell asleep quite quickly.

Nadia flopped into bed, cried a little and fell into a deep exhausted sleep.

The humiliation had only just started for Nadia. Having moved into a small apartment with Stella during the division of assets period, she gradually disclosed to her friends that they were divorcing. Then all these sordid stories started coming out. Their closest circle of friends had apparently been fully aware of his multiple cheating episodes and had withheld them from her. She was devastated. She felt her whole life unravelling. She was enraged at Sam, but also felt betrayed by their friends. His six-month relationship with a work colleague named Sacha was only the most serious, long-term affair. He had slept with women at various social gatherings, she would now have to replay over and over in her mind. How had she missed all those signals? She felt like such a damn fool. The German tourist girl who had stayed at his brother's place, the time in Whistler when he drove another girl home who said she wasn't feeling well, the weekend he went to his Uncle's cabin… it was all too much to process. Nadia retreated into loneliness and despair.

She could barely muster the strength to go to work and be a decent parent. After teaching all day she was exhausted. She would pick up Stella from day care, get her a snack and a drink, put cartoons on and fall asleep on the couch while she was playing. Then she would drag herself up to cook dinner, read her a bedtime story and tuck her in. She did not feel like a good mother, she felt abandoned and alone and cried herself to sleep many nights. She leaned heavily on her mother to take Stella on the weekends for a few hours so she could have a break from single parenting.

Meanwhile, as if to rub it in her face, Sam had met a new girlfriend almost immediately who had a daughter the same age as Stella and they were moving to England. Part of her was furious about how he could abandon his own child to go and raise somebody else's, but part of her was relieved; good riddance! She was tired of the miserable exchanges back and forth with him as he visited his daughter. Once, in a rage, she had told him she wished he were dead. She was not proud of this encounter, but she was shocked that he was turning out to be a deadbeat dad by not paying her child support regularly. It was only in dribs and drabs whenever it suited him.

The worst part was that Stella was suffering from his neglect. He would bring her home after an overnight visit all wound up, dirty, dishevelled and worn out. Nadia would have to pick up the pieces and get her calmed down, bathed and caught up on sleep for day care the next day. She was upset and would throw tantrums and scream for hours at a time. Nadia's lowest point ever was throwing a cup of water in her daughter's face once after an hour of screaming, to try and snap her out of it. She would never share this with anyone or forgive herself. She felt so ashamed of being a lousy mother in that moment.

Nadia ended up consulting a paediatrician and enacting some behavioural strategies to help her cope. Stella was responding well to her weekly rewards chart on the fridge and was happier focusing on helping mommy with getting dressed or ready for bed to earn stickers on her chart and a small prize of her choice at the end of the week. Perhaps it took her mind off her father. Who knows, but it certainly helped to curb the tantrums. Nadia felt like she was a better parent and back in control of her life.

Adding to her difficulties, Nadia couldn't stomach seeing Sam's mother Brenda anymore, even though she knew that Stella should maintain a relationship with both her grandmas. Brenda had obviously sided with her son in their divorce and had even gone so far as to tell Nadia that she was being too controlling in their marriage and that's what caused him to stray. That was rich! Talk about having blinders on. Nadia couldn't stand seeing her or even talking to her at this point.

She felt like her whole vision of family was crumbling around her into ruins.

Settling into their new life, Nadia gradually found the nearby grocery store, library, spray parks and recreation centre and settled into a routine. Life seemed tolerable again and they were having lots of happy parent and tot moments together.

One day, Nadia took her down to Trout Lake Park for a walk on a beautiful, sunny day. There was nobody around on the far side of the lake and they felt peaceful surrounded by nature. Nadia picked up a woolly bear caterpillar to show Stella and she was brave enough to let it run over her arm. She giggled and told her mom how it tickled her skin. You could feel the summer turning to fall and soon Nadia would have to go back to work; the first leaves were changing and beginning to curl.

They got about two hundred yards down the path and suddenly Stella dropped to the ground like a sack of potatoes right in front of Nadia. She went into panic mode and fell on her knees, bending over her daughter whose eyes were fluttering. Then her little girl passed out. Nadia's heart was racing! She bent down to feel her daughter's breath on her cheek and called her name repeatedly. She took her water bottle and wet her own hands and put cold water on Stella's cheeks and the back of her neck. Stella came to in about ten seconds, but still looked woozy and wasn't talking. With her adrenaline racing, Nadia scooped the heavy child up into her arms and began to run back to the car. Their medical clinic was only a few blocks away and she thought it would be faster than calling an ambulance, so she placed Stella beside her in the front seat and drove like a maniac.

She carried her in and said loudly to the group of women

working at reception:

"She just passed out. Please get a doctor to look at her straight away!"

They sprang into high gear and she was taken right in, despite a large group in the waiting room, where nobody seemed to object.

Stella was starting to wake up and look more alert and after a thorough examination, the doctor said she seemed fine, but he was concerned that her heart rate seemed to fluctuate a little and he wanted to get that checked out by a specialist. He got her a rushed referral to the hospital for the following day, told her to keep Stella resting and hydrated for the rest of the day and to sleep with her that night. He also said to call an ambulance if anything changed suddenly.

Nadia felt both relieved and worried at the same time. What if she had a heart problem? After all the stress of divorce, this would be so terrible she didn't know how she would cope. She tried to push it out of her mind.

The rest of the day Stella seemed normal. After she rested and watched TV for a while, she got up and played with her toys and appeared quite energetic again. She ate quite a bit of her dinner and the night went without incident.

The following day, they went for the hospital appointment and they gave her an ECG. Stella was fascinated by the suction cups all over her chest and the nurse was so nice and funny that she was relaxed and happy. Then the doctor met with them and said he noticed a small fluctuation that he wanted to examine further. He put a radio-halter on her body, which was like a little strappy jacket with a battery pack of some sort attached to it. Stella had to wear this for twenty-four hours and then bring it back the next day.

The follow-up appointment revealed that she had a heart murmur, but the doctor assured Nadia that this was very common in young children and that she would probably grow out of it by adolescence. Nadia was so relieved. She asked about any restrictions in activity and he said there were none, but Nadia knew she wouldn't be walking in the woods with Stella again any time soon. The whole ordeal had been terrifying.

After several months in hiding, Nadia started to confide in her most trusted friends, Susan and Lisa. Susan and Alex still lived close enough in East Vancouver to visit in the evenings after work. Sometimes Nadia would pick Stella up from day care and go straight there for supper. After they ate, Alex was kind enough to watch both kids and let them talk for an hour, uninterrupted on the back deck with a cold beer. Susan would naturally commiserate with Nadia over all of Sam's obvious shortcomings as a husband and father. She seemed genuinely disappointed in Sam for letting Nadia down so glaringly and abandoning his daughter. Even Alex concurred that, from a male perspective, this was shocking. He kept saying that he could never leave his kid, no matter how angry an ex-wife became.

Lisa and David's place also became a safe harbour during this difficult period in Nadia's life. Most weekends she would pack a bag and take Stella over there. Stella loved playing with Malory, which allowed Nadia and Lisa to talk for hours, relax by the kiddy pool or cook meals together. Isaac would entertain the two little girls by making funny faces or flopping onto the floor suddenly, barking like a dog. David would go mountain biking or just hang out with them. It was so nice of him to allow her to monopolise his wife's attention all weekend.

Lisa was a good ear. She knew all about Sam's penchant for running away, as Sam had left her high and dry, pregnant at age eighteen, while he tripped off to Africa for the adventure of his life. Lisa explained Sam's frequent bouts of depression since he was a child, possibly resulting from his father's alcoholism or from his mother's flighty affairs with much younger men that ended in a messy divorce. Of course, none of this excused Sam for being such a shitty father, but it helped Nadia to understand why. Nadia started to realise that running away was Sam's way of dealing with, or not dealing with, any problems in his life. He was a serial user of women with no sense of commitment or responsibility. She felt ashamed of herself for marrying such a loser. How could she have been so blind?

Sometimes Alex and David would be away at the same time on an out-of-town job, so the three moms would lean on each other for support. They became each other's lifeline by picking up groceries and medicine or babysitting. When the weather was nice, the three toddlers would play in the yard while their moms caught up on all their problems with husbands and ex-husbands and compared developmental milestones. It was a great trio of friendship and laughter that uplifted them all and helped Nadia overcome her feelings of loss. Thank God she had her parents close by and these wonderful friends to share her pain with.

East Vancouver was their neighbourhood during these challenging years. They all loved to push their strollers along Commercial Drive to get out of the house. There were lots of cool cafes where they could meet for a cappuccino. There were cheap greengrocers and Italian delis to shop in. Once in a while they would swim with their toddlers at Britannia pool or go to a read-aloud at the library there. They could walk around Trout Lake to commune with nature or listen to buskers or poets perform at outdoor summer gigs. It was a wonderful community to raise their kids in and they all felt like they were part of something bigger than their own little day to day problems.

Chapter Six
The Incident

One fine summer day at Lisa and David's house, Nadia was having coffee with Susan and Lisa in the kitchen while their three girls played in the bedroom. They were discussing the recent problems between Susan and her husband Alex.

Susan complained, "I'm fed up with Alex always mountain biking on Saturday mornings while I'm stuck at home looking after Raina. I feel like a bike widow."

Lisa concurred, "If my David did that, I would cut his balls off. No seriously though, have you told him how you feel?"

"Yah, I tried, but it's like he's not hearing me. He says it's important to blow off steam after a long work week to keep his sanity."

Nadia chimed in, "Maybe you should hide his bike at my place for a week to make your point."

Suddenly there was a blood curdling scream from the bedroom. They all ran in there to find Stella and Raina staring at Malory, who was lying on the floor screaming and holding her wrist, which looked distended and was starting to swell up.

"What the hell happened here?" Lisa asked.

Stella spoke up, "Raina pushed her and she fell and hit the dresser."

Susan was horrified. "Raina, why did you push Malory?"

"She pulled the head off my Barbie," Raina said sheepishly.

Lisa yelled at the top of her lungs, "Get the fuck away from my daughter you little bully!"

She grabbed Malory and ran out of the room to the bathroom, slamming the door behind her.

Susan implored Raina, "What were you thinking? You really hurt Malory. Let's go young lady. You can apologise later when things calm down. Sorry Nadia but we have to go."

She grabbed Raina, bundled up her clothes, and hurried to their car.

Nadia quickly got Stella dressed, gathered up her purse and left. She leaned against the bathroom door for a moment, where the crying had quietened to gentle sobbing, and tried to comfort her friend.

"Bye Lisa. I'm so sorry this happened. Let me know if there's anything I can do."

Lisa entered the hospital emergency ward looking completely harried. Her long blonde hair was dishevelled, and her mascara smudged under her eyes. She was carrying Malory, who had stopped crying but was now calm and getting sleepy.

"My daughter needs to see a doctor right away."

"What's the emergency?" the receptionist asked her, deadpan.

Lisa whispered, leaning across the counter, "My child has been beaten up and I think her wrist is broken."

"Oh dear, I'm so sorry. Please take a seat and fill out this form and we will get her in as quickly as possible."

After about fifteen minutes of Malory's quiet sobbing, they took her in.

"Hello there Mrs. Delaney and this must be Malory. Let's have a look at that wrist."

Lisa burst into tears. "Malory was playing with a few friends in the bedroom and one of the girls pushed her into the dresser."

"I'm so sorry dear. Let me examine her. Is it okay if I give her something for the pain right now?"

"Sure, sure, of course."

"Is she allergic to any medications?"

"No."

He gave a colourful, glass, holographic globe to distract her while he quickly gave her a shot. She didn't even notice or cry.

"Okay, I'm going to send her for an x-ray right away and then we will either cast it or she may need surgery to re-set the bone."

Twenty minutes later the doctor shared his conclusions.

"I'm afraid the bone is at a bit of a difficult angle, so we really do need the surgery. When was the last time she ate or drank anything?"

Lisa kept a brave face for her daughter, even though she was scared. Things started happening very quickly. She signed the consent form and they wheeled Malory off. While Lisa waited, she tried to get a hold of David, but he was working in a remote area and the office couldn't get a hold of him. They paged him for a call-back to his wife.

After the surgery, Malory came back with a cast on her arm and a prescription for pain medicine.

"Can I get a referral for some counselling for Malory, in case she is upset after this?"

"Yes, of course you can. I can you refer you to a local

child psychologist and reception will call you with an appointment."

"Thank you so much doctor. I really appreciate it. Okay Malory, let's go home and get you something to eat and you can watch your favourite show."

"Yay, you mean the Smurfs, right?"

"Of course, my love. We can have some chicken strips with your favourite creamy dip."

"Yay, I love chicken strips!"

They left the office and Lisa was feeling very relieved and exhausted.

This was just before everyone carried cell phones around, so Lisa had not been able to get in touch with her husband David at work all day because he was out in the field doing surveying. When he got home, he found Lisa asleep on the couch with Malory watching TV. This was a bit unusual because she usually had dinner ready when he got home from work. He kissed his daughter on the head and saw the cast on her arm. Lisa stirred.

"Holy shit! What the hell happened?" David asked.

"It was the day from hell," Lisa said. "You have no freakin' idea."

She proceeded to explain everything that happened, from the playdate to the doctor's office. David was understandably upset.

"Jesus Christ! What a little bully that kid is!" He scooped up his daughter and gave her a big hug.

"Are you okay sweetie?"

"Sure daddy. I just got an owie so the doctor gave me a 'noperation' and he said I was brave and gave me a candy."

"A candy, eh? Well that sounds nice. What flavour was

it?" David tried to deflect.

"Grape."

"Yum, that's my favourite. Maybe I should go to the hospital too?"

"Don't be silly daddy. You don't have a big owie."

"No, I guess I don't," he smiled at Lisa.

After Malory went into her playroom, David thought out loud, "What the hell am I going to say to Alex tomorrow at work? Christ this is awkward."

Lisa said emphatically, "Well I'm not going to see Susan or Raina anymore. I'm done! If she can't control her daughter better than that, I don't want Malory anywhere near her!"

"Damn it, Lisa, you're putting me in a very awkward position. Alex is my best friend."

"Well I'm sorry about that. You can still be friends with Alex if you want, but I'm not having that kid over here ever again."

David decided he'd better let things cool down a bit, so he changed the subject.

"Do you want me to order a pizza or something?"

"That would be great. I'm actually starving. I kind of forgot to eat all day with all this upheaval. I did manage to feed Malory when we got home though, but she'll probably eat again."

"I think we need a glass of wine, right now!" David went to the fridge and then phoned to place the pizza order.

Later that evening, he put his daughter to bed and tucked her in.

"Can you show daddy your cast?" he asked sheepishly.

"Sure daddy." She held up her arm.

"Oh dear, that looks sore. Can I draw a smiley face on it?"

"Yup, and mummy said if I let her give me more Ty-re-nol in the morning, she will make me a Minnie Mouse pancake."

"Well that sounds wonderful. I want one too."

"No daddy, you have to have a Mickey Mouse pancake because you are a boy!"

"Oh, alright then. I'm sure glad I've got you to explain all the breakfast rules. Nighty-night my little buttercup." He smiled and kissed her on the forehead and turned on the night-light.

The next morning, Alex came by at the usual time to pick David up but this time he honked the horn and waited out in the car, instead of coming in to refill his travel mug with coffee like he usually did. When David got into the car, he started in on Alex right away.

"So, what the fuck dude? This is such a mess. My wife is out of her mind, angry about what happened."

"I know. I'm so sorry man. I wish I had been there to separate the kids before they started rough-housing," Alex said.

"I'm actually kind of pissed that they were in the bedroom with the door shut in the first place," David said.

"Dude, they're only five! I think Raina just got carried away and got a bit too rough. She would never hurt Malory on purpose."

"Well I hope you're right, but I have no idea how I'm going to get Lisa to see things differently. She's calling it bullying."

"Bullying? That's insane! Raina would never hurt Malory on purpose!" Alex was getting really upset.

"Okay, okay, maybe you're right. I really don't know. But

she definitely seems to have some kind of anger issues. I'm pretty pissed that my daughter has a broken wrist."

"God, I'm so sorry man. That is just awful. I can't explain what was going on while they were playing that made her so mad, but Raina knows she's done something really wrong, believe me. She was quiet as a mouse when I got home yesterday. I couldn't even get her to smile and she refused to play Trouble with me after dinner and that is our daily routine. Susan feels so terrible about all of this. It's eating her up inside. She was crying off and on all evening. This whole thing's so messed up. Please David, I'm begging you, let's try and stay calm and be the rational ones here. There's enough drama between Lisa, Susan and Nadia that we should probably stay out of it as much as possible. Hopefully time will heal all wounds."

"I wish Sam was still around to help Lisa cope with all this. They have known each other since grade five. He could have played mediator between her and Susan. I think he would have understood better what to say to get through to Lisa," David said.

"Sam can go to hell," Alex blurted out. "He has hardly been a good dad to Stella this past year. What does he know about taking care of his little girl? Nadia has been doing everything on her own. Personally, I think he's as useless as tits on a bull." Alex suddenly heard himself and realised that this was in no way helpful.

David was losing patience. "Well let's get going or we'll be late for work. I definitely don't want to talk about this at work or in front of anybody else really ever, so don't bring it up," he said.

"I couldn't agree more." Alex drove away from the curb

and turned on some music to break up the tension in the car.

Up at the university library, Nadia was busy looking up some information to try and educate herself on child development to better understand what had happened between the children. This is what she found:

'Here's a list of what paediatricians say is normal rough play behaviour in young children:

Benefits of rough-and-tumble play:

•Children can develop key physical, cognitive, social-emotional and language skills.

•They can also practice learning balance and body control.

•Activities like wrestling help little learners refine arm and hand movements.

•Rough-and-tumble play nurtures body awareness.'[1]

So, the type of rough-housing their kids had been playing at in the bedroom was not aberrant for their age. That was a relief. However, something had just made Raina get too rough in that moment; but was it really bullying? Nadia felt completely out of her depth and realised she would probably need a PHD in child psychology to break this down. She left feeling overwhelmed but had to leave it to get to her next class on time.

That evening she called Susan.

"How are you girl? How is Raina doing?"

"Not great. She has been super quiet all day and won't eat much. I think she is still upset about what happened yesterday."

"Well that makes sense. Lisa's reaction was pretty harsh, and she can probably sense that you are upset too and feels guilty about what happened. It will pass, just give Lisa some time. I'm sure she will come around."

"She is so furious that she won't speak to me. I left a message on her answering machine saying how sorry I was. David told Alex that she doesn't want to see me or Raina anymore."

"Holy shit," replied Nadia, "she is so overreacting! They are just little kids. They are going to make mistakes and get hurt. What the hell?"

"She said she took Malory to the hospital and she had emergency surgery to place the bone and cast it. She said her daughter is traumatised, never mind how Raina is doing. She doesn't seem to really understand what happened. She says they were just playing Barbies and then Malory pulled off her doll's head and she got mad. Now I have to explain to her why she can't see her best friend anymore. I feel just terrible about the whole thing."

"Jesus, what a mess. Maybe I can talk to Lisa and try to smooth things over?"

"I wouldn't if I were you. I don't want you to get involved and then for her to be pissed at you too. Just stay out of it please, I'm begging you, for Stella' s sake too."

"Okay, okay, but at least let me help you cheer Raina up. I can take Raina to my place to play so she knows that she still has friends who love her," offered Nadia.

"Oh my God, thank you. That would be awesome. You are the best friend ever."

"Susan, it's a drop in the bucket compared to what you and Alex have done for me since my divorce. I would do anything for you guys."

For the next two weeks Nadia helped Susan almost daily. It was summer holidays, so she wasn't teaching, thank god.

Susan was able to make a doctor's appointment for Raina fairly quickly to get a referral to a child psychologist. She was worried about her because she seemed sad and quiet since the incident with Malory.

Nadia couldn't help worrying in the back of her mind about how she was going to reconnect with Lisa. She didn't know how long she should wait to call her and ask how Malory was doing. She was afraid Lisa somehow blamed her too, since she was Susan's best friend. Lisa hadn't spoken to Alex or Sam either, so it seemed like the husbands were somehow stuck in the middle of this drama.

One morning, Nadia was at Susan's place and she offered to go visit Lisa and act as a buffer.

"I will simply bite the bullet and ask her to come over for coffee."

She went into the other room to call Lisa privately. She came out minutes later with a sombre look on her face.

"What did she say?" asked Susan.

"She said no."

"What do you mean? What did she say exactly?"

"She said she wasn't up for seeing me today, that's all."

"What the fuck does that mean?"

"I'm not sure. Maybe she just needs a little more time to get over this thing. I'm sure she'll come around."

"God damn it." Susan was frustrated. "Why does this all have to be so complicated? They are just little kids. It's nobody's fault that this happened."

"I know, and I totally agree with you, but obviously it's a bigger deal for Lisa. Did you know she was bullied by this tough, older girl all through grade eight and was afraid to even walk home alone? This girl apparently spread nasty rumours and lies about her and would punch her in the hallway between classes."

"What the hell?" Susan was shocked. "No, I didn't know that! How the hell could I have known that?"

"I thought maybe Sam told Alex about it. He knew."

"Christ does everybody know about this except me? No wonder she is freaking out. This must have brought up all kinds of horrible feelings from her past. Now I feel even worse. Can you please ask Sam to call David and tell him that I'm sorry and I'd like to see Lisa soon, and I hope Malory is doing better," Susan pleaded. "God, how did this thing get so fucked up?"

Nadia gave Susan a hug and left with a sinking feeling in the pit of her stomach. Somehow, she sensed that this incident was going to grow into something more insidious.

Chapter Seven
The Rift

Several months went by and it became clear that Lisa had shut Nadia and Susan out of her life. Nadia had tried six times to procure an invite when Alex was going to see David, but she was consistently turned away. It became obvious that Lisa had created two camps in her mind and anyone who supported Susan was in the enemy camp. She even left the kitchen when Alex came to pick up David for work. Nadia couldn't help but try to psychoanalyse what was really going on for Lisa. Was there more to the relationship between the three couples than she knew? Or was this crisis due solely to Lisa reliving her own childhood trauma?

Nadia felt very hurt and disposed of by a treasured friend. Everything was weird now. This new dynamic created all sorts of social problems for their wider circle of friends. The whole party scene with the geologists and their wives became an intricate web of who's in and who's out. Nadia, Susan and Alex were sick about it and felt the incident had been wildly blown out of proportion, but nobody could say or do anything to bring David and Lisa back into the fold. It felt like the end of an era for Nadia's social scene and she was devastated.

Many nights, Nadia would lie awake and think of Lisa and her anger would turn to tears about their lost connection and the rift that it had caused among their network of friends.

There were fewer and fewer social gatherings now and Nadia felt her life getting smaller and smaller. Divorce also seemed to be a systemic affliction of their thirties, with many broken couples scattering to different parts of the city. The internet was in its infancy, so people still phoned each other. Now friends who used to call each other regularly had stopped calling. It seemed that the light-hearted period of their lives was over, replaced by the realities of working and motherhood. Nadia was always tired and received no support from Sam, who was still in England, living with the new girlfriend and her little girl. If it weren't for her parents living close by, Nadia would have had a complete breakdown, but somehow, she kept going, as all single mothers do.

Meanwhile Susan was dealing with her own fallout from that terrible day at Lisa's. Raina began showing signs of social anxiety. She was unable to mix in with other children in any group setting like a playground or party and she was afraid she would not be able to play with the other kids when she started kindergarten. She couldn't explain to her mom why she didn't want to join in. Luckily, Susan had access to counselling for her through work, and quickly got an appointment with a child psychologist who specialised in play therapy.

When they arrived for their first appointment, the therapist observed Raina in an empty playroom through a one-way glass window. Susan was also allowed to observe, but she was supposed to keep silent while the therapist took notes. Raina found a toy doll house and picked up a dolly. She began talking in a high voice about making food in the little kitchen. After five minutes another young girl entered, and then Raina became obviously stressed. She stopped playing altogether and just watched the other girl in fearful silence. When the second child approached her, spoke and picked up another doll, Raina backed off into the corner and sat on a beanbag chair. The other child was being very sweet and bringing her some tiny, plastic food and inviting her to come back, but Raina was frozen. Then a third little girl came in and began playing with the second one quite happily. She walked over and stared at Raina for a minute without saying a word and then went back to ignoring her.

After watching them for a while, the psychologist decided to refer Raina to one of his colleagues who practiced a specialised kind of treatment called Eye Movement Desensitisation and Reprocessing (EMDR). Susan described to Nadia what the therapy was like because she had never heard of it. The therapist began by meeting with Susan to discuss the traumatic incident of watching Lisa screaming at her mother to get out of her house. On the next visit he talked to Raina about the incident and asked her how it made her feel. Raina said it scared her and she felt bad in her tummy. The psychologist sat Raina down in front of a light bar and told her to picture that incident in her mind while following some flashing lights moving side to side with her eyes.

After a second longer meeting with the doctor, Susan was guided through developing a story script about the traumatic incident at Lisa's house and bring it with her next time. They ended the story with Susan and Raina feeling happy and visiting a playground, where she had fun interacting with other children. During their third session, the doctor had Raina draw out a safe space where she liked to go. He told Raina to go there in her mind whenever she felt overwhelmed. Then he sat Raina on her mother's lap and read out the trauma story while tapping rhythmically on Raina's knees. At the end of the story

Raina smiled and said she felt better.

Nadia felt sad for Susan that her child was suffering from the fallout of Lisa's rejection. This furthered her belief that the whole incident had got blown way out of proportion. She wondered what her sister would make of all this, so she decided to share a little bit of Raina's ordeal with her during their next long-distance telephone call.

Rosanne was still living in Alberta and working as a waitress at a busy truck-stop diner where the tips were amazing. She had recently ended her relationship with the older black guy she had originally followed there from BC because he was cheating on her. Now she had an apartment of her own.

"Hiya sis," Nadia began, "how's your life?"

"Good, good. It's getting cold already, but I can't complain. What's up with you? How's Stella doing?"

"Oh, Stella's awesome. She just started going down the big slide at Blue Mountain Park by herself without me standing at the bottom."

"Wow, what a big girl. Is mom gaga over her? I think she's half expecting me to come home pregnant one of these days."

"Oh yah, mom is loving the grandma zone for sure. She tries to get Stella to help her in the garden, which is pretty adorable."

"Any news from your stupid ex-husband?"

"He had the nerve to send Stella photos from England of his new instant family. Can you believe how insensitive that is? He's such an ass."

"Has he sent you any money lately?"

"Of course not. He's way too busy supporting her kid to

support his own. God, I hate him now."

"Yah, men are all shits. I think I'm going to become a lesbian."

"Well good luck with that. So, I have to tell you about the new drama in my life."

Nadia explained what had transpired between Susan, Lisa and their kids. She hoped to get some clarity from her older, more worldly big sister.

She was surprised that Rosanne seemed unmoved about Susan and Raina's plight and much more concerned about little Malory. It was as if she were siding squarely with Lisa.

"Don't you think that Lisa might be having a really hard time too?" Rosanne reminded her to see both sides. "She has to revisit something really painful from her past and try to help her own daughter with the same issues."

"But can you really call it bullying if it was an unintentional act committed by a five- year-old?" Nadia reasoned.

"The effects could be the same in little Malory's mind. How do you know it was unintentional? How can you inflict that much harm on someone without intention?"

Nadia considered this for a minute. "Well young children may intend to harm, but they surely don't understand the fallout past the next ten seconds of their lives."

"I'm not so sure," Rosanne pondered. "I believe we are born wanting control over our environment and understand these roles quite young. Look how some children boss each other around and try to dominate any game they play. That is no coincidence, because it repeats itself across every culture."

"Geez, I guess you have a point. This is a lot more complex than I thought. I don't know all the details of what happened to Lisa when she was young. I only know that she was bullied by an older girl when she was thirteen."

"Well that's enough to know that she must be really struggling," said Rosanne.

"Okay, I will try and be more open minded," Nadia promised, "but it's hard when Lisa won't even speak to me. I feel like my role right now is to support Susan and Raina. Those are the cards I've been dealt."

"Fair enough," Rosanne agreed. "But hopefully you can mend fences with Lisa sometime in the near future when everyone is feeling less riled up. I would like to be able to come back to Vancouver and hang out with all of you without all this fuss and weirdness going on."

"Me too sis. I hate all this drama and misery. I miss hanging out with them and all the girls playing together. It sucks! Well thanks for listening. I miss having you here to talk to."

They said their goodbyes and promised to keep in touch.

After that call, Nadia decided to do some more research into child psychology to clear up some bigger questions in her mind. She wondered if Raina could have intentionally chosen to hurt Malory that horrible day, or if she really didn't know what she was doing. She needed to know so she'd have some background information when dealing with kids in her career as well.

She looked up bullying in young children on the internet and found some pertinent information straight away. Apparently, bullying could not be an isolated incident. That, in itself, was interesting. Nadia scrolled down through the many available links and then chose the first one that looked simple and clear:

'For a situation to be considered a bullying incident, three indicators must be present:

1.Power — children who bully acquire their power through physical size and strength, by status within the peer group, and by recruiting support of the group.

2.Frequency — bullying is not a random act. It is this factor that brings about the anticipatory terror in the mind of the child being bullied that can be so detrimental and have the most debilitating long-term effects.

3.Intent to harm — children who bully generally do so with the intent to either physically or emotionally harm the other child.

A person who shows bullying behaviour says or does something intentionally hurtful to others and they keep doing it, with no sense of regret or remorse — even when it's obvious that they've hurt the other person or when they're asked to stop.' [2]

Raina definitely did not fit the profile. She was extremely affectionate with Stella, for instance, she would even give her kisses while they were playing. She rarely showed anger, so this seemed to be an isolated incident. In fact, she was socially withdrawn at times, especially if there was a gathering of other unfamiliar children, like at the park or at a birthday party. Sometimes this even looked more like extreme shyness. Mostly, she seemed overly sensitive, which was the opposite of this profile. For instance, Nadia remembered the time when she cried about her father gutting a fish he had caught. She thought it was cruel and refused to come to the dinner table while they were eating it. She was certainly the farthest thing from intimidating.

So how had she done this terrible thing to Malory? Nadia couldn't make sense of it, other than to wonder if she was jealous of Malory playing with Stella and wanted Stella all to herself. If Lisa was calling this bullying, at what point did the child's intention come into play?

That night in bed, Nadia was reflecting on the issue of bullying, when suddenly a memory came to her that she had pushed away, from her childhood. She was about fourteen years old and she was walking home with Susan from the corner store one night. They saw two grade twelve girls approaching and smoking cigarettes, who they recognised from the popular crowd at their high school. As they passed by, the one named Bonnie Carpenter brushed against Nadia, called her a dweeb and kept on walking. A few seconds later, Nadia felt a pinching sensation on her chest. She looked down to find the ember of the cigarette burning into her shirt. She panicked and flicked it away, but it had already burned a hole in her shirt.

Nadia never mentioned this to anyone. Several years later, she was in the kitchen with Rosanne and her mother making lunch. They were talking about a family who lived down the road, when her sister blurted out:

"Melissa Ferguson is a bully."

"Why?" Nadia asked.

"She tried to embarrass me by hanging my bra up in the girls' locker room for everyone to see, while I was in the shower after gym," she explained.

Nadia's mother didn't even blink. She seemingly ignored the whole conversation, but Nadia could tell she was listening as she stirred the macaroni and cheese.

"That's awful. She's probably just jealous because she's

flat," Nadia said.

"Something like that happened to me too," Nadia stated matter-of-factly. She told them the cigarette burn story.

"Really?" her mother sounded surprised. "I can't believe girls do mean things like that."

And that was the end of the conversation. Nobody told her to talk to a teacher or a counsellor about it. Nobody called it bullying. They just ate their lunch as normal. Nadia felt confused, but somewhat relieved that her sister shared a similar experience and it seemed like it was no big deal to her anymore.

Now, as an adult, Nadia reflected on this childhood experience and wondered how little Malory could have been so affected by such a minor play incident with five-year-old Raina. Surely at such a young age, she would have had no understanding of what was happening, other than general pain and then physical healing. Was it Lisa's own trauma from childhood that was being replayed at a louder volume? Is that why there was such a need for counselling? Nadia couldn't help feeling that the backlash against Raina had been much more damaging psychologically. Here was a little girl being rejected by some of her most trusted adults and playmates.

Furthermore, why did Nadia care so much about Lisa's rejection of her? Was it simply because she had lost a treasured confidante? Perhaps it was because she hated conflict and always did her best to mediate situations like this. She honestly felt angrier now that Lisa had such influence over their circle of friends, that she could pull strings and create divisions where none needed to exist. How could she selfishly allow her husband David to throw away his best friend Alex? Alex had even given his son the middle name David because they were such good buddies. It wasn't just the women who had suffered from this rift, it was the men as well; although they did a better job of pushing their feelings way down and pouring beer on them. It was difficult now to plan any social gatherings because they always had to weigh who was in and who was out.

Naida finally fell into a restless sleep and woke up feeling quite groggy. She dragged herself downstairs and poured a cup of coffee. Ten minutes later the telephone rang.

It was Susan calling her with some more bad news.

"Alex has a job offer in Nelson and we are going to be moving up there as soon as Raina finishes her therapy," she announced.

"What? No! This is so shitty Susan. How am I supposed to survive without you? God, I am so mad at you right now."

"Well to be honest, I am fed up with this whole Lisa scene and Alex is pretty fed up with it too. He says I am moping around all the time and he's sick of his daughter being stigmatised as some kind of deviant, bad kid. We need to get away from all this bullshit. It has been really draining for us."

"I know it has girl and I'm so sorry about that, but I will miss you terribly and Stella will miss Raina. How far is Nelson anyways?"

"It's like an eight-hour drive, so we can easily visit each other," Susan said.

"Well not easily because I only get school holidays, but summers for sure I can come up there. I guess you will have to look for a new job as well, right?

"Yah, I will take whatever's available. Maybe I will even get motivated and take a course to upgrade my computer skills. I feel like I need a change."

"Well I guess you can drop Raina off here on the weekends and I will watch the kids while you guys pack up your lives. God this is so shitty."

"Thank you, Nadia you are amazing. I know this really sucks, but we need to get out of the city. There are too many negative emotions here right now. I'm actually looking forward to slowing down, getting into small town life and having more wilderness around me. It will help me clear my head."

"Well I hope you guys are happy up there, but I know I'm really going to be bummed out for a little while after you leave. I will try and just focus on work and Stella and carry on without you. I love you girl."

"I love you too. I'm sorry it has to be this way."

Nadia hung up the phone, put her head down on the breakfast table and cried.

Chapter Eight
Nelson

The week before Christmas 1995, Nadia and five-year-old Stella drove nine hours east to Nelson BC to spend the school holidays with Susan, Alex and their daughter Raina. She had never seen their place and was curious to find out what their new life was like in the Kootenay Mountains. They had rented a little A-frame house just outside of town and Alex was working on the local ski hill as a liftie. Susan had part-time work in the after-school recreation program, but she had the school holidays off so they could hang out together with the kids.

When she arrived, there was quite a bit of snow and the driveway looked a little steep, so she parked up on the road. Susan came and hugged her and helped her with her bags. It was so great to see her after six months apart. They threw their stuff into the spare room while Raina and Stella were both buzzing around pulling out toys, excited to see each other. Susan reheated some pizza for their supper and they poured a glass of wine and sat down to catch up.

"So, how do you like living up here in the wild blue yonder?" Nadia began.

"We love it. The people are so friendly in a small town compared to the city. We have made quite a few friends already. Our neighbours are awesome. There have been a few fun, social gatherings like pot-luck dinners and music nights at the local cafe. They bring in live performers from the area every Tuesday night. It's a great place to hang and there's even a kids' play area. We should check it out while you're here."

"Sounds fun. I sure miss having you around though."

Nadia explained to Susan in great detail how life in the city was going. Alex came home from the ski hill and joined them for a toke and a beer. He rolled around on the carpet with the kids and made them squeal with laughter. He apparently loved his winter job and was looking for a surveyor job for the spring. After a couple of hours of catching up, they put the kids to bed and Nadia crashed too. After driving all day, she was bagged.

The next morning after Alex left for work, Susan and Nadia sat drinking coffee and talking for the longest time. It was wonderful to be together and their kids were playing happily with toys strewn all over the living room floor.

Nadia wanted to get some more feedback on the whole Lisa situation. She knew Alex had kept in touch with David and thought perhaps she could find out how they were doing.

"So has Alex talked to David lately?" Nadia asked.

"Yah, they spoke a couple of weeks ago. Lisa's doing better and Malory has finished her therapy and seems to be okay now."

"What kind of therapy did she need?" Nadia pressed.

"All I know is she saw the same counsellor that Lisa saw as a teenager who helped her so much. I think dealing with trauma is his specialty."

"So, do you know why Lisa has shut me out of her life as well?" Nadia couldn't help sounding hurt.

"I think she just needs time to heal and she feels that you

are my greatest ally in this situation. She says she doesn't have the energy to deal with negative influences right now."

"Negative influences!" Nadia felt betrayed. "I am not biased against Lisa. I think this whole thing got blown so out of proportion. Both moms and both kids have suffered equally and I'm trying to remain as neutral as possible, even though I'm obviously supportive of you and Raina. Can't Alex explain to David that I'm not holding anything against her?" Nadia implored.

"I really don't want to get involved in this," Susan admitted. "Lisa finally trusts me enough to talk to me about what happened and at least I can share this with you, so you know what's going on. I don't want to jeopardise Alex's friendship with David any more than I already have."

Nadia was getting frustrated. "So, you aren't willing to speak to Alex or David about getting me back into her life then?"

"Not really," Susan sounded a little pissed off. "How is that going to make things any better? Lisa just needs more time to heal and figure out what her priorities are. Try not to take it personally. It's more about her protecting her child than anything against you personally."

Nadia felt jilted by her most trusted friend. Her face was getting hot and she needed to walk away from the conversation.

"I'm going outside for some air," she announced emphatically. "I'll be back in a few minutes."

She got up and went outside, letting the screen door slam behind her. She walked quickly down the gravel driveway and out onto the road. She felt the adrenaline pumping in her veins and kicked a rock, forgetting she had sandals on. She swore out loud at the stupidity of hurting her toes. She stormed down the road for about ten minutes and tried to breathe the mountain air deeply, to calm herself. Suddenly she sensed the passing of time and realised it was unfair to saddle Susan with both kids and turned around.

When she got back to the kitchen, she gave Susan a hug.

"I'm sorry. I don't want other people's feelings to come between us or damage our friendship. It's just not worth it. You are too important to me."

"Thank you. I feel the same way," Susan looked relieved. "Let's just enjoy this time together and forget about Lisa and anything else that's a distraction. You are here in this gorgeous place to relax and unwind from work. Let's just have some fun."

Nadia agreed. They put on some loud reggae music and danced around the living room with the kids while they made them lunch. Then they set up some playdough for them on the coffee table with cookie cutters and geometric stamps.

Suddenly there came a knock on the door and a tall, lanky guy in Timberland boots strolled in.

"Hi Bruce," Susan greeted her neighbour, "this is my best friend Nadia from the city. You wanna cuppa joe?"

"For sure, that would be awesome," He was obviously very comfortable in her kitchen, like he'd been here a hundred times before.

The three of them chatted for about an hour before he left. He was an artist with a painting studio outbuilding beside his house. God knows how he paid the bills, but Susan admired his talent and encouraged Nadia to go over and check out his work before she left. There was a glint in Susan's eye that Nadia immediately picked up on when she talked about Bruce. Nadia knew it spelled danger for her marriage.

"Um, you and Bruce sure seem to have a good connection." She dared confront her friend.

"Yah he's a great guy. I really like having him around," Susan admitted.

"Yah, it looks like he really likes having you around too." Nadia pushed for more details.

"What are you getting at?" Susan replied defensively.

"Well should I be worried?"

Susan relented, "Yah, you could be right, I guess. I've grown pretty attached to him and you've got to admit, he's kinda hot right?"

"Oh God damn it girl, you're totally smitten! This is serious. I don't want all of my friends to be divorced. Why can't any of us stay together already?" Nadia lamented.

"Well calm down. I haven't left yet, have I? I haven't done anything wrong. We just like hanging out, that's all. Besides, Bruce and Alex get along really well. It's not like that."

"All right girl, I'll give you the benefit of the doubt."

They had a wonderful Christmas together with the kids. Nadia had packed a bunch of gifts in the bottom of her suitcase. The little girls were so excited to be opening them with a buddy and got to play with them right away. She and Susan had agreed beforehand to get two gifts the same for each one so there would be no jealousy or squabbling. They especially loved combining their building blocks to make something bigger. After all the morning fun and coffee, they crashed for a nap after breakfast, before starting to cook a big meal. Bruce was invited for supper, as well as one other older neighbour named Jocelyn, who was also alone for the holidays. She was a retired nurse whose husband had died, but she was very upbeat and social in spite of this. She talked about her travel plans and making changes to her house.

After a delicious turkey dinner, they all smoked a joint and had coffee; life seemed really spectacular when shared with friends. Nadia watched how Alex and Bruce interacted to see if there was any hint of suspicion between them, but she saw none. This settled her worries about Susan making a bad choice. She really valued their marriage and viewed them as a port of calm in the otherwise stormy friendship scene in Vancouver. Maybe she was reading too much into Susan's doe eyes for Bruce.

Boxing Day was sunny, so after breakfast, Susan and Nadia walked over to Bruce's studio to check out his paintings. Nadia was impressed with the lifelike quality of his work. There were some stark, local landscapes showing off the majesty of the Kootenay Mountains and lakes. There were some still-life works and some portraits. Moving slowly through the room, Nadia suddenly froze, slack-jawed, agog. There in front of her was a large canvas of Susan, sprawled out on a rug naked.

"Wow, that was brave," she grabbed Susan's cuff and gave it a hard tug.

"What? That's no big deal. We all go skinny dipping at the lake so it's nothing new. He has painted loads of nudes. That's what artists do!"

"I guess so." Nadia didn't want to sound like a prude in front of Bruce. "Beautiful work Bruce. You really have an eye for detail."

When they got outside, Nadia really let her have it.

"Are you kidding me, Susan? No wonder I am sensing sparks between you two. How many hours did he have to stare at you naked to complete that painting?"

"About four," she admitted, "but I felt really comfortable the whole time. We were just chatting like normal friends. It wasn't weird at all."

"Okay, if you say so, but I think you're playing with fire here girl! If you really care about your marriage, you should give him a wider berth. Besides, what does Alex think about that painting?"

"He thinks it's awesome. If he had the money, he would probably buy it."

"Yah, I can see why. I wouldn't want my naked wife on some other guy's wall either."

"Oh, come on. You're being so conventional. With all the porn on the internet, nobody's beating off to fine art, I can guarantee you that."

"Yah, okay, well you definitely have a point there." They both laughed at the ridiculousness of the thought and walked back home.

Three days later, as Nadia hugged Susan goodbye to begin the long drive back to the city, she whispered in her ear, "Behave yourself girl. I love you guys. Come and visit soon."

"I love you too. Stop worrying. Everything will be hunky dory."

But it wasn't hunky dory. Nadia's prediction came true and Susan would betray Alex on the down low for four months before she left him to live with Bruce, taking little Raina with her. Alex was so devastated that he moved to the other side of town so he wouldn't have to see them every day. Susan did her level best to keep a fair and open exchange of child-care with Alex, but he was understandably so angry that it was challenging. When little Raina talked about how much fun she'd had with Bruce it was even harder for Alex to stay positive around his ex. Finally, he took a job in Alberta to get away from the whole scene.

Nadia couldn't stay mad at Susan for very long. She had been through her own messy divorce and knew how it felt. Susan called Nadia frequently during the unravelling of her marriage. One night the phone rang at midnight and Nadia could hear Susan was crying.

"What's going on girl?"

"I'm a terrible human being Nadia," she sobbed. "How can I do this to Alex and my daughter?"

"You're not a terrible human being Susan, you're just in love with somebody else. It happens. The heart wants what the heart wants. You have to stop beating yourself up about this."

"I know, but Alex is so furious with me that we can't even talk right now. I feel bad that Raina has to see us like that."

"It's just a phase Susan, trust me. I couldn't even look at Sam for about a year, but then it passes and gets easier, I promise. You guys will both be excellent parents regardless, just not together. You just need some time to get over the shock, that's all."

"I hope you're right Nadia because I can't take much more of this silent treatment. When I drop Raina off, he just takes her and walks away. It's so cold and mean."

"He's just hurting right now Susan. Give him some time. He just needs some space from you right now."

"Okay, I know you're right."

"So how is Bruce? Are you at least happy with him? How

are you going to combine your two homes?"

"Yah, I am happy with Bruce actually. He just gets me, intuitively. I never have to explain what I'm feeling with him. It's so nice that way. He has more or less moved in here, but he goes next door to his studio to paint every day. I think we will keep both places for the time being and maybe rent out his space soon to make some extra cash. We just need to fix it up a little first."

"That sounds like a good plan Susan. Try and focus on the positive. You've got a great place, a great man who loves you and a beautiful daughter. Your life is actually pretty good right now."

"You're absolutely right, I do have a pretty good life. I feel like maybe I can sleep now. Thanks Nadia, for always listening to my problems. I don't know what I'd do without you."

"No worries, you can call me any time day or night. I love you."

"I love you too. Bye for now."

"Sleep tight sugar plum," she laughed, "sweet dreams."

Nadia continued to help guide Susan though the emotions of her divorce. They shared the same worries about how their young children would fare being away from their fathers for long periods of time. They lamented trying to collect child support on time or getting regular breaks from parenting. It seemed like the mothers always carried the bulk of the load, especially since Nadia had returned to full-time teaching and was also paying a whack of money for childcare. At least Susan had Alex living in Alberta to spell her off during his vacation time. Life seemed unfairly hard during this period in their early thirties and they longed for the carelessness of their youth.

Chapter Nine
A New Decade of Love

Nadia spent two years on the dating scene. Aged thirty, she bought her own motorcycle and joined a riding club where she hoped to meet new men. This had various effects on her life, both positive and negative. Sometimes she found herself in some dodgy situations, at biker bashes with unsavoury characters of all sorts. There were people at these events who Nadia would normally never hang out with, like drug dealers, gang associates and strippers. She had some interesting stories to tell around the school lunch table for a while. She would leave Stella with her mother for the weekend and go off to sew her wild oats. Mostly it was the riding she enjoyed, but she also met some really nice people who just liked to get into the mountains and lakes to camp out, laugh and drink a few beers.

At one of these biker bashes in the Okanagan she met an ex-army guy named Jared. He was jacked with muscles and had long, wild, black hair all the way down his back in a braid and complete sleeve tattoos on both arms. In fact, he looked very scary, but over the course of the weekend she discovered that he had a wicked sense of humour that was very attractive. They rode back to Vancouver together with a group of friends and much to her surprise, he called her the next week.

They started seeing each other. He was really sweet with Stella and introduced them to his brother Andrew's family, who also had little kids for Stella to play with. They spent quite a bit of time visiting with them on weekends and hanging out. But Nadia gradually discovered that he had to smoke pot constantly to feel normal. If they were out in a public place and he couldn't go for a toke, he became grumpy and despondent and wanted to leave. It was the first time she had ever met someone with a dependency on marijuana and was surprised because she thought you couldn't be addicted to this drug. Their sex life was pretty bad because he would often fall asleep on her in a smoky haze. He also had other friends who used harder drugs, which kind of freaked her out. She felt a sense of panic creeping in whenever they were at a party and someone was snorting white powder off the table. She didn't want to be raising Stella around this environment. When he finally admitted to her that he had been a heroin user in the army, she decided to end it.

Then she met another biker named Gary at a Toys for Tots ride around the city. They had an instant, strong chemistry and their sex life was good, but he turned out to be psychologically controlling. In the evenings, he wanted to talk on the phone way too long for her busy life and she couldn't cut it short without him getting offended. It was so childish and annoying. When she tried to end it multiple times, he would draw her back in with weird head games. Once he called her from work and let her listen in while he flirted with some other woman in his office to make her jealous. It was so warped and infuriating that she dropped his spare apartment key off the very next day. Then there would come the apologies and dramatic declarations of love to draw her back in. He even had her looking at houses with him and she knew he wanted to have a child, which terrified her. This toxic relationship lasted way too long, but Nadia was finally able to extricate herself after a very painful year. Every impulse told her to run.

Then, out of the blue, an old love came calling. It was her second boyfriend Charlie, who she was with aged seventeen to eighteen. She recognised his voice immediately on the phone message, even though she hadn't seen him in two decades.

"Hi Nadia. This is Charlie from twenty years back. I heard through the grapevine that you might be single and I'm wondering if you might like to go for coffee sometime?"

Nadia's heart skipped a beat when she heard his voice. She had nothing but fond memories of the time they spent together. He was caring, kind and had a terrific sense of humour. They had also enjoyed wonderful sexual chemistry and she remembered how much she liked his whole family. They were good people. She didn't hesitate to respond to the message and before she knew it, they were meeting at a coffee shop to talk. They recognised each other immediately.

"Wow, you look exactly the same." Charlie gave her a hug.

"You are being kind," Nadia replied, "but you look really good too." She loved his warm, light blue eyes and sandy, blond hair that was starting to show a little grey at the temples. He was heavier than in their twenties, but who wasn't? They settled into some tall lattes and started to open up.

"So, how's your life? I heard you have a daughter now. Do you have any photos on your phone?"

"Yah, her name's Stella and she's six years old. She's the light of my life." Nadia showed him some photos and he commented on how cute she was and how much she looked like Nadia.

"Not really," said Nadia, "she actually looks more like her

dad. He's living in England right now, so she doesn't get to see much of him unfortunately. He's also been really crap at sending me any money for child support."

"That must be tough. Well my ex-wife is living locally, but she wanted me to raise my ten-year-old son Ethan because she has gone back to school and really doesn't have the time or inclination."

"Wow, well lucky you, I guess. Is that what you wanted?"

"Oh, absolutely," Charlie was obviously a devoted father. This only made him more attractive in her eyes. They reminisced about their earlier relationship and all the good times they'd had. They recalled concerts, parties and camping trips. It was hard to believe that twenty years had passed, and they had been through so much. Nadia learned that Charlie was working in a warehouse as a forklift operator. It was a steady job with good pay. He lived about a half hour from Nadia in a townhouse. After chatting for over an hour, they came up with a plan for their next date and hugged goodbye. She was so excited she could hardly wait to tell Susan. She phoned her as soon as she got home to tell her the good news. Susan remembered Charlie and was delighted for her best friend. She made Nadia promise to give her an update after their next rendezvous.

They shared a babysitter at Charlie's place the following Saturday night and went out for burgers at a local pub. They ended up just talking for hours to reminisce about their past relationship when they were young and to catch up on the twenty years in between then and now. They complained about their exes and the trials of reaching a divorce settlement without killing each other. They admitted that being a single parent was hard, but they agreed that their children were their driving force to go to work every day and keep it together. They remembered each other's family members and asked how they were doing. Suddenly it was eleven o'clock and they realised they should let the babysitter go home.

When they got back, Ethan was in bed and little Stella was fast asleep on the couch. They looked at each other for about three seconds and Charlie pulled Nadia's hand and went up to his bedroom. They made passionate love and immediately clicked; like they were teenagers again. Every inch of their bodies seemed deliciously familiar as they explored the smell and taste of their skin and sweat. They took their time and discovered all the wonders of what promised to be a deeply satisfying sex life.

The next morning, the kids were both surprised and delighted to find that Nadia had stayed over. They began playing Legos and watching cartoons in the morning without missing a beat, while Charlie made scrambled eggs for everyone. Nadia and Charlie flashed loving looks over the edges of their coffee cups, while the children ate and laughed, oblivious to their parents' strong, new connection. It couldn't have felt more lovely to Nadia.

It was so easy with Charlie that they knew within a few weeks that marriage was on the cards. Stella and Ethan hit it off immediately. They would play together for hours whenever Nadia came over, which became more and more regularly. They moved in together after a passionate summer and the kids started attending the same school. Nadia was the happiest she had ever been and felt her luck was turning a corner. All the drama of her old group of friends seemed to melt into the distant past.

Nadia and Charlie got married and bought a house in the

suburbs in their early forties and the kids grew up fast. Soon their home was filled with noisy pre-teens who constantly needed rides to all their music lessons and sports practices. It was a hectic but satisfying life. Nadia's teaching career was going well, although she was often very tired at the end of the day. Charlie and Stella had a strong, natural bond. He was more of a father to her than Sam would ever be. However, it was more difficult for Nadia to form a bond with Ethan. He was somewhat resistant to letting her in. He seemed to resent the fact that she had replaced his real mother, even though they made sure he had regular visits with his mom on weekends. He had a hard time dealing with his parents' divorce, so Nadia often felt like she was walking on eggshells. Charlie had to act as peacemaker on occasion, when they disagreed over house rules or boundaries. Ethan would get sulky and then retreat to his room whenever Nadia tried to discipline him.

Several years flew by and Nadia and Charlie bought a bigger house in the suburbs. When Stella turned ten and Ethan was fourteen, Nadia and Charlie sent them off to summer camp together. They were super excited to go because other than single night sleepovers, they had only ever been away from home to stay with their respective other parents. Now they were up near the town of Squamish, in real cabins by a lake, with bunkbeds and new kids from all over the lower mainland around Vancouver. It was a big adventure.

Of course, Nadia and Charlie were jazzed to get some alone time as well. They took a drive to Harrison Hot-springs and spent a romantic night soaking in the mineral pools, dining on sushi and making love in a hotel. It was a great recharge for their marriage, and they were very happy with the outing, until the drive home when Nadia's cell phone rang in the car. The call display read Forest Rangers Camp.

"Hello?"

"Hello Mrs. Lewis. I'm afraid there's been a bit of an incident here at camp involving Stella. Don't worry, she is fine, but we just thought we should let you know what happened."

"Okay…" Nadia naturally sounded apprehensive.

"She was in the washroom building alone and a boy came into the girls' washroom and groped her breasts. She screamed and he ran away quickly and hid in the bushes. The camp counsellors brought him into the office and he has been disciplined now."

"Holy shit, is she okay?"

"Yes, she fine, just a little shaken up. Would you like to speak to her?"

"Yes, in a moment. First, what do you mean by disciplined? Is the boy being sent home?"

"No, we've given him some counselling with one of our male staff and we've reported it to his parents. We wanted to give him a second chance. He's only twelve and we feel that he needs to learn to interact with girls in an appropriate manner."

"Well how are you going to keep the little freak away from my daughter?" Nadia couldn't help herself from getting angry.

"We've implemented a camp-wide buddy system for going into the washrooms now so nobody will be open to such an incident again. It will be safer for everyone."

"Well okay, I guess so, but let me talk to Stella first please."

"Of course, Mrs. Lewis, thank you for your patience and understanding in this matter. The boy's family will really appreciate this."

"Yah, I'm sure they will be, given that she could have pressed assault charges against him. All right, put Stella on the phone now please."

"Sure, just a moment."

"Hi Mom."

"Sweetheart are you okay? "

"Yah, I'm fine. Please don't worry. That little perv is keeping ten miles away from me now, he got in so much shit."

"Good, he deserves it! I'm proud of you for screaming and reporting him right away. Good job! At least all those talks paid off and you're not still hiding in the bathroom stall keeping this a secret. Well done! But don't be surprised if you feel upset again in the next few days or need to cry. I want you to go and get your stepbrother or talk to a female counsellor if you feel upset and call me right away. I can come and pick you up if you want. Do you want to come home now?"

"No mom I'm fine. I have made a really good friend here named Marcie and I'm actually having a lot of fun. Ethan is here and he's got my back. He loves it here too. This camp is awesome."

"Okay, well can you text me and let me know how things are going every night before bed?"

"We're out of service range here mom, so I can't, but I'll call if I need anything, I promise. Please don't worry."

"Okay, I love you sweetheart and Charlie sends his love too. Give Ethan a hug from us. We'll see you on Sunday then. Take care of yourself."

"Thanks mom, I will. Bye for now."

Charlie had pulled over and they sat in the car talking for

a while. Nadia was in shock and needed comforting and her husband reassured her that Stella would be able to handle it and enjoy the rest of her camp experience. They were both really glad that Ethan had gone too.

That night, lying in bed, Nadia couldn't help but make the connection between what had happened to Stella and what had happened to Malory all those years ago. She suddenly had a better understanding of how Lisa might have felt under the circumstances. She felt bad for not being more empathetic towards her friend at the time. After her mama-bear hackles had been raised so quickly, she finally had insight into those raw emotions Lisa must have felt towards Raina, even though she was so young at the time. She had immediately decided that the boy at camp was some kind of future paedophile, without any hope for rehabilitation. She had even pictured him in her mind as some trailer park trash with a bad upbringing and an abusive, misogynistic, macho father. Now she realised this stereotype could be so far from accurate.

As a teacher, she had seen plenty of really good parents trying to deal with their own child acting out in all kinds of horrible ways at school. She knew first-hand that if she gave up on these kids, they would have no hope of learning to change their behaviour in a prosocial way. But when her child suddenly became the victim, it was so hard not to just react and lash out. Maybe she should have cut Lisa some more slack after Malory got hurt. Perhaps she had been a shitty friend to Lisa after all? She felt uneasy and it took a long time to finally fall asleep.

Chapter Ten
Sam in Crisis

The following year, when Stella was eleven, her father suddenly returned from England without warning. Sam called Nadia and said that his relationship had fallen apart. She realised that he was repeating his old pattern of running away from commitment. Nadia arranged to bring a very excited Stella to see her dad in a restaurant for lunch and then she was going to spend the afternoon with him in Vancouver.

When they arrived at the restaurant, Nadia was shocked to see that Sam was thin and gaunt looking and had shaved off all his curly locks. He looked very unwell and was unusually lacking in energy. After he hugged his daughter for a long time, they ordered food and Sam said he needed a smoke. Nadia asked Stella to give them a moment alone outside.

"What's going on with you?" Nadia had to know. "Are you okay. You don't look well. "

Sam was reluctant to share. "I'm just going through a rough patch right now. Things will get better soon."

"Well I don't think I should leave you with Stella until you're feeling better. I've seen your rough patches and they usually end up in the foetal position in bed for a week or more. When are you going to get some medication for this depression you've been struggling with for years?"

"Okay, okay, you're probably right. I will make a doctor's

appointment tomorrow," Sam agreed.

"I would like you to tell Stella that you're not feeling well so that I don't have to be the bad guy who disappoints her today. We can stay at the restaurant for a longer visit and then I'll wander down the street and look at the shops to give you some alone time with her, but don't make any promises you can't keep."

"Okay, sounds good. Thanks Nadia. "

"Where are you staying right now?"

"I've rented a room in an old four-plex at the corner of King Edward at Main. The address is actually one hundred King Edward. I'm in unit four."

"Do you have enough money to feed yourself?" Nadia was really concerned that he might not be eating. He was so skinny that she wondered if he was a drug addict. He had been known to dabble in illicit substances in the past, but only recreationally.

"Yah, I had a good job in England, so I have a bit of savings. I should be fine for a few months at least."

"You're not using drugs, are you?" She had to ask. "Because I won't have Stella around that lifestyle."

"No, no it's nothing like that, I promise. Just one of my regular low periods. My life just feels like shit right now since everything fell apart in England."

Nadia couldn't help but think of the other woman he had lived with and her child and wondered what kind of mess he had left behind him.

"Well let's get back in," Nadia said. "I don't want to leave Stella alone and our food will be coming soon."

They enjoyed a subdued meal together and Sam asked his daughter twenty questions to catch up on her life. She was

120

delighted to have his full attention for the first time in six years. Nadia left for a bit, as promised, and came back thirty minutes later. They were looking at Stella's art scrapbook she had brought along with her and he was praising her talent. Sam understood the look Nadia gave him and told Stella that he wasn't feeling well enough to walk around the city today, but he'd see her again very soon. They hugged again and headed home.

Shortly after midnight, when Nadia had just fallen asleep, the phone rang. It was Sam and he was crying.

"Take good care of Stella," he said and hung up.

Nadia flew into panic mode. Her mind was racing. She recognised his sentiment as suicidal right away, but she wasn't sure what to do. She grabbed her address book and called his mother. A sleepy, bewildered voice answered.

"Brenda, it's Nadia. I'm sorry to call you so late. Sam just called me and sounded very upset. He was crying and he told me to take good care of Stella and hung up. I think he might be suicidal."

"Oh, my God! I don't have a car. Where are you?" She was freaking out.

"I live forty-five minutes from the city. I can't get there fast enough. I think I should call the cops. What was that address he told me today?"

She suddenly remembered, one hundred King Edward, unit four. "I will call you back after I talk to the police."

The police said they would send someone over right away. Thirty minutes later they called Nadia back and confirmed her fears that he had tried to take his own life. There was an empty bottle of pills beside his bed and Sam had been taken by ambulance to the hospital to get his stomach pumped. Brenda was on her way in a taxi.

When Nadia hung up the phone, she sat there speechless. She couldn't believe that Sam had nosedived into such a desperate state of depression. She pictured poor Stella hearing the news that her father was dead of an overdose and started to cry. Charlie was now fully awake and comforted Nadia, who was shaking. She cried on his shoulder for a while and eventually they fell back asleep.

The next morning, after Stella left for a friend's house, Nadia called the hospital for an update. Sam was fine, but he was sedated and sleeping. His mother promised to stay with him for the foreseeable future and agreed that the doctor's recommendation of antidepressants was a necessary first step towards healing. Nadia told her she would bring Stella to see him once he was released and stabilised. The invitation came from Brenda a week later for tea.

When Nadia and Stella arrived at Brenda's small apartment in Kitsilano, the story for Stella was that her dad had just recovered from a bad flu. Stella brought his favourite strong, black liquorice and a CD they enjoyed when she was young. His eyes welled up when he greeted her.

"What's the matter daddy?"

"I have just missed you, that's all sweetheart," he lied.

Brenda brought out the teapot and four cups on a wooden tray. She surprised Nadia:

"You just missed Lisa. She brought by these flowers and a card for Sam. Wasn't that nice of her?"

Nadia felt her face awkwardly turning red. "Yes, that's so nice." She tried to hide her nerves. She had no idea how she would have spoken to Lisa. She didn't think Sam even knew about their falling out and she didn't want to upset him with any drama when he was just starting to feel better. Perhaps it was for the best that they had just missed each other.

They made small talk and Brenda promised to look after Sam until he was feeling strong again and to make sure he was eating and taking his meds. Nadia promised to bring Stella over frequently to visit him. She hugged her daddy for a long minute, and then they said goodbye and left.

So began Sam's road to recovery. Six months later he was able to find a job and reconnect with his old life in Vancouver. He was taking his medication and had gained weight and energy. His curly locks had grown back in and he had colour in his face again. Stella was able to see her dad regularly now and could even sleep over at his new apartment on weekends. She was thrilled to have her father back in her life and Nadia was so happy for her. Sam even started to pay her some child support regularly and their communication was positive and caring. Nadia could feel Sam's ever-present underlying gratitude for saving his life, even though he had not uttered the words.

However, Sam felt overwhelmed by city life, so he moved up to Nelson and got a job as a carpenter building houses. A year after his breakdown, he had settled into a quieter, happier small-town life. He was even able to reconnect with his old buddy Alex, who had moved back there from Alberta because he missed his daughter. Together, they could commiserate about their ex-wives, divorces and sporadic parenting duties. Nadia was relieved that Sam was healthy again and that he had managed to build a good relationship with Stella. All her old anger towards him had melted away with time and became water under the bridge.

Chapter Eleven
The Forties

Before long, Stella and Ethan were teenagers, hanging out with all their lanky, zitty friends and being loud. They had a happy home with a pool table and a rec room downstairs where their friends were always welcome to hang out. There was enough money coming in with two incomes to pay the mortgage and life was sweet. There was so much joy and laughter during these busy years.

It seemed like Nadia and Charlie were always busy driving them to activities, like Ethan's trampoline and piano lessons and Stella's soccer and guitar. Then there were the constant rides to friends' houses. They couldn't wait until these kids were old enough to drive themselves. It seemed like there were school functions, birthday parties, movies and sports tournaments every weekend. Life was very full but exhausting. Nadia longed for those rare, quiet Sunday mornings with no commitments, when she could just sit and drink coffee and stare at the trees in the backyard, stroking a purring cat's fur on her lap.

But despite this overall happiness, every now and then the thought of Lisa and her old circle of friends in Vancouver would creep into her mind and she would feel a wave of sadness come over her. Ironically, now that Facebook was around, Lisa had 'friended' her, and this felt awkward. She could never muster the courage to message her and tell her how hurt she was by Lisa's rejection ten years ago. So, they simply carried on 'liking' each other's posts and acting like nothing had happened. It was weird. Nadia wondered how their kids would have gotten along as teenagers and was sad that they didn't know each other. Stella was the same age as Malory and she imagined they would have been quite compatible if they had grown up together, since they both had feisty, outspoken mothers.

Susan and Nadia were still very close friends and always made sure they saw each other a couple of times a year. They would also talk on the phone long distance regularly, to keep track of each other's lives and children. The two women occasionally wondered what was happening with David and Lisa's children, Isaac and Malory. They saw their photos on Facebook, but never really knew them past the tender age when the life altering incident had occurred. It was sad that the children who had played together so often as toddlers, no longer shared any real friendship with each other.

Susan had moved in with Bruce and Raina had made a strong connection with her new stepdad. Susan became pregnant shortly thereafter, and they welcomed a son, Eli. After some time off for maternity leave, she was back to working two jobs, one at the local rec centre and one with the city council transcribing minutes of their meetings. Nadia tried to visit Susan at least once a year but found, as time went on, that they were spending less and less time together.

Occasionally Susan would come to Vancouver with her young son and stay with Nadia and Charlie for a weekend and catch up on all their news. The felt more like sisters than friends because no matter how long they were apart, they could instantly pick up where they left off without a hiccup. Susan and Bruce were struggling financially, so Nadia felt bad for her, especially because it was causing stress in their relationship. Bruce had just started a new party rentals business and she wanted to give him a chance to get it off the ground by being supportive, but it was hard when they couldn't pay their bills. Sometimes Nadia would slip her a fifty or a hundred-dollar bill, but she could tell that Susan felt embarrassed whenever she did this. Susan was a proud woman who wanted to be self-reliant.

Raina and Stella remained friends who could talk easily, even as teenagers. They had shared a special bond since babyhood, as well as a lot of common history. They were almost like sisters. Nadia never told Stella about the 'incident' from childhood, even though Stella knew that her mother had been hurt by Lisa's rejection, but she never really understood why.

Raina, now fourteen years old, was also oblivious to the childhood trauma she and Malory had endured. She had little memory of the therapy she had received afterwards, when she had withdrawn into social anxiety. She had felt, for a long time, that she was to blame for her parents splitting up. She could sense there was some sort of friction between her mom and Lisa whenever her name came up. She even asked her dad about it once, but Alex didn't want to share any details.

At least Nadia had found the most supportive husband ever, who listened to all her feelings about the past and was smart enough not to interfere. Charlie said that whatever course of action she wanted to take to try and mend these old friendships, he would support her. She just couldn't muster the courage to call Lisa and invite her to a coffee shop in the city to talk. This would have been the logical first step to finding some neutral ground. They could start again fifteen years later and just call it 'so much water under the bridge'. Nadia figured that should be easy enough for both of them.

Then she had another memory of how cruel kids could be. When she was in grade six, she had gone to the skating rink with her best friend from class, a girl called Gillian Sharp.

She had even played at Gillian's house many times over their primary years and felt they were close. At the rink, they had run into another prettier, more popular girl from their class called Shelley. They had skated with her for a bit and then caught the bus home together. When they got to the agreed bus stop, Gillian and Shelley had exited the back door of the bus as normal. When Nadia tried to follow, they pushed the door shut so she couldn't get out and then ran away, cackling. Nadia knew at that moment that her friendship with Gillian was over and that Gillian had chosen Shelley over her. They barely said hi to each other at school after that and so ended six years of friendship in a single moment of cruelty.

Nadia wondered if, like her marriage, all the time and effort spent in forming a bond with someone was pointless. It seemed that love could turn to hate, or even worse, indifference, in the blink of an eye and without warning. Didn't children feel remorse for their actions? She had seen many times, as a teacher, how the previous day's events were forgotten. She had always thought this was a positive trait, because children moved on without carrying grudges. Each day was a beautiful, clean slate; unlike her adult colleagues, who could bicker and stew about a misplaced stapler for months. But was there also some pathological disconnect between their actions and how they affect others? Perhaps what Raina did to Malory was actually wiped clean from their memory banks. Nadia wished the parents could find this same knack for leaving the past behind and just getting on with it. Why did she always have to keep repeating this lingering sadness and resentment towards Lisa? It was a waste of her energy.

And why was it so difficult to initiate? Was she afraid of rejection? Yes, that was it. But she was also afraid her anger might boil up and she'd say something to blow the whole reconciliation. Who was Lisa to write her off as an expendable friend in the first place? Did she think she was better than Nadia? What gave her the right to assume that Nadia was unsympathetic to her plight? Nadia was surprised that her own anger was still there bubbling just below the surface. She was hoping to feel more compassion and forgiveness by now. She always ended up feeling too frozen between sorrow and bitterness to pick up the phone, and so life went on.

It was during this time that Susan's mom was diagnosed with Multiple Sclerosis and her mobility soon became quite impaired. Her parents had divorced a few years earlier and she now had a very strained relationship with her dad, since he shocked the family by taking up with another woman aged seventy-five. Susan suggested that her mother come and live with her in Nelson and Bruce added some adaptations to their home to accommodate her. He put in handrails in the spare bedroom and bathroom and built a ramp to the front door. She was already using a walker, but the need for a wheelchair seemed imminent. There were several teary phone calls from Susan during this time as she came to terms with her mother's illness. Nadia would listen and offer advice as best she could, like encouraging Susan to join a local support group for caregivers, which seemed to really help her emotionally. However, the care needs eventually became too much for Susan and she found her mother a bed in an assisted-living facility nearby.

Susan got really pissed off when Nadia suggested that she reach out to her father to tell him about her mother's illness and rapid decline.

"He doesn't give a shit about my mom," Susan blurted out in anger, "so what would be the point?"

"Well he spent like four decades of his life with her. There's got to be some level of caring between them still." Nadia tried to calm her down.

"Well there isn't," Susan insisted. "And he can go to hell as far as I'm concerned. He doesn't deserve a phone call from me. He hasn't reached out for the past year, not even a fucking birthday card!"

"Okay, okay, I'm sorry Susan. Obviously, I have struck a nerve. I didn't know he had been such a shitty father lately. That's terrible. This new woman must have really changed him. Growing up, I always thought he was a nice guy."

"I thought so too. He was good to us as kids, but now it's like we are his old family that he wants to forget. He's too busy traveling the world with his newer model wife to care about us. Even my brother Peter has written him off."

"I'm sorry Susan, that's really sad. I hope he comes to his senses one day soon. It's a shame that your kids don't have a relationship with their grandfather anymore. Eli looks just like him too."

"I know, it sucks. When Raina was little, she used to go fishing and camping with my dad and they really had a bond. Now it's as if he has forgotten he even has two grandkids. Do you know that for Christmas last year, all he sent them was a stupid t-shirt from Barbados? It was the lamest gift ever. I was so ashamed of him. He has lots of money and he's spending it all on her, while I am struggling to make ends meet. "

"That's terrible Susan. I'm so sorry. If I see him, I will give him a piece of my mind," Nadia said.

It seemed that the trials and tribulations of being part of the sandwich generation were already well upon Susan. Nadia could only watch and learn about what was inevitably coming for her as well. Caring for teenagers and parents at the same time seemed so unfair. For right now, she decided it was best to change the subject to something lighter, so she made Susan laugh with a story about how a kindergarten kid asked if she ever brushed her teeth. They chatted for a few more minutes and rang off.

After Susan's mother settled into the assisted-living facility, she was quite happy with the new arrangement. Susan reported back that her mother had made a bunch of new friends and was often joining in social activities and outings. She was eating better, taking her meds on time and doing physiotherapy. Everything seemed positive, then Nadia got an alarming phone call.

"Can you believe this Nadia? My mom has been sexually assaulted by some old geezer in her care home!" Susan was livid.

"What? Are you kidding me?"

"Nope, he came into her room last night and climbed into her bed and rubbed his flaccid penis all over her! When she woke up and realised what was happening, she hit the call button and the staff came and pulled him off."

"Jesus Christ! What a mess. So, what happens now?"

Nadia asked.

"Well they asked her if she wanted to press charges and of course she said no because she feels sorry for him and thinks he must be out of his ever-beloved mind."

"Is she physically okay though Susan? Did he hurt her?"

"No, she's fine. She's just a little shaken up and has a bruise on her hip. They have moved him to another wing for flight risk patients with a buzzer on his door so he can't just wander anymore."

"God, I'm so sorry Susan. What a bizarre situation. Please give your mom my love."

"Thanks Nadia. I just had to vent to someone. It's been a really weird day."

Things got even weirder when two months later Susan's dad suddenly died of a heart attack. Susan told Nadia that she felt torn about her father's passing. It was a strange mixture of anger and sadness at the same time. The hardest thing was dealing with his new wife Priscilla, who Susan couldn't stand. They had to meet with his lawyer to go over the will. When Susan had entered the office with Priscilla, they got her brother Peter on a Skype conference call from Alberta. The lawyer read out her father's wishes:

"To my wife Priscilla, I leave my house at 845 Granger St. in Kelowna, BC and all its contents. To my children, Susan and Peter, I leave all my bank accounts and my investments."

Susan was flabbergasted. She told Peter she would call him after she got home and then they chatted for a long time. Apparently, there was roughly eight hundred thousand dollars for them to share. It was a life changing amount. She could pay off her mortgage, pay for both her kids' educations, buy a newer vehicle and still have money left over. She was understandably thrilled.

Two days later, after talking over her budget with Bruce, she phoned Nadia to tell her the good news.

"Wow Susan, I'm so happy for you. That's wonderful!"

"Yah, who knew the old fart actually did care about us after all? You should have seen the look on Priscilla's face. She was not happy."

"Too bad. You are his kids and you deserve a break after working so hard to raise your boys and struggling to make ends meet all these years."

"Well Nadia, I was talking to Bruce last night and we've decided that we need a vacation. We are going to book an al-inclusive hotel in Mexico at Christmas break with the kids."

"That's a great idea Susan. You haven't been away in like, forever."

"But that's not all. We want you, Charlie, Ethan and Stella to come with us and I am paying for all of us, no questions asked. That's what I want and I can afford it now."

"Oh Susan, that is so nice. I am really touched. Are you sure you can afford that?"

"Absolutely! It will be so much fun for all of us to go together."

"Well, Ethan might prefer to house sit and hang out with his friends though. I'll let you know, but Raina and Stella adore each other and they can keep an eye on Eli while we drink pina coladas all day by the pool. It sounds amazing; thank you so much. I will let Charlie and the kids know so they can book time off at school holidays. What an amazing gift. I love you girl."

"I love you too. I will email you the booking details once I've made a reservation. Talk to you soon."

That Christmas, they had a wonderful week in Puerto Vallarta. Nadia and Susan did water aerobics every morning with a hot Latin instructor named Sergio. The parents napped and made love in their air-conditioned rooms while the kids swam all day in the pool. They ate and drank to excess and watched the lavish theatre and dance shows at night. The kids went parasailing off the back of a speed boat, Charlie and Bruce went fishing and caught a huge marlin, while Susan treated Nadia to a luxurious spa day. That evening, looking out at the sunset, Charlie gave Nadia a beautiful gold and garnet ring she had been eyeing in the gift shop.

"I am the luckiest man alive," he told her, stroking her wavy hair back off her neck and kissing her lightly on the nose where her freckles had long since vanished.

"I feel the same way my love. You have made me the happiest I have ever been in my whole life. I have to pinch myself sometimes." Nadia looked into his pale blue eyes and kissed him deeply.

Every night the two teenage girls would dance in the on-site disco and they met lots of other teens. Stella fell madly in love with a Mexican boy from the dance troupe and Eli walked in on them making out in the kids' hotel room. He was concerned about Stella, so he told her secret to the parents. Nadia had to talk to her daughter about personal safety. When they left, Stella cried all the way to the airport. Raina and Eli rolled their eyes at each other, but secretly felt jealous of Stella's little romance. Nadia cuddled her daughter in the back seat of the taxi and thought the whole situation was pretty adorable.

Chapter Twelve
Teaching Crisis

In 2006, Nadia already considered herself to be an experienced teacher. She felt she had mastered the art of managing a classroom, including most of the details of handling more challenging kids, like those with behaviour issues or special needs. This year, however, she got more than she bargained for, with a very hyperactive boy named Kyle, whose parents refused to give him ADD medication, even though the paediatrician and school strongly recommended it. To make matters worse, she had a girl with severe autism who was non-verbal and required the constant care of an education assistant (EA). She was a lovely child but very needy, so Nadia felt she always had to be on high alert. By the end of every workday, she was exhausted.

Before the school year even started, she had planned a field trip to Lynn Canyon Park in North Vancouver to visit the ecology centre and to take a small hike along the trails. Now it all seemed a little daunting, but she had a good relationship with her Education Assistant and plenty of parent volunteers, so it was all set. The visit to the ecology centre went well. Kyle was in Nadia's small group as planned and he only had to be told about ten times not to touch the exhibits, interrupt the guide or wander off. Things were going well, and the kids were visibly loving the experience.

Then, as they moved to the hike portion of the morning, Nadia stopped to check in on the EA and the little girl to see how she was coping.

"How are you liking the forest walk Tammy?" she asked the little girl.

Tammy pressed her voice box buttons on the fanny pack around her waist. She selected the recording for, "I like it." The EA reported that she was keeping up fine and seemed to be enjoying herself, so Nadia was pleased.

As Nadia turned back to re-join her small group of boys, she couldn't see Kyle. Suddenly she spied him about fifteen feet up on the rocky bank above them.

"Kyle, get down right now!" she yelled, but he ignored her and kept climbing higher.

"Kyle, get down here this minute or you will be going home immediately!" This warning had been spelled out to him before the trip and a parent was prepared to drive him back early for non-compliance.

Kyle stopped and looked down at her to show that he understood and was ready to listen. However, he was having difficulty finding his footing to work backwards. Nadia tried to guide him.

"There's a big rock by your right foot. Take a step onto that now. Good, good. Now place your left foot onto that big reddish-coloured rock that's sticking out. Well done. Now slide along a bit more to the left."

It was then that Kyle lost his balance and fell backwards onto the ground right in front of everyone, hitting his head hard with an ominous thud as he landed. Everyone panicked and gathered around him. He was conscious, but he looked very woozy and out of focus for what seemed like a very long minute.

"Kyle, Kyle, are you okay? Say something to me. What is your last name?" Nadia was freaking out.

"Franklin," he finally responded, to her great relief.

"Damn it, Kyle, why can't you listen sometimes?" Nadia couldn't help swearing inappropriately in frustration.

"I'm going to have to get him checked out," she announced to the parents," he might have a concussion. I'm calling an ambulance. Listen kids, don't be alarmed, he's probably fine but it's important that he's looked at by a doctor. You might hear a siren coming here in a few minutes." She grabbed her cell phone and called 911.

"Can everyone please follow the moms back up to the ecology centre and Mrs. French, please stay with me. Mrs. Jones please take Mrs. French's group with you and tell the EMT's exactly where we are."

Everyone moved quickly as directed and Nadia kept Kyle stable on the ground and did not move him. In ten long minutes, the EMT's were there. They took him to Lions Gate Hospital for a thorough check-up. Nadia called the school and his parents were leaving work immediately to meet him at the hospital.

When Nadia got everyone back onto the school bus, they were all hushed and subdued. She reassured them that Kyle was getting the best possible care and that his parents were with him. He might not be at school tomorrow, but she would phone his parents to get a report later and let them know first thing tomorrow how he was doing.

When she got back and the class had gone home, she broke down and cried in the staff washroom. Then she dragged herself into the Principal's office to fill out the required accident report. Her boss was sympathetic, but it had been the worst day of her career ever.

When she got home, she told Charlie what had happened, and he hugged her as she cried again. After supper, she mustered the courage to phone Kyle's parents.

"Hello Mrs. Franklin. How is Kyle doing?"

"Well, he has a concussion, so we have to keep him awake all night and report any changes to the doctor. They gave him a Cat-scan and there's no significant brain injury, thank God. How could you let this happen?" Her tone was accusatory.

"Mrs. Franklin, Kyle disobeyed my instructions to stay with the group and climbed up the rock face, which was clearly against the rules."

"But you were supposed to be watching him!" she barked.

"I was watching him, but I also needed to watch out for my little girl with autism. He's not the only kid I am responsible for, Mrs. Franklin."

"Well I will be reporting this to the school board," she snapped. "Good evening Ms. Lewis," and she hung up on Nadia.

"Holy shit," she told Charlie, "she's going to report me to the school board! She thinks it's my fault that her annoying little brat fell off the rocks. She's unbelievable!" Nadia could feel her face getting hot with rage.

"It's okay Nadia," said Charlie, "your boss will back you up and so will your union. You did nothing wrong. It was clearly his fault. Everything will blow over. She's just upset right now. Give her a couple of days to calm down."

"I hope you're right," Nadia took a deep breath to slow down her racing thoughts.

"I'm getting you a big glass of wine." Charlie headed for the fridge. "We are going to relax and watch a comedy show to get your mind off this shitty day. Come and sit down." He knew exactly how to help her when she was upset.

Unfortunately, things didn't just blow over in a couple of days. A week later, Nadia had to appear before a disciplinary hearing at the school board office with her union rep. She had to explain in painstaking detail everything that happened that day. The parents were threatening legal action. Nadia couldn't believe what was happening.

Finally, a ruling came back from the board office. Nadia was found at fault because it was clearly outlined in Kyle's behaviour plan that he was to stay with the teacher at all times during field trips and she had walked too far away from her group of students. Nadia would receive three days off without pay and a black mark on her record. The board had reached a settlement with the parents that they would cover all Kyle's medical expenses and for private tutoring while he was off school. Nadia was devastated.

When she got home that night, she collapsed into Charlie's arms and wept like a baby. She felt so ashamed and defeated. She couldn't face going back to school the next day, even if Kyle would be away for a while. Charlie advised her to call in sick, go to the doctor and take a stress leave, so that's what she did.

Nadia spent her days curled up in her pyjamas watching game shows and sleeping as the days off work turned into weeks. Charlie and Stella tried to console her, but she was clinically depressed. Even though she heard that her substitute teacher was doing a good job, she couldn't help feeling overwhelmed with guilt and shame for abandoning her class. Her colleagues sent her flowers and cards with supportive messages and even the class parents sent emails reassuring her that none of this was her fault. Nadia's union rep told her that the employer ordered her to go for counselling as part of the requirements to return to work. Her doctor put her on anti-depressants and gave her the referral.

When Nadia entered the counselling office for the first session, she did not feel like talking to a total stranger. Charlie tried to reassure her that it would be helpful, but she just wasn't feeling it. A younger woman dressed in business attire greeted her and introduced herself as Marion. Nadia couldn't help feeling prejudiced against her because of her youth. How could she possibly have enough life experience to know what she had lived through?

Marion began by asking her why she had come, which took Nadia aback. She assumed erroneously that her employer had sent details of the incident over ahead of time.

"No, that would be illegal disclosure of your personal information," Marion stated calmly. "It's completely up to you to share whatever you want to share."

"Oh, well honestly I don't feel much like sharing at all," Nadia sulked.

"Am I sensing some anger that you don't want to be here?" Marion asked.

"You're damn right!" Nadia blurted out.

"And why is that?"

"Because I've done nothing wrong. I got blamed for this badly-behaved, little boy hurting himself when it wasn't my fault."

"Okay, can you please describe to me what happened?"

Nadia reluctantly went through that horrible day in detail again. Then Marion's next question took her by surprise.

"Have you ever been wrongly accused of something before in your life?"

"Yes, as a matter of fact I have!"

"Tell me about that."

Nadia retold the whole incident of Raina hurting Malory and how she was pushed away by Lisa as a result.

"How did that make you feel?"

"Angry and sad. I really loved Lisa as a friend, and I was suddenly shut out for something that I didn't do."

"Why do you think she shut you out?"

"Because she felt I was taking sides with Susan and her daughter Raina."

"Were you taking sides?"

"I just felt like I had to protect Susan. She had done nothing wrong. She was a good mother."

"Why did you have to protect Susan? Wasn't Susan an adult who could look after herself?"

"I suppose, but her daughter suffered through the incident and needed therapy and really struggled emotionally afterwards."

"And you felt like that was Lisa's fault?"

"Yes."

"What should Lisa have done ideally in your opinion?"

"She should have accepted Susan's apology right away and allowed everyone to work through what happened together as a team. There was no need for her to be divisive."

"So how do you think this relates back to your field trip incident? Is there a connection to the way you're feeling about that now?"

"I never thought about it. Maybe you're right. I'm not sure."

"Isn't Kyle's mother blaming you in just the same way that Lisa blamed Susan?"

"Jeez, you could be right about that. Let me think about it."

"Well I think that's a good place to pick up our next session."

Nadia left the office feeling like this Marion might be worth her salt after all. The following week she came in and sat down more willingly.

"So, what did you figure out about the connection between those two incidents that have both been upsetting for you?" Marion started.

"Well, I guess this time it has brought the old hurt and anger back to the surface, I won't deny it."

"Okay, well that's a good start. So why was this Lisa so important to you?"

"Well, we had a ton of shared history. She was my first husband's girlfriend in high-school, and she helped me a lot during my divorce from him. She became a safe place for me to go to with my new baby and talk to when things were really shitty. She knew all of Sam's failings and idiosyncrasies and she loved us both, so she could be unbiased and fair."

"Okay, well that does sound like a really good friend. Have you considered what you could do to try and make amends with her?"

"Maybe she's the one who should try and make amends with me?" Nadia shot back.

"Well somebody needs to extend an olive branch at some point, or you will both remain entrenched in this same spot."

"I suppose that's true. I will think about it."

"So, let's get back to your need to rescue Susan. Where does that come from? Tell me about your family. What was it like growing up with your parents and siblings?"

Nadia launched into her entire background, including her father's story as a Holocaust survivor, the fact that he was never happy; her mother sticking by him even when she and her sister begged her to get a divorce so they wouldn't have to live with his misery any more. She explained how Rosanne had been the rebellious one, leaving her to be the good girl.

"So, you became the keeper of the peace whenever Rosanne went off the rails?"

"I guess so, although I never really saw it that way."

"Well did you always try to please both your parents? How was school for you?"

"I was a straight A student."

"So, a perfectionist then? That is a good way to please your parents."

"Yah, I guess you're right. I did suffer from a lot of test anxiety and worried that I would not get high marks."

"Perhaps you needed to rescue your father from feeling miserable all the time by being the perfect child with perfect marks?"

"Well that's a stretch. I was more concerned about my mother having to live with his verbal abuse every day."

"Ah, so you needed to rescue your mother from an unhappy marriage. Do you think that's fair for a child to have that kind of responsibility?"

"I suppose not, but whose life is fair? Don't we all just have to play the cards we're dealt?" Nadia asked.

"Yes, up to a point. But perhaps your mother should have

taken more responsibility instead of letting you worry about your father's state of mind all the time."

"Maybe she stayed because she couldn't afford to raise us with one income? Who knows? I certainly never blamed my mother. She was the victim in my eyes."

"Exactly, you had to rescue your mother, just like you had to rescue Susan."

"Wow, I never considered any of this. Come to think of it, I was always trying to protect my sister from my parents' anger when she did crazy things."

"See, you are a rescuer!"

"Okay, okay, maybe you're right."

"So how do you think this affects your situation with this boy's accident at work and his parents' complaint against you?"

"I don't know. I guess I'm upset because I couldn't take care of everybody in that moment. I felt helpless and powerless. I feel like I did the best I could so they shouldn't blame me."

"People like you who have been rescuing everyone around them their whole lives have difficulty giving up control. It's part of the perfectionism. It's very hard to accept that something went wrong on your watch, even if it was purely an accident and beyond your control. It sounds like you did everything in your power to take care of your class. Can you accept that it was impossible to please this parent under the circumstances?"

"Okay, but how does this help me?"

"Well if you say to yourself, I cannot make these parents happy no matter what I do… I cannot fix this… then perhaps you can just give up control, forgive yourself and move on?"

"Okay, well I can try it I guess," Nadia said.

"I want you to think about it this week and we will talk more next session. In the meantime, I want you to try getting dressed and going for a walk outside every day like we discussed. Take care Nadia."

Nadia considered all week what it might be like to stop trying to fix everyone around her. The idea of it seemed liberating, but she worried that she wouldn't be able to put it into practice.

During what would be their final session, Marion walked her through what it would be like to face Kyle and his parents when she returned to work. She made Nadia act it out in a role play and presented all the possible accusations and solutions she could to help Nadia to move on. Afterwards, she encouraged Nadia to get back on the horse and return to work as soon as possible. She said that delaying her return would just make it harder. Nadia followed up and made a plan with her union rep to return right after Christmas break.

When she got back, the kids in her class had hung a banner reading, 'Welcome back Ms. Lewis; and they all hugged her and told her how much they missed her. She got tears in her eyes and thanked them all and told them she missed them too. She was so relieved and felt loved and appreciated again.

Her colleagues greeted her with open arms and offered lesson plans and guidance to help her get her class up and running again. The parents expressed their support for her over the next few months in various ways that made her feel validated. By the end of the year, she was gradually able to wean herself off her medication.

Nadia was especially nervous, about facing Kyle again. She was surprised to learn from her principal that Kyle's parents had reconsidered the medication option for their son's ADD, since he was having real difficulty getting along with his peers. Her boss said that his behaviour had really improved since her leave of absence. He wasn't bouncing out of his seat and blurting out inappropriate comments every few minutes and he was actually getting some schoolwork done now. Nadia was relieved to hear this.

She decided to make a real effort to reconnect with Kyle in a positive way upon her return. After all, it wasn't his fault that his parents had been so challenging. She invited him to join a lunch club playing computer games in her room and even gave him the responsibility of checking members on a list when they arrived. He started opening up to her more and sharing his feelings. It made both their lives easier on a daily basis.

However, she noticed that the other kids in class still weren't including him in their free time play at recess and lunch and he often walked the playground alone. He was also last picked for teams in gym and for project partners in class. She decided to ask her principal what he thought might help, since she liked and trusted her boss.

"Well Nadia, I'm afraid the problem is bigger than just your classroom. Apparently, he accidentally hurt Kevin Duncan's little sister while they were having a playdate and Mrs Duncan has made it into a huge deal. Now there's a whole group of neighbourhood coffee moms that have decided that Kyle is a bad seed and should not be invited for playdates or birthday parties."

"That's awful," Nadia said. "He has been making such good progress lately. Poor Kyle, I can't believe I'm saying this, but I actually feel bad for him. He's really a nice kid inside and I know he's trying."

"I'm considering calling Mrs Duncan in for a meeting to try and shift the tide of public opinion, but it's going to be challenging for sure. Once the rumour mill gets going, it's hard to turn around."

Unfortunately, there were only three months left in the school year and they were unable to improve matters. Kyle's mother had been just as challenging with her neighbours as she had been with Nadia and the family ended up moving at the end of the year and placing him in a different school. Nadia wondered if this kid would be running away from his mother's failed relationships for the rest of his school years.

Something in all this reminded Nadia of the rift between Lisa and Susan over Raina and Malory's painful encounter all those years ago. Why would parents not forgive each other's children for their mistakes growing up? Couldn't they see that all this blaming and anger would cause even more harm to their kids? They needed to give them an opportunity to learn from their mistakes, make adjustments to their behaviour and move on. It made Nadia feel frustrated and helpless. All these petty grudges held for years did nothing but entrench the bitterness and hatred felt by everyone involved. It had been a lousy end to a lousy year of her career, and she wished to put it all behind her.

Chapter Thirteen
The Fire

One Saturday morning in 2008, Nadia was half asleep when her phone rang. Rolling over and looking at the screen she saw it was her mother Josephine, so she answered it.

"Hey Mom, what's up?"

"I'm sorry to call you so early but Sam accidentally dialed my number this morning trying to get a hold of you. Apparently, there was a fire last night at his mother's apartment building and they're saying it was arson. I told him I would call you because he was rushing to get to work."

"Holy crap, is Brenda okay? Did they catch the guy?"

"Yah, everyone is fine, but her place is badly damaged, so she has to find another place to live and a lot of her stuff got ruined. They haven't caught the guy, but there's been a string of arson attacks in the neighbourhood in the last year so it's a big police case now for sure."

"Wow that's terrible! And it's so hard to find rentals in Vancouver. Where is she going to stay for the rest of the month?"

"She's at John's place. I already spoke to him and got a list of household basics they need. I was going to call around and try to gather up donations for her this weekend. Would you be able to come over and help me for a couple of hours?"

"Sure, just let me talk to Charlie about what's happening this weekend and I'll call you back with a time. Does she need any kitchen stuff? There is that whole extra set of dishes and cutlery from grandma's place."

"Yah, I'll dig that out for sure. Look I know you and Sam have had your differences over the years, but Brenda's a nice lady and she's still Stella's grandma, right?"

"Yah, of course mom. It's absolutely the right thing to do. Actually, it will be good for you to see her again. You do know that Stella has seen her regularly over the years and they have a great relationship? I am sure Stella will want to help out too."

"You sound sleepy honey. Call me back when you're fully awake."

"Okay Mom, I'll talk to yah soon. God, this is such shitty news."

When Nadia, her mom and Stella arrived at John's place on Sunday morning, they had a trunk full of household gear. They also brought enough Danishes for everyone, hoping to visit for a bit. After exchanging long hugs at the door, they went into the kitchen and sat down. Brenda looked exhausted and shellshocked; John was making coffee. They had already been visited by the police crisis response counsellor the day before and had been given a list of services. There was also a case worker helping Brenda find a new rental accommodation.

Brenda started by thanking them for all their kindness and Nadia told her what was in the bags and boxes they had brought.

"The only things we couldn't find were a bathing suit for you and a small bedside lamp," Stella explained.

"Wow, that's amazing. You guys are wonderful. I can't believe you found all this so fast. The bedding especially will be a huge help right away," Brenda said, sounding overwhelmed.

"Everyone feels terrible for you. It's the least we could do. So is Sam coming down to the city to help you?" Nadia asked.

"He said he couldn't get away from work right now, but he will come down in two weeks and help me get moved into a new place, if I can find one. A few friends have offered to help me, like my old work colleague Darlene, of course John, and also Sam's ex-girlfriend Lisa."

Nadia bristled at the mention of Lisa.

After discussing the arson investigation and their insurance coverage, Nadia, her mom and Stella left to let them get on with their day. They had a million little details to sort, like filling out claim forms and contacting their employers to get some time off. Thank goodness Brenda had her son John in town to help her out in this situation.

Out in front of the building, Nadia kissed her mom goodbye and Stella gave her grandma a big hug.

As soon as they got in the car, Nadia's couldn't stop thinking about Lisa. Stella noticed how her mom was lost in reflection and asked her what was on her mind.

"So, what happened between you and Lisa anyhow?"

Nadia hesitated to share her most vulnerable feelings with her daughter. She was also worried the story might get back to Raina, but she just couldn't hold in the secret any longer. It was like a levee breaking and the past game gushing out. She even started to get teary, which took Stella by surprise.

"Well you can't help feeling how you feel mom." Stella always knew just what to say to console her. "Don't dismiss your feelings, just observe them and try to figure out why you still get so riled up at the very mention of Lisa's name. If you can unwrap that mystery, it will be healthier for you."

"You're right. Of course, you're right. You always get me. I think it's her rejection that still stings. I thought I meant more to her as a friend than that. It's stupid, I know it's stupid. God, it's almost like she broke up with me through a bad text or something. I'm being ridiculous. I need to get over myself already!" Nadia suddenly felt embarrassed of her own behaviour. But then she remembered. "Please don't share that story with Raina though, sweetheart. I'm worried that it might upset her."

"It's okay mom, I won't. Now forget about it. Let's go to Granville Island market and pick up some yummy treats for Charlie and Ethan."

Chapter Fourteen
Stella's grad

The year 2009 brought joy to Nadia's family because Stella was graduating from high school. It was also the year of Raina's graduation in Nelson and luckily the two events were staggered so they could attend each other's celebrations. Susan and Raina drove down for the weekend and then Nadia and Stella drove up to Nelson three weekends later. Stella had her first boyfriend, a boy called Trevor, who looked adorable in his rented, blue tuxedo. Raina didn't have a boyfriend, so Ethan went as her date and got to wear the fancy blue suit they rented for him.

Both Charlie and Sam attended Stella's big do and they actually got along really well. They treated each other with mutual respect, with Charlie insisting that Sam take the first dance with his daughter, but then Sam invited Charlie back to take over halfway through the song to acknowledge him for being a great stepdad. After the dance, Sam even leaned on Charlie's shoulder and thanked him for raising his daughter for all those years when he was in England. They both started getting a little emotional. It was a beautiful moment and Nadia suddenly felt grateful for these two men in her daughter's life.

"I hope Bruce and Alex can share something like this in three weeks' time," she told Susan.

"Don't count on it," Susan warned, "Alex still feels a lot

of bitterness over the way Bruce stole me away from him."

"Yikes, is it going to be awkward then?"

"I don't know," Susan confessed, "I doubt it though. They will both want to be on their best behaviour for Raina's sake."

"Well thank God for that." Nadia wanted the night to be fun.

They all stayed up late for the dry grad festivities, all the parents even volunteered to help out. Charlie was a dealer at the poker table. Alex helped the grads get into these giant bubble-balls for hilarious combat in a boxing ring. Susan and Nadia worked at the food counter selling pizza slices, candy and cold drinks. Everyone had a great time.

At five in the morning, the grads went to a friend's place for breakfast and the adults went back to Nadia's to sleep. Susan had the spare room with Raina and Sam crashed on the couch downstairs. When they woke up at noon, Nadia was surprised to find Trevor and Stella together asleep in her bed. She decided not to make a big deal about it, but when they finally walked into the kitchen just in time for supper, she greeted them warmly.

"Well top of the morning to you two lovebirds."

Trevor blushed and Stella groaned, "Mom, please! Can we just get some coffee?"

"Well sure, I'll put on a pot, even though it's dinner time. No problem. I'm glad you guys had so much fun last night. It really was an awesome party."

The next day, Nadia decided she had better have 'the talk' with her daughter, just to make sure.

"So sweetheart, would you like me to take you to the doctor's office to get some birth control?"

"Oh Mom, we haven't done anything yet."

"Okay, but it's better to be prepared right? It's only a matter of time."

"I suppose… but you're not coming in with me. No way!"

"Sure honey, that's fine. Whatever makes you most comfortable. I will take you as soon as classes are finished."

So, Stella went on the pill and Nadia reminded her that she could still get S.T.D.'s if she didn't use a condom.

"I know Mother. I'm not an idiot."

"Okay, I know you're not an idiot. I'm just making sure you don't forget in the heat of the moment."

Stella plugged her ears, "La-la- la- la-la," and walked away with her long, wavy, brown hair trailing behind her.

Nadia tried to remember what it was like to have that first love. It seemed like a lifetime ago. She had dated a boy named Shawn before Charlie and lost her virginity to Shawn on the sofa in his parents' basement. The whole experience had been embarrassingly awkward and uncomfortable. She hoped it was better for Stella the first time.

Three weeks later they drove up to Nelson. Raina and Stella looked so cute together in their fancy dresses. Stella wore her hair in a chignon with one long curl on each temple, and sparkly, pale, green eyeshadow made her look like a pixie elf. Raina looked cool with her dark bangs that swooped down over one eye, long, dangly, Celtic cross earrings and a silver brocade dress.

Sam dropped by the see Stella and introduced his pretty new girlfriend Andrea. Susan and Nadia took tons of photos of the girls before they left. They expected them to party afterwards with friends because there was no dry grad organised, so they gave them cab fare, told them to be safe and stay away from any pills that were offered.

"You can drink booze or smoke weed, but no ecstasy, no molly, no special K or whatever you call it, no toxic chemicals of any kind. You can't tell what they are laced with and they can kill you!" were Nadia's last words as they left the house.

"Okay mom, we got it." Stella shot back with half a smile.

Nadia and Susan drove over to the dinner portion of the grad thirty minutes later, but they had promised to leave before the dance portion so their kids wouldn't feel embarrassed. Bruce and Alex sat at opposite ends of the table to avoid awkwardness. Susan was surprised to see that Alex had brought a new girlfriend along named Jessie. She wondered if this was a real relationship or just for shock value. Jessie was definitely hot as hell and Susan had to tell herself not to feel bad that she wasn't wearing much make-up or high heels. She felt like the practical mom versus sexy new girlfriend. Nadia shot her a raised eyebrow look that told her in a split second that she was stunned at how Alex had raised his game, but cynically didn't believe it

They chatted about their kids' future plans over dinner. Raina said she wanted to travel before she went to college. She was interested in taking the hotel management program because she loved to golf. She already had a summer job lined up working reception at one of the local hotels. Stella wasn't sure what she wanted to do for a career, but she was definitely headed to university in the fall. She would live at home to save money and use public transport. She also planned to find an evening job waitressing as soon as possible to help pay for her studies. Raina teased her about getting serious with her new boyfriend Trevor, but she brushed it off by saying she was already interested in someone else and planned to end it with

Trevor soon. Nadia told her to be nice to Trevor and let him down easy, but she already knew Stella would break his heart.

After dinner, all the parents left for the dance portion of the evening and Nadia went back to Susan's, where they talked into the wee hours. They patted themselves on the back for raising such great kids and coming out the other side with some shred of sanity left. They laughed about their exes' new girlfriends and how they would probably screw up these new relationships with younger women, but then admitted that maybe they were just jealous because Jessie and Andrea were prettier than them. They cursed their tight asses and firm breasts and wished for them to get pregnant so that Alex and Sam would have to be dads all over again in their old age. This thought made them roll off the couch laughing hysterically like they did in high school.

The next morning Nadia phoned Charlie to see how things were going back home. She was surprised to hear that he had some big news for her.

"Last night Ethan came into the kitchen and said he needed to talk. He told me that he's gay."

"Holy shit, this is huge!" Nadia said.

"Yah, well I just told him that I was proud of him for telling me and that we would love and support him no matter what. I gave him a big hug and that was pretty much it."

"Wow, well done super dad. That is awesome. I bet he feels so much better getting that off his chest. I know you've had your suspicions for a while now, right?"

"Oh definitely. I think I've known for years, but I wasn't ready to admit it to myself. I mean there has only been one girlfriend and that whole thing seemed pretty awkward. I don't even know if he even slept with her, but I doubt it. I just wasn't getting that vibe."

"Yah, me neither, poor girl. She probably wondered the whole time why he just wasn't that into her," Nadia laughed.

"Well I guess I'll see you tonight then?"

"Yah we will be hitting the road shortly. We're just cleaning up breakfast and packing up the car. Well, you'd better educate yourself about Aids prevention so you can talk to your son."

"Yikes, no thank you. I will leave that for you to bring up. You are way better at that stuff than me anyhow."

"Okay, I get it. I will just prepare an information package and leave it for him to read," Nadia promised.

"Thanks teacher," Charlie sounded relieved, "see you tonight. Drive safe. I love you."

"I love you too."

Nadia told Susan and Stella the big news. Raina was still sleeping but Stella was excited for her stepbrother. She said she had figured out he was gay a while ago, but she was waiting for him to come out on his own terms before bringing it up. Nadia was impressed with her maturity. She knew she would be super supportive of Ethan because they got along so well.

They hugged Susan good-bye and left a note for Raina with little hearts around it saying how great it was to see her. They drove the eight hours back to Vancouver, stopping for burgers in Merritt to break up the journey. When they got home, they both gave Ethan a big hug and told him they loved him. He looked a little embarrassed that they had both heard his big news already from Charlie. Stella pulled him aside for a private chat while Charlie made dinner.

"He's already seeing someone," Charlie told Nadia.

"Wow, who is it?"

"A guy from work named Darren. They are both baristas at Starbucks. Apparently, they have been together for about two months."

"Well did you invite him over to meet us?" Nadia asked.

"Oh no, I didn't even think of that," Charlie admitted, "I just told him I was happy for him."

"Okay, well let's tell Ethan over dinner that we would love to meet this Darren."

"Sure, good idea," Charlie agreed.

Nadia pushed him a little harder. "So how would you feel about him sleeping over?"

"Wow, I had never considered that. I don't know. How would you feel?"

"Well we already let Trevor stay over here once with Stella so I guess it would be hypocritical if we said no to Ethan."

"Yah, I guess you're right, but I don't really want to think about them having sex in the next room. That's gross." Charlie was having more of a hard time with this than he was letting on.

"Now you know how they must feel about us having sex. Anyhow, they wouldn't be in the next room. They could sleep downstairs on the pull-out sofa. I'm afraid you're going to have to open up your mind my darling. He needs our support."

"Okay you're right. I will get on board. Just give me a little time to take all this in please."

So, Darren came over for dinner a week later and they tried not to grill him with too many personal questions. He was a really nice Asian man who was a couple of years older than Ethan. They shared a mutual interest in alternative music like

Radiohead and Moby and both loved a computer game called Fable. He still lived with his family and was studying business at university.

After Darren left, Nadia had to ask Ethan if Darren had already come out to his family.

"Oh yah, but it's only his mom and sister. His dad lives in Newfoundland and they don't have much contact. His mom has known for a few years and she's been really cool about it."

"Have you met his mom yet?"

"Yah, I've been over there a couple of times. They live close to the Coquitlam Centre mall in an apartment."

"He's really nice and he is welcome here any time," Nadia added. "Your dad and I have even agreed that he can spend the night if you want to sleep downstairs on the sofa bed."

"Really?" Ethan looked sheepish. "Is Dad okay with that?"

"Yup, we've decided to try and be twenty-first century parents and keep it fresh." She smiled at her stepson.

"Yay then. Thank god for you guys." Ethan looked happily surprised.

"You're welcome, now help me dry these pots and pans," Nadia smiled back at him. It was one of those rare moments when she felt really connected to him.

Chapter Fifteen
The Funeral

Several years later, in 2015, Nadia went on Facebook and discovered there had been a terrible accident. Lisa's son, Isaac, from her first marriage had died in a car crash on the Coquihalla highway over the weekend. There were outpourings of grief posted under a beautiful photograph of him as a child with his baby sister Malory. Nadia recognised Lisa's children instantly and she felt a huge wave of sadness. But the grief she felt was for her lost friendship with Lisa and not just for the dead young man.

Nadia wondered if she should go to the funeral, but she wasn't sure if she'd be welcome there. Of course, she knew that funerals were public events that anyone could attend. How awkward would it be to see Lisa and her family in their hour of grief after all these years? Who else from her old circle of friends would she meet there? Could the funeral serve as a kind of healing of broken friendships or was this just a self-serving outlook?

Nadia called Susan to tell her the news and she was surprised to find that Susan intended to attend the service. She did not seem afraid of what the consequences might be. Susan seemed quite shaken at the death of the boy who had played with her daughter so many years ago. That was at the time when Susan had been blamed and ostracised for having a bad child.

"I think you're very brave to just show up there after twenty years," Nadia praised.

"Some things are more important than my feelings about the past," replied Susan. "Besides, Lisa needs our support, regardless of what happened between us back then."

"I don't know if I can muster the courage to go," admitted Nadia. "What if she still hates me?"

"I don't think she ever hated you Nadia," Susan reassured her. "You were just caught in the middle of our feud and forced to take sides. Nobody should ever have to take sides when young children are involved."

"You're definitely right about that," Nadia agreed, "things just got completely out of hand. Do you know that it still hurts to this day to think about our broken friendship? Maybe I should take the high road and go with you to the funeral?"

"That would be awesome," encouraged Susan, "think about it and let me know when you decide. Bruce is trying to get someone to cover his shift so he can come too. We will drive down next Wednesday. Eli has to work, but I doubt he remembers playing with her kids anyhow. They were so little."

"Do you need a place to stay?" Nadia offered.

"No, we will stay at my dad's in the city, but thanks for the offer. It will be so weird to see everyone together again after so long."

"Yah, no kidding. I am a little nervous about seeing Lisa. I hope that all is forgiven after so many years."

Nadia walked through the rest of that day like she was in a fog. So many memories wafted in and out of her mind of wild parties in their twenties and all the good times with their young children. She had trouble focusing on anything else while she folded laundry and cleaned up the house. Charlie came back from golfing and noticed she was far away in her thoughts. When he asked her what was up, she burst into tears. She shared all her feelings about young Isaac's death, the upcoming funeral and all the unresolved hurt from the past. Charlie hugged and consoled Nadia and told her that whatever she decided, he would support her and offered to go to the funeral with her, even though he didn't know Lisa's family.

That night, Nadia fell into a deep sleep and dreamt of a big, empty house with broken toys strewn across the floor. There were dolls with the arms and legs pulled off, trucks with no wheels and tangled marionettes. There was a wooden kitchen with the doors hanging off the cupboards and a smashed-up tea set on the little table. She was desperately trying to sweep everything up and get it all into black plastic trash bags before the guests arrived. The alarm clock was beeping loudly in the distance and she woke up in a panic.

She dragged herself out of bed, made a cup of coffee and sat in a vegetative state at the kitchen table reflecting on the bad dream. Charlie had left to visit his mother, so the house was quiet until the telephone rang. Nadia recognised the voice instantly; it was her ex-husband Sam. He was calling from Nelson, where he had been living for the past five years with his new partner Andrea.

"Have you heard the terrible news about Lisa's son, Isaac?" he asked Nadia.

"Yah, it's so awful. She must be devastated."

"I'm coming down for the funeral. I just thought I should let you know in case you planned on going. I didn't want it to be a nasty surprise for you running into me there."

"Oh, I think we are way past that now," Nadia replied calmly. "Our kids are grown now and it's so much water under the bridge, seriously."

"Okay well are you planning on going then?" asked Sam.

"I'm not sure yet, but Susan is going, so that will be interesting. If she can make peace with Lisa then anyone can," Nadia pondered.

"You should come," offered Sam, "it would actually be nice to see you. How's Stella?"

"She's great. She's still up north tree planting with her cousin, as you know. Last I heard they were just north of Prince George, but she has no cell reception up there so you can't call her. She said she's planning to visit you at the end of August before she comes home."

"That's great. I can take a week off to spend time with her then. They owe me some time off for all the overtime I've been putting in lately." Sam sounded tired.

"Stella says she really likes Andrea and enjoyed getting to know her over spring break. I think they really connected over the jewelry making thing."

"Yah, I'm glad they hit it off. I knew they would, she's pretty chill."

Nadia couldn't help thinking, "She'd have to be to live with you," but she resisted the urge to be nasty.

"Have you seen Susan lately?"

Sam replied, "Yah, I ran into her at the bakery yesterday and told her about the accident. She said she was going to call you today. I think she and Bruce are planning to come down to the funeral."

"Yah, we just talked. I'm looking forward to seeing

them," Nadia explained. "They are planning on staying with Susan's dad in Vancouver because he lives closer to the mortuary."

"Well, I guess I will see you there then," said Sam.

"Yah, if I can muster up the courage to go. Thanks for calling." Nadia rang off.

Nadia felt more positive for the rest of the day. She hadn't spoken to Sam since Raina's graduation and it was good to reconnect with her daughter's father. She had tried to be patient with his many shortcomings as a father over the years, and they had often had harsh words, but things were getting easier now that they had both moved on with other partners.

Nadia finally mustered the courage to go to the funeral. She met Susan and Bruce beforehand at a coffee shop. Charlie had an important meeting that day so she told him she would face the music without him.

When Nadia walked into the coffee shop, Susan looked exactly the same as when they were twenty, except for a few wisps of grey hair at her temples. She had managed to keep her young figure without ever exercising. "Good genes," thought Nadia. She looked happy leaning on Bruce's shoulder. He was a big teddy bear of a man who kept her grounded.

"Hey guys," they all exchanged hugs, "we'd better get going because the service starts in twenty minutes."

When they entered the funeral home, Nadia could see Lisa and David up at the front with Malory and their extended family. It was already quiet inside and the director was ushering people to take their seats. Sam was sitting three rows ahead of Nadia and she was struck by how good looking he still was in a shirt and tie after all these years. He was alone, so Nadia guessed that Andrea couldn't get the time off work. Nadia also noticed some of their other old party friends from the eighties sitting near the front who she hadn't seen for years. She was surprised that David was already completely grey, and Lisa had put on some weight, but still looked elegant. Alex came in and walked straight up to the front to hug David, which made Nadia and Susan both tear up.

The soft music that had been playing suddenly stopped and a minister came to the alter. He spoke solemnly of a young life cut too short by tragedy and Lisa and Malory both sobbed quietly in the front row. Isaac's father, Lisa's first husband, was there wiping tears, but David somehow remained stoic. A few of Isaac's friends mustered the courage to say a few words about his success in lacrosse and hockey and his love for a girlfriend who looked on, sobbing uncontrollably. Lisa's father spoke of his beloved grandson who he'd hoped would one day take over his auto parts business. Afterwards the director invited everyone to stay for coffee and sandwiches.

Nadia asked Susan to accompany her to the front to face Lisa; her heart was racing as they approached. Lisa was talking to an older woman, but she saw them coming out of the corner of her eye and broke away from her conversation.

"Wow, this is a sight for sore eyes," Lisa spoke quietly, looking emotionally and physically drained.

Nadia couldn't help herself, "I've missed you terribly all these years," she blurted out and squeezed Lisa hard.

"I've missed you guys too," Lisa admitted. "Sam and Alex have kept me in the loop and told me when you both remarried. Where are these wonderful husbands that I keep hearing about?"

"I'm sorry, Charlie couldn't get out of work today, but I would love for you to meet him sometime. Maybe we could have you and David over for dinner at our place?"

"Well I'm not up for doing anything right now, as you can imagine, but maybe in a few months. It would be a nice distraction."

Susan introduced Bruce to Lisa and then she offered her condolences.

"We are so sorry about Isaac. I can't even imagine what you're going through. Please let us know if we can help you in any way. I mean it," she said.

"Thanks, I will," replied Lisa. "I'm sorry, but I have to greet all the other guests right now."

"Can I get your number?" asked Nadia tentatively.

"Sure, just message me on Facebook," replied Lisa. "Take care you guys, and thanks for coming."

And so, with five simple minutes of conversation, the wounds of thirty years began to heal. Nadia turned to Susan and said, "I can't believe it was that easy. What a fool I have been not to reach out sooner."

Susan replied, "Don't beat yourself up Nadia, she could have just as easily reached out to you, but she didn't so…"

"Yah, I guess that's true. Why are we so stubborn? Children don't get hung up and hold grudges like we do."

"That's true," agreed Susan. "We should try to live in the moment and keep an open heart because, obviously, any day could be our last. Well I'm going to try to see you guys more often. Maybe we should have a reunion? I could host it up in Nelson."

"That's a fantastic idea. It would give us all an excuse to get away for a weekend and let loose. Let's plan it for next summer."

They decided to make it happen and invite all their old friends from their twenties. It was a happy outcome from the devastating event.

Chapter Sixteen
The Reunion

The following year, in Nelson British Columbia, they all met at Susan and Bruce's property for the reunion. There were about thirty people total, including their adult kids. They had a large yard with plenty of room for camping out and playing games like badminton and horseshoes. Everyone brought food and they lit a fire in the evenings to hang out and talk. Nadia and Susan were both thrilled with the turnout and they reconnected with many old friends from their twenties. It was amazing to see how ex-husbands and ex-wives and their new significant others all got along famously now. Gone were the petty jealousies and grudges of earlier cheating scandals and divorces. The years had gradually washed them all away.

Lisa and David set up their Winnebago and a full-size barbecue grill for everyone to use. Alex brought his small stereo with a karaoke machine so there would be music, and everyone embarrassed themselves thoroughly with a turn at the microphone around the campfire in the evening. Raina, now twenty-five, told great stories of her recent travels to South America, which made everyone jealous of her youth and freedom. Susan and Bruce brought pot brownies to put them all in the spirit of 1980. Sam came with his girlfriend Andrea, who Nadia really connected with, in spite of the fact that she was dating her ex-husband and was years younger than them and very pretty. Susan's ex-husband Alex was still with his girlfriend Jessie, who had proven to be a really good person. Susan had grown to like and respect her. Nadia introduced Charlie to those who had never met him, and he fitted right in immediately because he was so easy-going and friendly. By the end of the weekend, it felt like he had known them as long as she had.

After they set up a badminton net, they played doubles games that were hotly contested. Alex and David cooked up some burgers and hot-dogs for everyone and several people had brought Tupperware containers full of various salads. They all pulled up their lawn chairs and feasted.

On that first night, they lit candles and held a short vigil for the one-year anniversary of Isaac's passing. Lisa cried and David spoke of their family's attempts to heal through supporting a few of Isaac's closest friends, who were also struggling emotionally. They also adopted a large, shelter dog named Rufus, who kept them very busy.

Then, to get back to a happier mood, they all got drunk and sang karaoke. Susan and Bruce sang 'Stop Dragging My Heart Around' by Tom Petty and Stevie Nicks and surprisingly, they really pulled it off. Then Sam made everybody laugh singing 'Bad to the Bone' by George Thorogood, because he couldn't hold a note if he tried. Nadia gave him full credit for making a complete ass of himself for everyone else's enjoyment. Then Lisa sang 'I Love Rock and Roll' by Joan Jett and the Blackhearts and tried to mimic that mean and raunchy swagger, to laughable effect. Charlie sang 'Everybody Wants to Rule the World' by Tears for Fears and had a really good voice. Nadia decided she had to drag Susan up with her for a B52's number and they sang 'Love Shack' together, bopping around joyfully. All their children were either killing themselves laughing, videotaping them or dying of embarrassment to some degree. It was such good fun.

On Sunday morning, everyone suffered from severe hangovers. They were thankful to their grown children for putting on the coffee and firing up the grill to make their parents a nice, greasy breakfast. As the elders slowly pulled themselves out of the haze, Lisa reminded them that they were all supposed to bring some old photos to share, so she now called upon them to spread them out on a large, plastic, folding table.

The parents all gathered around the table now, pointing and laughing and recalling shared memories.

"Look at you Nadia, in that ripped concert t-shirt and cut-off jean shorts. What a badass!" Susan said.

"I know right? I would have slept in that Bruce Springsteen shirt if it didn't need washing occasionally."

Alex showed Jessie a photo of himself skiing at Whistler wearing a red mac jacket and a ball cap with the band Green Day on it.

He said proudly, "I was so radical back then dude!"

David pointed out his old truck that he was so fond of and recalled the four of them sleeping in the canopy after skinny-dipping at Meager Creek Hot springs.

All the twenty-something children were gathered round marvelling at their parents' days of being relevant and cool, and laughing at their long hair, stoner vibe and laid-back attitude.

"Geez mom, you look like a total hippy in that sundress," Raina remarked.

"I know Raina. I pretty much was I guess."

"You and Lisa are both basically wearing the same outfit. I guess you shopped at the same thrift shops together back then?"

"Yah, we were pretty inseparable for a while there," Susan mused distantly.

Stella had been listening to this conversation and she suddenly realised that Raina had no idea about the childhood incident that had torn these women apart. Only Stella knew from what her mom had told her in the car that day after Grandma Brenda's house fire. She looked at her mom to gauge her emotions and could sense that she felt a little uncomfortable, so she quickly changed the subject.

"Dad, you look so ridiculous in those red Adidas short-shorts. Is that really what guys wore back then?"

"I'm afraid so Stella. We wore it loud and proud too."

Everyone chuckled. They continued looking at the photo table for another twenty minutes while they finished their coffee and then began to clean up their camp, in preparation for the long drive back to the city.

As Raina and Stella were putting away the horseshoes into a small shed at the back of the property, Stella suddenly lapsed on her promise to keep her mother's secret.

"So, Raina, do you have any memory of what happened between you and Malory when you were little kids?"

Raina was taken by surprise. "What are you talking about?"

"I mean the time when you were kids and you hurt her so badly."

"What the hell are you talking about?" said Raina, sounding more alarmed now.

"Well, apparently when you were five, you pushed

Malory into a dresser and broke her wrist and she had to go to hospital and have surgery."

"What the hell?" Now she was really freaking out. "Who told you this?"

"My mom did, a couple of years ago. That's why my mom and your mom never spoke to Lisa for years," Stella explained.

"Oh my God! I've got to go." Raina backed out of the shed in a panic. She ran into the bushes and doubled over, hyperventilating and feeling sick. So many thoughts and questions raced through her mind at once. Had she really done this terrible thing, and if so, why was it kept a secret all these years?

Was there something wrong with her that she would hurt another girl like that? She remembered their family moving to Nelson very suddenly when she was young. Had she caused them to leave Vancouver and eventually get a divorce? Had she single-handedly ruined her parents' friendships? She ran to her mother and pulled her over to the car.

"What's wrong?" She could see that Raina was upset. She started crying and Susan realised that they needed a private space to talk so they went for a quick drive a few blocks away and parked down a gravel road. She turned to face her daughter, very worried.

"What's going on? You're really scaring me."

Raina finally stopped crying and pulled herself together enough to speak.

"Stella just told me that I hurt Malory when we were five years old and she had to go to the hospital. Why am I just hearing about this now?"

"You were five! Children that young make mistakes all the time. Who knows what triggered you to hurt her? You kids were playing happily in the bedroom one minute and we moms were having coffee in the kitchen. Apparently, Malory pulled the head off your Barbie and you got mad and pushed her. It was an accident. Nadia and I all felt that Lisa completely overreacted due to some past experience of her own."

"But why would I hurt her like that? That's so twisted! What kind of a freak does that?" Raina implored.

Her mom vehemently denied the sentiment. "You're not a freak honey, you were a perfectly normal, well-adjusted kid. You probably didn't even realise you shoved her so hard. You must have felt provoked in that moment. Who knows? Like I said, we didn't see what happened. Besides, you needed as much therapy after the incident as Malory did."

"Therapy! What kind of therapy? I can't remember any of this." Raina was really freaking out.

"After that incident, you became very withdrawn and anxious. You wouldn't participate in any play dates with other kids. You would just stand back and watch from a distance. You couldn't handle birthday parties at all. You received some state-of-the-art light therapy in a special room they had. It was supposed to desensitise you from the trauma and it really helped. It was a very tough time for you."

Raina suddenly remembered the room with the funny, flashing, coloured lights. She recalled a man's face with glasses and a grey beard. The man was wearing a white coat and telling her to raise her hand and press some buttons. Raina started to feel a little calmer, however there was still a question burning in her mind. Without any inhibition, she blurted it out, "Was this the reason you and dad split up?"

"Oh my God no! Your dad and I had plenty of our own problems, but you were the one good thing in our lives that we always agreed upon. You were our greatest joy, honey. Never for a minute think otherwise."

"But what about Malory? Was she okay?" Raina implored.

"Well I don't really know. Lisa never told us what happened after the incident. I only know that Malory got a cast on her wrist and got some kind of treatment afterwards. I know her mom was already in counselling for some past bullying that she suffered as a young teen, so maybe she took Malory to that same psychologist. All I know is that she seems like a happy, well-adjusted, young woman who has plenty of friends. So, let's just hope that she is fine, and we can finally put this behind us."

"Should I apologise or something?" Raina worried.

"Well, that's up to you love. It's whatever you feel comfortable with. Maybe you could write her a letter telling her how you just found out about this and how you honestly feel. It's much easier to express yourself on paper than in conversation. But just take some time and think about it first. It may reopen old wounds, more than help. I'm really not sure. God honey, I'm so sorry this is upsetting you twenty years after the fact. I really thought with the reunion we had finally put this issue to rest and were moving on. This reunion has been so positive for me to reconnect with my old friends. Really, I want you to let this go and just get on with your life and be happy."

After Susan reassured her that none of this was her fault, they cried together, hugged and Susan called Nadia to explain why they had left the party so suddenly without saying goodbye.

Nadia was shocked. "Jesus, why did I tell my daughter

about all this? I'm so sorry Susan. She should have never shared that with Raina."

Susan replied, "Maybe she thought Malory was harbouring some old wounds from that time that needed to be resolved? It's okay Nadia, don't blame Stella. I do feel bad for Raina, but honestly, I'm kind of glad that it's finally all out in the open."

Nadia promised Susan she would reach out to Raina when she got back to the city to explain their side of the story. She would include Stella in the conversation as well, so that Raina would keep trusting her to lean on. They bid their farewells to Lisa and David, Sam and Andrea, Alex and Jessie and the other guests and began the long drive home.

Susan and Nadia were fifty-two years old now and everything had come full circle. Of course, each person's version of the past was slightly different, and they all blamed each other for their own hurt and pain, as people do. Nobody had healed entirely, but they were now on their way towards carving out a new version of happiness, with new friends and partners. Their children were adults and had lives of their own, but this new revelation had no doubt helped them to piece together their parents' history. The saddest part was that their lives had been shaken by such child's play and that it had taken twenty years to come full circle and find closure.

Chapter Seventeen
Bruce

Exactly one year after the reunion, Susan called Nadia with some bad news.

"Bruce has prostate cancer."

"Oh Susan, I'm so sorry. What stage is it?"

"Stage three. He hadn't been for a physical in three years, so it has progressed further than if they caught it earlier. I bugged him to go, but he hates going to the doctor and he's so stubborn. Part of me is mad at him, but I can't tell him that of course."

"Oh, I'm sure he already knows and feels bad enough about it already. So, what course of treatment are they recommending?"

"Surgery and then radiation. He will have to go to Kelowna for the surgery. They don't have an oncologist surgeon here, but we do have the radiation available here. Luckily his sister lives there and we can stay with her."

"So, when is this happening?" Nadia asked.

"Right away. We are just waiting for the call for scheduling and then we have to hit the road. Raina can look after Eli, but Alex has offered to keep an eye on both of them as well."

"That's good. So how are you getting time off work to deal with all this?"

"They gave me a leave of absence for the next week and then we'll see after that. I should be able to drive him to radiation, since my rec centre job is only before and after school."

"Do you need money to make up for the lost week?" Naida offered.

"God, I am pretty worried about paying the bills this month. Could I borrow a bit?" Susan sounded sheepish.

"I'm sending you a thousand dollars and you don't need to pay me back. I won't hear another word about it," Nadia insisted.

"Oh my God, you are the greatest friend ever! I love you Nadia."

"I love you too girl. Just keep me posted on how you are doing, even if you just feel scared and you need to call at three in the morning to cry it out."

"Thanks Nadia, I would be lost without you."

"You would do the same for me. I know you would, so forget about it."

A week later, Bruce had had the surgery and was back in Nelson starting radiation. He was feeling okay and Susan was able to go back to work. Nadia called her every week to get an update. Three months later, there was a setback.

"The cancer has metastasised to his colon as well. He is so dejected. He has to go for chemo now. I'm really scared this time Nadia."

"Shit girl, I'm so sorry. Things were sounding so positive last week."

"I know, but then he got a scan and now this showed up. It's awful. I don't know how I'm going to tell the kids."

"Just be honest with them. They are old enough to

understand and they would want to know. It's worse if you don't tell them because they won't have time to process their emotions. Call Eli's school counsellors and get them on board. Raina will support her little brother too you know. They can lean on each other."

"Yah, you're right. That's a good idea. I will call the school as soon as I talk to the kids. Maybe I'll take them out for supper tonight, just the three of us, if Raina isn't working."

Several months later, the chemo hadn't been successful, and Bruce was in a palliative care unit. He declined rapidly and died just before Christmas. Nadia took Stella up there for Christmas break to cheer Susan up. She knew that Stella was good at talking to Raina and could lighten Eli's mood as well.

Stella took Raina out for coffee one morning and began the conversation.

"I'm so sorry about your stepdad. He was a really nice guy."

"Yah, he was. It's been really hard on my little brother."

"Eli is stronger than you think. He will be okay, especially because he has you and Susan to lean on."

Then Raina surprised her by bringing up the childhood incident with Malory. Stella felt bad that she had burdened her with this information back at the reunion.

"I have written a letter to Malory," Raina began, "but I'm too afraid to send it. Could you read it and let me know what you think?"

"Sure, if you're comfortable sharing that with me, I'd be happy to."

Raina produced some folded papers from her back pocket and handed them across the table. Then she went up to the counter to order some food, leaving Stella to read the letter.

'Dear Malory, I know this is twenty years too late, but I have to get this off my chest or I will never be able to live with myself.

I have very little memory from childhood about what happened between us. I can only remember flashes of going to see a therapist with my mom and looking at some flashing lights in a strange room. Unfortunately, I can't remember hurting you. It was Stella who told me what happened, from a conversation with her mom. I was totally shocked and devastated that I could have done something like this to you. I want to tell you that I am truly sorry for any pain or emotional distress I have caused you. I would never dream of hurting a friend like that. I don't think that I had any weird intentions when I was five, but I still feel ashamed that this happened. I really hope that you are okay and don't feel permanently scarred by this event.

I also feel bad that apparently this caused some kind of rift between our moms. I know they were close friends before this happened because I have seen so many photos of them hanging out when they were younger. I have overheard my mom saying that she misses your mom and wishes they could still see each other. Maybe we can somehow help them bridge this gap and get together? I don't want to meddle in their affairs, but if you know of any way to help that along, that's up to you. No pressure, of course.

Well, you don't need to reply to this letter, but if I run into you at our future functions, I would hope that you can at least feel safe and comfortable around me. I am not a monster, I promise. I have a really sweet boyfriend named Jason who can vouch for that. Please let me know if there is anything else, I can do to make this right.

Thanks for listening, Raina.'

When Raina came back to the table with a banana-chocolate muffin, Stella told her the letter was perfect and she should definitely send it.

"Really? You think so? I was afraid it was too much."

"No, I think it's really nice and I'm sure she will too. Go for it. What harm can it do? Even if you never talk to her again, you'll feel better knowing that you set the record straight. And who knows? Maybe our moms can all get over themselves and spend more time together. I know my mom would love to see Lisa as well."

"Great, thanks Stella. You're awesome. I'm so glad I can talk to you about anything."

"No worries man, I will always have your back. Now, tell me all about this boyfriend."

They chatted for a couple of hours and went for a long walk in the snow around the town of Nelson. Raina wanted to spend as much time with her as she could and with her little half-brother Eli, who was now in grade nine, while he struggled with his dad's passing. Stella suggested they go skating with him after supper at the local rink. She knew Eli was a hockey player, so he could show off his skills to her and this would give him a boost. Raina agreed and they went back to Susan's place.

The next day, Nadia helped Susan sort through Bruce's clothing and belongings and make a donation bin for the Salvation Army thrift store. They asked Eli which shirts he wanted to keep, and Susan kept his favourite brown flannel so she could smell his scent whenever she needed a good cry. They shared many memories of Bruce and many tears while they went through the closet. It was good therapy.

When Susan and Stella left to drive back to Vancouver, they extended an open invitation to all three of them to come and stay whenever they wanted. They had a spare room for Susan and a couch and air mattress downstairs for the kids. Susan promised she would take them up on the offer real soon. Nadia slipped the cheque for $1000 under her friend's coffee cup, which she discovered when she went back inside and shook her head, smiling.

Two months later, Raina received a letter from Malory.

'Dear Raina, Thank you for your recent apology letter. It was very sincere, and I appreciate the gesture. I am actually doing fine and like you, I also have very little memory of that event. I have seen my medical chart, which says that I had counselling at that time, and I know the counsellor because my mom still sees the old dude once in a while. However, I don't recall the actual event itself. Maybe I blocked it out because it was painful? I'm not sure. Anyhow, I accept your apology and please don't worry about running into me at our functions. It's all good. I am very happy, and I also have a boyfriend who loves me, so I guess we both turned out okay, right?

As for our moms, I am going to stay out of it. I'm sure they can solve their own problems. I don't think my mom has anything against your mom or Stella's mom anymore, as the reunion went so well last year. You shouldn't worry about them. They are big girls who can fight their own battles. Well, take care and see you around.

Hugs, Malory.'

Raina felt so relieved. She texted Stella right away to tell her the good news. Stella shared this with her mom and then Nadia called Susan to pass it on. The two women were very pleased that this had come full circle and worked itself out. They were thrilled to hear that Lisa felt no ill will towards them any longer. It was a great relief for everyone.

Shortly after returning to the city, Nadia discovered online that Lisa had started a charity in her son's memory called Isaac's Smile, whose goal was to raise scholarship funds for local lacrosse players to start post-secondary education. Nadia saw an opportunity to reach out and re-connect. She sent Lisa a message that she would like to offer some help over the summer break. The following day, Lisa called her.

"Hi Nadia. How are you? I really appreciate your offer to help out with the charity."

"I'm doing fine. Yah, well it's school holidays now so what kind of help do you need?"

"Well ideally, if you could call around to some local businesses out where you live to solicit donations, that would be awesome. I don't know anybody else in your part of the city."

"Sure, I can do that. How much money are we talking about?"

"Well, we have already raised $6000, but I'm hoping to double that amount to be able to support two boys and two girls with their tuition from Isaac's old team and the sister team."

"Wow, okay. I guess any donation is helpful right?"

"Oh, for sure. Some smaller businesses may offer only $50, but if you can ask the bigger places, like builders, real estate agencies, lawyer's offices, they may be able to give more. Any amount is good, and I will send you my tax receipt template so you can just enter the amount and print them a copy."

"Sounds good. Say, did you know that Susan's husband Bruce died recently?"

"Oh my God, no. What happened?"

"He had prostate cancer, which turned into colon cancer and then he went fairly quickly."

"Oh, poor Susan. I will have to give her a call. How is she holding up?"

"Well not too great, as you will fully understand. Maybe you can offer some insight into the grieving process and how to cope?"

"Sure, I will try, but everyone is so different. I went to a support group and it really helped. Maybe she can find something like that in her small town."

"Well Lisa, it's great that I can help you with the charity, but I'd also love to get together sometime."

"For sure. We hold a monthly meeting of volunteers for the charity, so in two weeks you can come to my place for that. We usually end up having a couple of glasses of wine and some snacks afterwards."

"Sounds great. Send me the details and I will be there for sure. It will be great to see you."

"Okay perfect. I will email you an information package for the charity in the next few minutes. Let me know if you have any questions after you read through the material. Talk to you soon Nadia."

"Okay thanks and do give Susan a call. She would love to hear from you. Bye Lisa."

Two weeks later, Nadia was on her way to Lisa's for the meeting. She had managed to collect eleven hundred dollars from community sponsors. Lisa was thrilled and gave her a big hug when she told her the good news. There were six other people there, one being the lacrosse coach who had brought forth a short-list of names of possible worthy recipients on the teams.

They chose two boys and two girls whose families were on low incomes and made plans to publish their success in the local papers. They brainstormed a few more businesses to target to reach their goal. Afterwards, Lisa brought out appetisers and wine and they mingled.

David came back from the gym and gave Nadia a big hug. She hadn't seen him since the reunion and she missed his warm presence and humour in her life. She invited him to bring Lisa over for a barbeque sometime soon and he promised he would.

"How is Malory coping with her brother's passing?" Nadia asked.

"Oh, pretty well, all things considered. She gets teary sometimes, but less and less often. She saw a counsellor after his accident because she was afraid to drive for a while. That really helped," David explained.

"So, have you seen Sam since the reunion?" Nadia asked.

"Oh yah, but just once. I drove up there for a weekend of golf with him in April. We had a great time. He seems really happy living in the Kootenays."

"Yah, I think that girlfriend of his is awesome. She keeps him grounded and Stella really likes her too. She is calling her step-mom now." Nadia wanted David to know that she was fine with him moving on with his life.

"Yah, Andrea is awesome. He is drinking way less now. I think he has really got his shit together."

Lisa left a conversation with the coach to come over and greet her husband.

"Hey there buff guy, look who stepped up and raised eleven hundred dollars for our boy."

"Wow, nice job Nadia. You must have good people skills or something. Who knew?" he laughed.

"Yah, I guess so," Nadia enjoyed the flattery. "I should try out my charms on you two sometime? Maybe I could get myself a free meal?"

"For sure," David offered, "the door is always open."

Nadia tried to gauge how Lisa felt about the open invitation, but she kept a pretty good poker face.

"Well next time I'm in the city, I might take you up on that." Nadia decided to hold them to it.

She had already made good progress with Lisa, so she figured she may as well keep the ball rolling.

After saying good night, she drove home to the suburbs feeling very positive. Her goal to reconnect with Lisa had been realised and they were feeling more comfortable with each other. The small group setting had smoothed things over and taken the pressure off, and they had managed to avoid any heavy conversation about the past or about the huge passage of time they had allowed to slip between them. Maybe next visit they could talk about their kids and the recent reconciliation between Malory and Raina.

When Nadia got home, she called Susan to tell her the good news. Susan was relieved to hear this, but she sounded sad at the same time.

"What's wrong Susan? Have you been crying?"

"Maybe a little," she admitted. "I am having a hard time financially since Bruce died. I paid off the mortgage after my dad died, but the bills have mounted up again. Raina is going to move in with her boyfriend anyhow, so I'm thinking of selling the house and renting. I only need two bedrooms for Eli and me."

"I'm sending you some money. How much do you need to get through the month?" Nadia insisted.

"Maybe four hundred? I feel terrible taking your money Nadia. You have helped me so much these past few years."

"Don't worry about it. You've been through a lot Susan. It's not your fault your husband died and left you with only one income. Eventually you are going to meet somebody nice and things will get easier."

"God, I can't even wrap my head around that idea. I'm just not ready to get out there again. My children are my only priority right now."

"It will happen, it just takes time. I am e-mailing you four hundred right now and I won't hear another word about it. Lisa suggested going to a support group for grieving spouses. I think that would be a good idea. Ask your doctor or community centre where to find one."

"Maybe you're right. Okay, I will try. Thanks Nadia. You're a lifesaver. I'm so glad you reconnected with Lisa. That's wonderful news. Talk to you soon."

"Hang in there, girl. Things can only get better."

Chapter Eighteen
Susan Moves In

A few months later, Nadia woke up with an idea she just couldn't shake. She sat down at the breakfast table with a cup of coffee and shared it with Charlie. She kissed him on the forehead.

"Good morning sunshine. I have a proposal for you, but feel free to shoot it down if you don't like the idea."

"Okay… what's on your mind sweetheart?"

"Well you know how Susan has been struggling to make ends meet since Bruce died right?"

"Yes."

"And you know how Ethan has moved out with Darren and Stella is on her way out soon and we hardly ever use the basement rec room anymore?"

"Yes… I think I can see where this is going."

"Well, what if we put in a dividing wall to make a bedroom for Eli and let them live in our basement?"

"Wow, well that's really sweet of you and I think you're an incredibly supportive friend and while I really like Susan and Eli, I need to think about it and look at the cost of putting in a bedroom wall."

"But you're not saying no?"

"I'm not saying no, but I'm not saying yes, just yet."

She jumped up and gave him a big hug. "I love you. You're the best!"

"Uh huh, I don't know if I'm the best, but would they be living here for free?" Charlie asked.

"Oh, we could work that out. I was thinking of some sort of sliding scale. Like when she finds more work, she can pay more according to her ability. We don't really need the money, right?"

"Well, I do like money," Charlie smiled.

"I know, I know. They would definitely pay for their own food and phones and anything they need."

"Okay honey, I will look into it and get back to you really soon, but please don't make her any promises just yet okay?"

"Okay, I promise not to mention it until you approve."

Nadia couldn't contain her excitement though. She was buzzing around the basement looking at options all morning. She figured the bathroom was adequate for them, but she would need to get rid of some excess furniture and some of the kids' old junk like toys and sports equipment that was cluttering up the space. She would ask the kids what was really important to keep and then make a donation bin for the local thrift store and move some into the garage. The blinds needed fixing in one section, so she would call her friend Darlene who installed them. She had plenty of bedding for them, but she would need a single bed for Eli. Susan could use the pull-out sofa, which was actually very comfortable. They would share the kitchen and cooking duties, which Nadia would like, given that Susan was a much better cook than she was. It would be fun to have a teenager around again. She missed having that energy and laughter in the house.

Charlie got his construction friend Steve to come over and

look at the space. He said he could put in a wall for four thousand dollars. Being the sweetheart that he was, Charlie agreed. Nadia was jumping up and down to call Susan.

"Hi there. I have a proposal for you!" Nadia couldn't contain herself.

"Okay, I'm listening, what's going on?"

"How would you and Eli like to move into our basement suite? We would be putting in a wall to make a bedroom for Eli and there's already a bathroom with a shower and a really comfy, pull-out double sofa bed for you. You could pay whatever you can afford, based on whether you're unemployed or working part or full-time. What do you think?"

"Wow, Nadia that's an amazingly nice offer. I will have to think it over and talk to Eli. I don't think he'd be thrilled about leaving his friends, but he might be psyched to move to the city. Is Charlie okay with all this?"

"Yah, he is totally on board, I promise. We would love to have you here. Can you imagine how great it will be for us to be living together Susan? We could go out and do things around the city whenever we felt like it, just like old times!"

"Well, I will have to find a job Nadia, but sure, it would be awesome. We could hang out and drink coffee and talk or go to yoga together. I can see how it could be so much fun. But let me talk to Eli and I'll call you back in a few days okay?"

"No problem girl, and please don't feel pressured either way. I know I sound excited, but I can handle a no answer, if it's not going to work for you guys. Be honest, okay?"

"For sure Nadia. I so appreciate the offer. It's unbelievably nice of you and please thank Charlie for me as well."

"Will do. Talk to you soon."

Four days passed by and Nadia assumed it was a no go, but she was wrong. Susan was moving in at the end of the month and they were both so excited. Charlie went ahead with the work and the bedroom was framed off and then he painted it pale green to match their decor. They bought a cheap bed and dresser set from a friend and Nadia got her mom's old TV set up downstairs for them. She enjoyed decorating the space and put up a few old photos of her and Susan when they were in their prime. She even found a photo of Eli when he was little and hung it on his bedroom wall as a welcoming surprise.

When they arrived, Susan was overwhelmed with the change for the first little while. She had lived in a small town for almost twenty years, so it was a big adjustment. The traffic alone was shocking, even in the suburbs. She had to register Eli for grade eleven at the local high school, find a family doctor and generally get her bearings in this part of the city that she was unfamiliar with. Then she had to look for work. It was all very challenging, especially since she was still grieving Bruce and now also dealing with the emotions of leaving their shared home behind.

Stella came over to take Eli out a few times. She showed him the sites of Vancouver and even took him to a party with her friends, which he thought was very cool because they were all about seven years older than him. She introduced him to a neighbour and family friend his own age, who agreed to walk to school with him for the first week and help him find his way. The two boys hit it off and started hanging out, playing X-Box together.

Nadia was thrilled to have Susan around and they fell into a comfortable routine. Susan would cook for all of them three times a week and they would share grocery shopping duties by keeping a joint list on the fridge door. They would clean their own living space and do their own laundry. Susan and Eli would come upstairs for movie night on Fridays and they would all sit down for dinner together on Sunday nights, which seemed kind of old fashioned, but it was the only way they could all connect with Eli once a week.

Susan found work fairly quickly at the local newspaper managing their website and was also on-call for keeping the minutes at town council meetings until a more permanent position became available. They worked out a fair scheme for paying rent and everybody was happy. Susan could even visit her father more often now, who lived across town with his new wife. Her mother had died a few years before, after a long struggle with multiple sclerosis.

After Susan got settled, Nadia wanted to invite her to Lisa's monthly charity meeting for the Isaac's Smile. She got the okay from Lisa and they headed into town together one evening.

"I can't believe I feel nervous about seeing her," admitted Susan.

"Well, I'm not surprised," Nadia understood," I felt the same way the first time I went, even though the reunion two years ago was great. When you get to her place though, there will be five other volunteers to act as buffers, so that will make it easier."

When they arrived, Lisa gave Susan a warm hug and said she was happy to have her back in the city once again. Susan was thrilled to see David as well and they caught up on news about Alex and their kids. Alex was still living in Nelson with Jesse and working as a surveyor for a local forestry company. David and Lisa's daughter Malory had just finished her degree in counselling psychology and was going to be starting work in a high school the next week. Susan's daughter Raina had moved in with her boyfriend in Nelson and was still working at the hotel. Stella wanted to follow in Nadia's footsteps, so she was just finishing her teaching practicum and wanted to work at middle school, specialising in physical education. All their kids had turned out just fine, or so it seemed.

After the meeting, Lisa was thrilled that Susan could ask her connections at council meetings to solicit donations for Isaac's charity. It wasn't the time or place to address their past conflict over the childhood trauma between Malory and Raina, but both Susan and Nadia wished to clear the air with Lisa at some point in the near future. They agreed in the car on the way home to bring it up the next time the three of them got together in a more private setting. This would bring their healing full circle and allow them all closure, once and for all.

At this point, Susan's son Eli was a striking kid at sixteen, with his dad's black hair and wide nose and his mom's doe eyes. He was muscular from hockey and wore his hair buzzed all over except for a long swoop of bangs that he brushed straight back, gelled into place like the old pompadour style. He looked like a young, Italian, stallion without the Vespa; he naturally possessed that kind of swagger. After four months of school, Eli was fully settled into his new environment and had a group of friends from the hockey team he joined. Three of the team boys were in his classes and they got along really well. They were constantly flirting with various girls and having little get-togethers on the weekends; Susan was thrilled that her son seemed happy after the move.

Susan's life was also settling nicely. She had found all the local services and established a routine. It even looked like there may be a full-time position opening up in the local city hall administration office because a woman was retiring. Susan planned to apply and felt hopeful, since she knew the interview team from her job recording the minutes at their council meetings. She took some on-line seminars in the evenings to improve her computer skills and polished up her curriculum vitae. She even bought a new business outfit for the occasion.

Four days later she got the job, so they all drank a glass of champagne to toast the occasion with dinner that night. "Congratulations girl, you did it! Now all your money worries are over!" Nadia said.

"Thanks Nadia. I couldn't have done it without you. Really, and you too Charlie. You guys have been my greatest cheerleaders throughout this whole process."

"Well, now you will have medical and dental benefits for you and Eli, as well as a pension plan. I'm so happy for you."

Eli looked pleased with his mother's success. He had no doubt internalised her struggles since his dad had died and worried more than any teenager should have to. He gave his mom a hug and she teared up a little.

"Yah, I guess it's been a hard road for a while now. I couldn't really see it at the time, but I'm glad this phase is coming to an end. I feel like I can breathe for the first time in maybe two years," Susan admitted.

Christmas with Eli and Stella was fun, and Stella even brought her new boyfriend over for dinner. His name was Brian and he was from Ontario. He was currently doing a master's in computer science at her university. They seemed fairly compatible to Nadia, but it was still early days. They all did a small gift exchange before dinner and then enjoyed a turkey feast. Eli got some new hockey equipment from his mom, now that Susan had more money. Nadia gave Stella her grandmother's sapphire ring, which she was thrilled with.

After Christmas, Eli started staying out late with his friends, even on some school nights, and Susan was getting worried. She laid down a rule that he needed to be home by ten o'clock and he broke it repeatedly. She wondered how to discipline him appropriately, because he was six feet tall and growing facial hair already. She wanted to respect his privacy, but his school performance was slipping. His math teacher had called about several missed assignments and after a heated argument one night, he slammed the door and left to sleep at a friend's place.

Susan was very upset.

"Nadia, I'm at my wit's end. What am I going to do with this kid? If he ruins his grades, he won't be able to get into the tech programs that interest him in college. Do you think maybe Charlie could talk to him?"

"I will ask him, but he might want to keep out of it so that Eli has a neutral supporter, who is male, in the house. That way, Eli might confide in him when he really needs help."

"Hmmm, that's a good point. I never thought about it that way. Do you think he's hiding something from me?" Susan was worried.

"They are all hiding something at his age girl. They want to get away from any parental control so badly. It's totally normal. But I have to say that he does seem quiet and moody lately. I can't even get a 'good morning' out of him at breakfast and that's not like him," Nadia replied.

The next weekend, Eli didn't come home at all. He texted his mom and told her he was staying at Paul's place until

Sunday night.

"I don't trust this Paul kid," Susan told Nadia. "That guy has got a dark side. He just looks like trouble with his tattoos and piercings. I'm going to look in Eli's room and check out his laptop," Susan couldn't help herself.

"Jesus Susan, are you sure you want to go that route? If he finds out, he'll be furious. Besides that, how do you know his password?"

"It was the condition of me buying him the laptop. He had to agree to a shared e-mail account. There's been too many cases of disturbing webcam sextortion between teens lately. I just wanted to be sure everything is above board. I told him I wanted to use the laptop as well for my computer course, which was true."

"Okay, well good luck girl. I truly hope you don't find anything."

Susan came back upstairs half an hour later looking shaken. She held up a small baggie containing about ten pink and blue pills stamped with a butterfly.

"What the hell is that?" Nadia asked.

"I have no idea, but it's nothing any doctor prescribed for him. I'm guessing it's Ecstasy or Molly or some other party drug."

"Shit Susan, I'm so sorry. What are you going to do?"

"Confront him, obviously. What else can I do? Will you guys help me sit down and talk to him?"

"Sure, sure, I will talk to Charlie. We can say that he's not allowed to bring this stuff into our house. Hopefully that will put some pressure on him to clean up his act. Have you seen him look high lately?"

"He seemed a little out of it last Friday when he came back

to get his wallet. He was with that Paul guy, big surprise. I wonder if Paul even has parents. I don't even know if he goes to Eli's school or he's older."

"Well, we can all sit down on Sunday night when he gets home and have the talk. God, this is so shitty. I never pictured Eli taking drugs. He's so into his hockey, I thought it would be more of a health concern for him."

"Yah, me too," Susan agreed, "but it's everywhere nowadays. When we were his age it was just weed and booze mostly. Acid was the only real hard drug around our party scene. Now there are all these other scary addictive options. I hate this!"

When Eli showed up on Sunday night, he looked tired and was reluctant to sit down at the table. Nadia expected this, so she made his favourite triple chocolate cake to coax him. Charlie came and joined them and after the cake, Susan pulled out the baggie.

"Eli, what's this?" she asked.

Eli turned red and blurted out, "You have no right going in my room!"

"I'm your mother. If I don't have the right, then who does?"

"Nobody," he shouted, "it's my only private space!"

"What is this stuff?" Susan was yelling now too.

Charlie stepped in at this point. "Look Eli, you know we all love you, but we have to set some ground rules if you're living here under our roof. You can't bring drugs into this house. I'm guessing it's Molly or MDMA or Ecstasy, right? Also, the thing that worries us the most is that you seem to have more than just a personal use quantity here. Are you selling this shit now?"

"No, I just share it with my friends at parties and stuff. It's not that expensive." Charlie knew Eli was lying because he didn't have a job to pay for it.

"It's more money than you have, son."

"I'm not your son!" Eli lashed out.

"I know you're not my son, but I care about you," Charlie tried to calm him down. "Your mom is just worried because your schoolwork seems to be sliding and you won't be able to go to college without good grades. Your friend Paul also seems to be a bad influence on you at this point."

"Does he even have parents?" Susan asked.

"Of course, he has parents. They live in Langley, just over the bridge. But he has his own apartment."

"Ah, and there it is," Susan understood, "the parent-free zone where anything goes. So that's why you've been hanging out there all weekend. Well this is stopping now. You can't see Paul anymore and you're grounded for a month. No more going out after school. You come straight home, do your homework and get your act together."

"Or what?" Eli was defiant.

"Or I guess you will have to move out." Susan called his bluff, "and no more hockey or rides anywhere either." She knew he didn't have the means to make it on his own. Eli looked shocked. He sat there silent for a few long minutes, pondering her ultimatum. Finally, he gave in.

"Okay mom, you win. But can I still have friends over here?"

"Sure, one at a time. No problem. Just not Paul. He is too old to be hanging out with high school kids anyhow. He needs to get a life. Now, I'm going to flush this shit down the toilet. Put your cake plate in the dishwasher and do your math homework."

Eli slunk downstairs, and Charlie and Nadia congratulated her on the win. They decided to inform his school counsellor and his hockey coach about the drugs and ask them to keep an eye on him more closely, to make sure he was on the right path with his schoolwork and attendance. Gradually, things did turn around, but it was a scary time for Susan. Nadia felt she had dodged a bullet because she never had to go through this with Stella. She had lucked out in that department. Now if she could just make sure Stella didn't get pregnant until her career was off the ground, she would be satisfied she had done a fairly good job of single-parenting.

Chapter Nineteen
B52s

One Saturday morning, Nadia suggested to Susan that they should do something fun with Lisa, to really have a chance to talk and clear the air once and for all about any old issues. Nadia had found out that the B52s would be playing a concert soon in Vancouver. It was the music they had all loved to dance to the most when they were in their twenties, so they figured it would be hard for Lisa to resist the invite, especially if Nadia bought her a ticket.

Lisa agreed and the three of them met at a Greek restaurant for dinner downtown beforehand. It was an authentic looking whitewashed decor with vines hanging from the ceilings and fake, classical busts overlooking the diners. The three women were led to a cosy corner table with a red checked tablecloth. Once the starter pita bread and hummus dip arrived, Nadia took a chance.

"So, Lisa, I really wanted to make peace with you about what happened all those years ago with the kids. I'm guessing that you know about the letters that Malory and Raina exchanged recently right?"

"Yes, Malory told me. I thought it was good for both of them and Malory really appreciated her initiative on that."

"That's awesome," Nadia continued. "I just want you to know that we never felt like blaming the kids for their behaviour was the right way to go. Susan and I never felt that Raina was acting maliciously with the intent to harm Malory. We both felt terrible that it caused our friendship to be damaged and we never wanted to stop communicating with you. It all just kind of got out of hand and we are sorry."

"Well thanks," Lisa accepted the apology, "but I don't know how you can hurt someone that badly without intent. I think that young children understand a lot more than we give them credit for sometimes, but let's not rehash. The important thing is that they both worked through it and grew up to be happy, healthy adults."

Nadia felt her ire rising again at Lisa's refusal to take responsibility for blaming a five- year-old for her own issues. Susan sensed Nadia's frustration and jumped in to save the moment.

"I couldn't agree more. Thank you for allowing us to move past this and rekindle our friendship. You are so important to us Lisa. I really missed having you and Malory around these past twenty years."

Lisa agreed, "Yah, it was really hard, especially for David, Alex and Sam too. They were kind of caught in the fallout and I always felt bad about that. But it seems like they managed to keep in touch and ignore all our drama for the most part."

"Yah, I think men are better at letting things go than we arc," Susan said.

They enjoyed the rest of their meal and kept the conversation light by revisiting old memories of all the fun times they had shared in their twenties. Afterwards, they walked to the concert, which was a fantastic show. Everyone was out of their seats and dancing. Lisa bought them all t-shirts as a thank you for the free ticket. At midnight, Susan and Nadia hugged Lisa good-bye and caught the Skytrain back to the suburbs.

Exhausted but happy, Nadia leaned her head on Susan's shoulder and congratulated her for their breakthrough.

"Well that went about as well as it could have, right?" Susan asked.

"Well it wasn't perfect, but it was a pretty good outcome. I'm ready to close the book on that whole chapter, even though I doubt she will never see things the same way I do. I have tried for two decades to secure a five-year-old's redemption and now I'm giving up. We just have different views on child development, but I still love her as a friend and want her in my life. Jesus, live and learn I guess."

The next day, Susan phoned Raina to tell her the good news. She was very relieved to hear that her mom and Lisa had made amends. Stella was also updated and was thrilled that her mom sounded at peace and had her old friend back in her life for real, especially since her dad and Lisa had always kept in touch. Now there would be no more friction among her parents' friends and her buddy Raina could really move on. Everyone was glad to put it behind them.

Eli was also staying on a good path lately. His grades at school had improved and he'd been promoted up a level in hockey, to the rep team. The friend called Paul, who had led him down the garden path, was no longer in the picture and Susan was so relieved. Eli had earned back all his household privileges and had reconnected with his more positive hockey buddies.

Soon after this, Nadia got a call in the middle of the night from her mom, Josephine, who was sobbing. Apparently, her father had fallen down in the bathroom and had gone into respiratory distress. When the ambulance came, they worked on stabilising him and got him into the ambulance, where Josephine was allowed to accompany him. Upon arrival, they had used paddles to try and revive him, but he was already gone.

Nadia told her mother to wait where she was, she woke up Charlie and got him to drive her to the hospital. When they arrived, her mother was understandably in shock. She was sitting beside her husband's bed staring into space blankly. Nadia held her for a long time and reassured her that everything would be alright, she and Charlie would take care of her and make all the necessary arrangements.

Thankfully, they had not moved his body yet, so Nadia got a chance to kiss her father on the forehead. Then she sobbed uncontrollably and fell into Charlie's arms. Even though she had never had a very close relationship with her dad, the sight of him lying there, lifeless, was completely overwhelming. Nadia had never seen a dead body before and was shocked by how cold his forehead felt already.

Charlie spoke to the nurse about getting the death certificate and then drove both women to Nadia's mother's place to rest. Nadia wanted to stay with her for the day and slept beside her for a few hours, making sure she was eating and functioning again before heading home in the early evening. She promised to call her at bedtime and see her again the next day.

When Nadia got home, she felt numb. Charlie tried to get her to watch television to take her mind off things, but she couldn't. She just sat on the back patio staring at the trees and wondering what she could have done differently to connect more with her father. She knew the outline of his life through World War II and then coming to Canada, but he had never expressed any emotion about being displaced and losing his parents at such a young age. She felt deeply regretful for only scratching the surface of who her father really was and how he had suffered. Now she would never have the chance.

The next few weeks and months proved challenging. Her mother wanted to remain independent in her own home, but she was clearly not up to the task. Her arthritis was bad so she could barely lift a pot of water to boil on the stove. Nadia was afraid she would spill it and burn herself. After she convinced her to get a walker and install a stair-chair in the house, she realised that it wasn't enough. The pain in her knees was a safety issue for driving and she couldn't carry her own groceries anymore. Nadia knew that some sort of care situation was imminent but convincing her mom of this was another matter.

"Mom, how would you feel about someone coming in twice a week to help you with cleaning and bathing?"

"I don't want some total stranger seeing me naked and mucking about in my kitchen. What if they steal something?"

"They're not going to steal something mom. They have to be bonded to get the job and they would be fired instantly for stealing. They have seen hundreds of older people naked who have all the same bits as you, so you don't need to put on airs about that. I'm just worried about you falling in the tub. Please mom, won't you consider it, for my sake?"

"Oh, all right. I'll give it a try. But I don't want any man giving me a bath!"

"That's fine mom. I will insist on a female caregiver. Now what about some help with cooking? Can I set up a meal delivery service?"

"Those meals aren't healthy. They are all pre-packaged junk. I want real steamed vegetables and fresh fruit and not gravy and sauces on everything."

"We can order whatever you want mom. There are all kinds of healthy meal options available now, I promise. Let me just bring over some menus to show you."

"Won't it be too expensive? I'm not rich you know."

"I know mom, but dad left you enough to afford proper care. There's no reason to skimp on yourself when you need it the most. Take advantage of what's available. I can even get your groceries delivered now."

"Really? But how do I know the delivery person is safe?"

"They are vetted carefully by the company, mom. If it makes you more comfortable, I will get you one of those alarm bracelets so you can call for help whenever you feel worried. They just talk to you through a two-way intercom and then decide if the police or ambulance need to come out."

"Well alright dear, whatever you think is best. I'm too tired to argue with you right now. Set up whatever you want." She was being dismissive now.

"Okay thank you mom, but I'm still going to ask for your input. I'm not going to force you to do anything you don't want to." Nadia found the whole conversation exhausting.

When she got home that night, she vented to Charlie and Susan. It seemed that Susan's mother had been much more reasonable about setting up care, perhaps because she had an identifiable disease and her doctor had recommended assisted living. They both reassured Nadia that she was handling it as best she could and that she should focus on the positive. The small steps she had already accomplished were to be viewed as a triumph, not a failure.

Susan's full-time job was going well, and she had been putting away some money in the hopes of moving out and getting her own place. Even though she had enjoyed living with Charlie and Nadia, it was time. She needed more privacy if she was ever going to move on from Bruce's death and meet a new man. She had met someone nice in the maintenance department at work and sensed there might be a spark. She finally felt ready to dive in again and this seemed like the right time to move on.

"Listen guys, it has been amazing staying here for the past year and a half, but it's time for me to get my own place. I can afford it now and I want a little more space and, who knows, maybe even some privacy in case I meet a man."

"Oh, wow Susan, have you got your eye on someone in particular?"

"Yah, there's this guy at work, Kevin, who is really nice. He keeps coming upstairs and chatting with me. He pretends it's because our coffee is better upstairs, but I'm getting a vibe that there may be more to it."

"That's awesome girl. I'm so happy for you. Go for it!"

"All right Nadia, cool your jets. So, what I'm saying is, why don't you have your mom move in downstairs when I find a place?"

Charlie jumped in. "Woah, hold on there, toots, don't I get a say in this?"

"Of course, you do," Nadia said, "but you do get along great with my mom, right? She really wouldn't be that much trouble. She just does crosswords and watches TV all day. I promise she won't get in your way much at all."

"Well let me think about it before you go making any

promises please. This is a big decision. She could live another ten years or more."

"Okay, of course. Take all the time you need, but I promise I will take care of her and you won't have to do a blessed thing."

Charlie eventually agreed and three months later, Susan and Eli were moving into an apartment close by and Nadia's parents' home was sold. It was a ton of work for everyone to move Susan and Josephine both to their new homes, but Nadia found it to be a cleansing process. Her mom was quite amenable to her daughters sorting it all out, so Nadia's sister drove home from Alberta, to help out.

Nadia was a little nervous about how separating her parents' belongings might lead to conflict with her sister. She had heard of so many friends feuding with their siblings over estates and she didn't want this to happen to them. She decided to have a talk with Roseanne before they even started.

"So Rosey, I just want to say that you are important to me and I'm worried that we could end up fighting over mom and dad's stupid belongings, so let's just try and keep some perspective on what is really important here okay?"

"Yah, of course. I really don't want to take much stuff with me back to my small place in Alberta. It's already too cramped. Maybe just a few mementos. Don't worry about it. Actually Nadia, I'm really grateful that you are taking care of mom. That can't be easy having her living in your house. She can have a pretty harsh tongue sometimes."

"Yah, just yesterday she told Charlie she thought his sports card collection was a ridiculous waste of time and money."

"Oh my god, she can be so awful. How did he take it?"

"Like a champ. He is so patient with her, it's unreal. He's way more patient than I am."

"Well that's because she's not his mother. There's that five degrees of separation."

"Yah, you're right, but he's still a bloody saint. So how are we going to split up the photo albums though?"

"You keep them for now. I don't have the space. We can do that some other time. Let's just focus on donating or throwing out as much as possible. Who needs a box set of Beautiful BC magazines from 1968 anyhow?"

"Or Architectural Digest?"

They both laughed. After their talk, Nadia felt much better and they got started with the cleaning. They had rented a giant truck-sized bin that had been delivered and sat in the driveway now. Roseanne had an old friend who ran a second-hand furniture store who was coming by later with his own truck to pick up any pieces they didn't want. They shared a few heated moments over the jewellery, but generally it went quite smoothly. Roseanne took a few pieces of jewellery, some artwork, a blender and a good set of knives. Nadia also chose jewellery, as well as some bedding, a lamp, an antique side table and the silverware. She would hold for safekeeping the photo albums and her dad's war memorabilia and coin collection. At the end of the weekend, they hugged it out and promised to keep in touch about their mom's health.

Back at Susan's workplace, it turned out that she had been right about Kevin's interest in her. He finally mustered the courage to ask her out. Susan called Nadia to tell her the news.

"That's fantastic girl! Tell me about him. What does he look like?"

"Well he's tall and well-built with straight, sandy, brown

hair mixed with grey. He has nice, dark blue eyes and a goatee. I'm guessing he's a few years younger than me."

"Nice, you cradle robber you! Has he got any kids?"

"Yah, one daughter who lives in Burnaby. She's twenty-eight."

"Well that's good. At least he understands kids, so he will hopefully be able to make a connection with Eli. Does he know Eli still lives with you?"

"Oh yah, for sure. I figured it was pretty important to spell that out before he comes over here thinking it's going to be all loud sex on the couch and whatnot."

They both laughed.

"Well it's a good thing you've already started menopause girl. No more birth control for us, right?"

"Yah, thank god for that. Periods are highly overrated," Susan said.

So, three months later, things were moving fast for Susan. She and Eli moved into Kevin's small house nearby and Nadia and Charlie were introduced to him. They all got along well and began hanging out regularly for Friday movie nights with a bottle of wine and some take-out food. Eli seemed to like his mom's new boyfriend and his independent daughter Sarah, who dropped in occasionally for a meal on the weekends. Mostly he was happy to have a bigger bedroom space downstairs with a rec room attached to it for his friends and a yard. Kevin's house was way better than the small apartment Susan had previously rented for just the two of them.

Stella was now in her second year of teaching middle school P.E. and was settling into her career. She still looked more like her dad, with her curly, brown hair in long waves.

Her eyes were an amber mix of his brown and Nadia's green tones. She had turned out to be a beautiful woman aged twenty-six, especially since she got tons of exercise at work every day, which gave off a healthy radiance.

Stella had broken things off with Brian and was now seeing a young French-Canadian teacher named Dominic Colbert. Things had gradually become more serious and it seemed like they could be headed for marriage. Nadia and Charlie really liked Dom and he had already attended a few family dinners. He looked typically French, with his dark hair and eyes, neatly groomed beard and he had a wicked sense of humour. Nadia and Charlie agreed that they were a good match, so it was no surprise when they moved in together after six months of dating.

One day Stella called with some big news.

"Mom, are you sitting down?"

"Why, what's wrong?" Nadia replied.

"Nothing, I'm pregnant!" Stella sounded excited.

"Holy shit! I'm going to be a grandma! Wow this is amazing. Charlie, come here quick! Stella and Dom are having a baby!"

Then Nadia ran downstairs to tell her own mother, Josephine, that she would be a great-grandmother soon.

"That's such wonderful news dear," she beamed and gave Nadia a hug.

Nadia sprang into high gear, planning to make the spare room into a nursery so she could take the baby overnight to give Stella a break once in a while. Nadia began planning her retirement from teaching at the end of the year so she could spend more time with Stella and the baby.

"So, are you two planning on getting married?" Nadia

asked her daughter over herbal tea and scones the next Saturday morning.

"Well we don't see any rush, but it's on the table for discussion right now. Do you think it would look tacky to be showing already at my wedding?"

"Of course not, sweetheart. Susan did it, so why not you? It's totally fine. I think most people have moved past those traditional ways of thinking by now, especially your friends, my God. We could have it in our back yard if you want to keep it affordable. I would pay for some catering and you could just get a Justice of the Peace to officiate."

"That sounds pretty good mom. Let me run it by Dom and I'll get back to you."

So that summer, the wedding took place and Sam came down from Nelson to give his daughter away, although there was no aisle to walk down, just a small piece of grass to walk across. Stella invited about twenty close friends and Dom's large family flew out from Quebec. Nadia wanted to include Lisa, David and Malory in the party, mostly so that David and Sam could catch up, but also to cement the healing process between the families. Stella agreed to make her parents happy.

It was a lovely day, and everything went according to plan. The only real issue was their dog trying to get into all the photos. After the father-daughter dance in the garden, Sam surprised Stella and Dom with two tickets to Mexico for a week's honeymoon and they were thrilled. She was five months along, with a cute round belly, but still enthusiastic to go on the trip right away. Dom's parents gave a speech saying they were eternally grateful for all the love and support Nadia and Charlie had given their son since he moved to British Columbia. It was a wonderful night.

Naturally, Susan and Kevin came with Raina, Eli and Kevin's daughter Sarah. Raina brought her Australian boyfriend Jason. It seemed they were also getting serious after moving in together back in Nelson. Stella teased him that he would be the next one to get married and she was right. The following year they all took the eight-hour car ride up to the Kootenays for another wedding.

In early October, they were expecting Stella to give birth. Dom called Nadia one evening around nine o'clock to tell her that Stella was having contractions, but her waters hadn't broken yet. They were talking to the doctor, who told them to head into the hospital and they would break the amniotic sac for her to get things going.

Charlie tried to convince Nadia to get a few hours' sleep because first babies take a long time to arrive, but there was no way she could sleep. She was way too excited, so he reluctantly drove her straight away. He said he was going to come back and sleep and come in the morning, always being the reasonable one.

When she got there, Stella already had a bed and the nurse started her on an Oxytocin drip and they used what looked like a crochet hook to break her water. Nadia thought this was premature, but Stella had apparently been having contractions all day and wanted to speed the process up.

Things moved along quite quickly from there, but she was having terrible back labour, which was really hard for Nadia and Dom to watch because she was in so much pain. Finally, the obstetrician came and recommended an epidural to give her some relief and a rest before full dilation and pushing. Stella emphatically agreed with this idea and was amazed at how her pain disappeared, even though the contractions could still be seen spiking on the monitor. Nadia was so relieved to see her semi-sleeping. She told Dom to take a break and go get himself a snack and a coffee and she would text him if anything changed.

About an hour later, the epidural was wearing off and Stella suddenly felt the urge to push. Nadia texted Dom, who came running. Stella proved herself to be a championship pusher, as the baby was progressing nicely down the birth canal. Suddenly there was a moment of panic as the baby's heart rate dropped. The doctor somehow attached a monitor to the baby's scalp and said if the heart rate didn't stabilise, they might have to do an episiotomy, but thankfully a few minutes later it became regular again. Ten minutes and five great pushes later, a healthy baby emerged.

"It's a girl!" the doctor announced. Nadia and Dom were both crying and hugging each other. The nurse wiped off the baby's slippery coating, took her vitals, swaddled her and placed her gently on Stella's chest. Now it was her turn to cry.

"Oh mom, isn't she beautiful?"

"Yes, she is," Nadia beamed and kissed her daughter's forehead. "I've never seen anyone more beautiful in my life, other than you, of course."

Dom took his new daughter to let Stella rest and he stared at her with loving amazement.

"So which name did you guys decide on?" Nadia asked.

"Well we are leaning towards Madeline. what do you think honey?" he asked Stella.

"Yes, she looks like a Maddy to me."

Nadia was thrilled with their selection.

"Dom, can I hold her for a minute?" she asked hesitantly,

not wanting to interfere with his precious daddy time.

"Of course," he passed her over gingerly. "How does it feel to be a grandma?"

"It feels amazing. It's the best thing ever!" She smelled the baby's wispy ginger-brown lock of hair and inserted her pinkie finger into her curled up tiny grip. She marvelled at the miniature eyelashes and fingernails and recognised the same shaped head and pointy ears that Stella had, but her facial features were more like Dom, with a wide forehead and pouty lips. Waves of memory rushed over her from the moment she gave birth to Stella twenty-seven years ago and she was fighting back the tears again. This sleeping angel was the greatest gift her daughter could ever give her.

Charlie came into the room. "Good morning my lovelies. Well isn't this a precious sight to behold. Who is this tiny new person?"

"It's Madeline," Stella gushed. "Isn't she perfect?"

"Of course, she's perfect. How could she not be with a mother like you?" Charlie joked. "No seriously, congratulations Dom and Stella, she's really lovely. Well done. I brought you guys some coffee and donuts."

"Thanks Grandpa, you're the best," Nadia teased him.

After twenty minutes of fawning over the baby, they moved Stella and the baby upstairs to a room, where the nurses took over. Charlie took Nadia and Dom home to sleep for a while. It had been a truly amazing day.

Nadia was looking forward to building a connection between her own mother and the new baby. She was hopeful that Maddy might remember her great-grandmother Josephine as she grew up.

Unfortunately, this was not to be. Nadia's mother started

to lose her memory shortly after the baby arrived. Her mental health rapidly declined over the next few months. Charlie became frustrated with his mother-in-law because she started coming upstairs and wandering around their space, frequently criticising him for trivial things, like the kitchen being messy or the garden needing water. She would go into the fridge and start pulling out food and wiping down the shelves while he was trying to relax and watch a baseball game. She would mutter to herself incoherently the whole time, complaining that baseball was a stupid waste of time and he should get busy and do something productive. Finally, he lost his patience.

"Nadia, I'm sorry, but your mother is getting really hard to handle. I'm worried that she's going to do something erratic one day and hurt herself. Did you know she wandered down the road to the McTavish's house this morning and left a box of cookies on their porch? Mrs McTavish phoned to ask me why and I said I had no idea, so she brought them back."

"Jeez, that's not good. Yah, I have noticed some strange things downstairs in her room as well," Nadia admitted. "Yesterday, she had her silver cutlery all spread out on the bed and was polishing it with an old pair of socks, but she was using facial cream instead of silver polish. It was really odd. When I asked her, she said she needed to get ready for Christmas dinner, even though it's September. I also found her dish soap in the shower caddy and her dirty laundry under the sink. I had better take her to the doctor for an assessment."

"Good idea," Charlie sounded relieved, "and we might have to start looking at other care options Nadia. She can't live here if we have to watch her every move. It will wear us both down, until we're frazzled and fighting with each other and I don't want her to come between us."

"You are right. Of course, you are. I'm sorry I didn't notice this sooner honey. You have been a total champion with my mom." Nadia started to cry, so Charlie came over to give her a hug.

"It's okay, everything will work out. It's not your fault that your mom's getting old. It's just what happens to all of us eventually, but that doesn't make it any easier to watch and accept," he consoled her.

After the doctor's assessment, they got Josephine onto a wait list for a care home bed and three months later they got the call. She was to be moved into Sunny Cedars the following Saturday. Nadia quickly began painstakingly going through her clothes and asking what her favourite things were, but her mother's opinions were sketchy. She often couldn't recall where a certain knick-knack had come from or whether a blouse fit comfortably, so Nadia mostly had to take her best guess. She would gather up bags of her belongings and hide them in the garage while her mother was watching television in the evenings. She carefully left enough things in her room and closet so her mother wouldn't get stressed about sleeping in an empty room before moving day.

Moving day for her mother was a nightmare, mostly because Josephine had no idea what was going on. They had to pretend it was an outing to the garden shop to get her in the car. Once they arrived, Josephine got agitated so Nadia changed the story to visiting a friend while they spoke to the manager in the lobby. Then, once she was safely upstairs, she finally explained that this was her mother's 'new apartment'. Josephine said she wanted to go home. Charlie set up her TV as quickly as possible and turned it on to distract her while Nadia put up her family photos and artwork and got her clothes into the drawers. A caregiver brought her mother a nice lunch and they left her watching game shows. Nadia kissed her mother on the forehead and promised she would come by to visit her every day, which she knew was an exaggeration. Then she cried all the way home.

Two weeks later, Raina's wedding was a welcome diversion after a lousy, few months of settling Josephine into the care home. They all piled into two cars and headed up to Nelson for the weekend. The big event was taking place in Alex and Jessie's back yard. The Australian groom's family was flying in and his uncle was the officiating minister. Raina sweetly asked her younger brother Eli to be a groomsman and Susan looked so proud when he appeared with Jason's Australian mates dressed in their fancy-dress suits. Eli had grown up too quickly and was now a handsome, young man.

Lisa and her family had been invited but couldn't make it because David's father's funeral was being held the same weekend in Ontario, so they had to fly back east.

When Raina appeared in her gown, everyone gushed at how beautiful she looked. She was wearing a white, off-the-shoulder gown with her hair styled in long waves. Jason was already starting to tear up but managed to keep it together to say the vows; but Susan was a hot mess. Nadia had to keep feeding her Kleenex and she blew her nose so many times that their whole row was laughing at her. She kept apologising and passing her phone to Nadia to take pictures because she couldn't focus through all the tears.

Afterwards, they drank champagne and milled about in the garden. Sam and Alex were bonding over their shared plans to retire from geology work in the coming months. Stella chatted with Kevin's daughter Sarah, about how Eli had matured so much in the past year that she hardly recognised him. He was even sporting some scruffy facial hair now. Nadia and Charlie relaxed and watched Susan fussing over the photographer as he snapped shots of the large Australian family. She kept butting in to straighten out Juliette's train on her dress. Nadia finally stuck a glass of champagne in her hand and told her to relax already.

The weather held out and they were able to eat their dinner in the garden as planned. After the roast beef and chocolate mousse, Stella made a funny speech about her dear friend Raina who she had known since babyhood. She told stories about her many mishaps as a young girl, like when she belched loudly in class in grade two and when she lost her bathing suit bottoms jumping off the high diving board at the local pool. After she was thoroughly embarrassed, she touched everyone by saying that she was like a sister to her and she loved her dearly. Susan and Nadia leaned into each other and shed a few happy tears.

They danced and drank all night and then walked down the road to their hotel rooms. The next morning, they returned to Alex's for brunch and the gift opening. Nadia and Charlie bought Raina and Jason a spa and yoga weekend on Salt Spring Island, since he had decided to live in BC with her. Stella gave them a framed photo of Raina from childhood, doing a flip off the dock at Kootenay Lake. Susan and Kevin gave them some cash, and Alex and Jessie fixed up their old Toyota for them. The newlyweds planned to take a driving honeymoon to the Gulf Islands so Raina could show him all the natural beauty of his new home.

It had been a great weekend and they all left on a high, feeling like life was wonderful.

Chapter Twenty
Malory Escort

That year, Nadia's stepson Ethan got a job working downtown at a fancy hotel at the front desk. He was taking the commuter train into work and working a steady day shift. He loved meeting people from around the world and helping them find their way around the city.

One day at work, he saw Malory in the dining room having lunch with a much older man. Malory had her back to Ethan, so he didn't recognise her at first. As he got closer, he realised that she really looked like Lisa, her mother, since she was dressed older in business casual attire with her blond hair pulled up into a neat chignon. She was wearing heavy black framed glasses to accentuate the look. She wore a short, cropped, burgundy blazer over a black, pencil skirt and white blouse with the neck wide open. Her lipstick was dark and fetching for daytime and it looked like she'd had her lashes and nails done professionally. Her shiny, black, patent stilettos polished off the whole look.

He went over to say hi and she introduced her companion as her friend George. When Ethan asked them how they met, she stared back at him deliberately and said in a strangely calm, slow voice that they met on-line. Ethan was baffled by this response and didn't know what to make of it.

The following week he saw her again. This time she was

with a different man in a dark suit. Again, they were having lunch. Ethan said hi and she smiled at him in a bizarre way and asked,

"How come I keep running into you here?"

"I work here," he stated matter-of-factly.

"Oh, I didn't realise that. You're not wearing a uniform."

"No, we just have to dress business casual with black pants. So, do you work around here too?" he asked.

"Um, sort of," she said, without explaining further. There was an awkward silence and she did not introduce her Chinese companion.

"Okay then, it was nice to see you." Ethan went back to his work, checking on tonight's dinner specials.

When he got home, Ethan called Stella to tell her what had happened. After some banter back and forth, Stella put it all together.

"Oh my God, she's working as an escort!"

"No way? You're kidding me. How do you know?"

"Well that's what you're describing to me. She's meeting different, random, older businessmen in a hotel on a regular basis. What else could it be?"

"That's wild!" Ethan was shocked.

"Are you going to tell my mom?" Stella asked.

"How can I not?" Ethan said. "This is too juicy not to share. Your mom will be amazed."

"Okay then, but it's on you if this ends up causing a problem between her and Lisa," Stella warned.

"I don't care. We're all grown-ups now. Maybe Lisa already knows."

"I very much doubt it," Stella said. "Don't you think she would drag her daughter off the booty call train pretty fast?"

"Yah, I suppose you're right. Oh well, who cares. I love me some juicy gossip."

"All right bro. Let me know how it goes with mom."

Ethan went home that weekend for dinner so he could borrow Charlie's car to use on Sunday to go visit a friend who lived outside the city. At dinner he broke the big news to Nadia.

"So, guess who I saw at work?" he asked.

"Who?"

"Malory."

"Oh, that's right. Lisa told me she was working at a hotel, but I never thought it could be the same one you work at. What are the odds?"

"Oh, she's not working there, or rather she is, but not as an employee," Ethan was speaking cryptically.

"What the hell are you talking about son," Charlie asked.

"She is working as an escort!"

"What? How do you know that?"

"Because she's sitting there all dressed up dining with these different old farts in the middle of the day. It's pretty obvious what she's up to."

"Holy shit!" Nadia was shocked. "God damn it, I'm going to have to tell Lisa now."

"No, you don't," Charlie warned. "You don't want to mess with that Nadia. You're just going to end up sabotaging the friendship you just rescued after twenty years."

"But if Stella was turning tricks, I'd want to be told about it," she protested.

"She's an adult. Let her fight her own battles," Charlie said.

"Dad's right," Ethan said, "you should leave it alone."

"God damn it Ethan! Why did you have to tell me this?" Nadia said, sounding defeated.

"Sorry," Ethan said, "it was too juicy not to share with you guys."

That night Nadia had trouble sleeping. She was still torn about what to do with this information.

The next morning, she called Susan to ask her advice.

"Hi there, how are you?"

"Good, but I only have ten minutes left of my coffee break. What's up?"

Nadia told her the whole story. Susan gave a little chuckle.

"Who's the bad kid now?" she asked, referring to the irony of the situation. Here was Lisa, who had squarely placed the blame on Susan's son Raina for her childhood incident with Malory, now having to deal with her own daughter's questionable behaviour. Susan was enjoying the moment, in spite of her better judgement.

"Honestly, I think that Lisa would want to know, for her daughter's own safety. Despite how hard it will be for her to hear; we would be irresponsible to let Malory keep putting herself in harm's way going into hotel rooms with perfect strangers. Who knows what could happen?"

"Okay good, that's what I was thinking too. Will you help me break the news to Lisa? I'm really scared of how she might react," Nadia admitted.

"If you insist, but it won't be much fun," Susan reluctantly agreed.

So, the following Saturday, they met Lisa for coffee at the Granville Island market. As they ate fresh cheese bagels and drank their cappuccinos, Nadia began hesitantly.

"So, Lisa, I have something to tell you, but it's of a very

sensitive nature and I'm afraid of how you might take it."

"Okay?" Lisa put her food down and gathered herself together for what might be coming.

"You know how Ethan works downtown at the Luxe Hotel?"

"Yes."

"Well, he has seen Malory there a few times in the middle of the day."

"So what? That's where she works as well," Lisa stated matter-of-factly.

"No, she doesn't. That's what Ethan thought too, but she is not on their staff."

"What do you mean? Malory has been going into town every day for the last three months to work there. I have even dropped her off at the Skytrain myself."

"She is meeting men Lisa. I'm afraid that she is working as an escort."

"What the fuck Nadia? Why are you making this shit up? Are you trying to drive a wedge between us when we just got back on track?" Lisa was getting mad. Susan squirmed uncomfortably in her seat.

"No, I swear Lisa, it's true. The last thing I want is to cause you any grief. Your friendship is so important to me. I wasn't even going to tell you, but because Stella is the same age, I tried to put myself in your shoes and I figured you would want to know. I'm worried that Malory might be putting herself in a very dangerous situation and I want her to be safe, that's all."

"God damn it, you two. How can I even know if this is true or not? And if it is, how the hell am I supposed to tell her father? David will freak right out and lose his mind if she's really turning tricks. I have to go. This is all too much for me."

"I'm so sorry Lisa," Nadia implored. "If you want, I can get Ethan to talk to her about it. Maybe he could convince her to stop?" She knew as she said this she was grasping at straws.

"Never mind Nadia, I will handle this my own way. I will simply have a heart-to-heart with her and find out what's really going on." Lisa got up to leave in total frustration.

Susan reached across the table to grab her hand.

"Please don't go Lisa. We love you and we're so sorry if we hurt your feelings. We would never judge you or Malory, whatever the real story is. We only want her to be safe."

Lisa sat back down. "Okay, okay, maybe I overreacted. I will finish my coffee and try to think this through."

"Thank you," Susan said.

Nadia offered her some hope. "Hopefully there's some innocent explanation for all this. Maybe Ethan got it all wrong. Maybe the men he saw were just her college professors or something. Who knows?"

"You two are killing me slowly," Lisa said. "Honestly, with friends like you two, who needs enemies?"

Nadia and Susan looked at each other and felt terrible. Nadia wondered if she should have kept her big mouth shut. This whole situation felt too familiar, like a repeat of when the kids were five.

"Please don't tell Stella, Raina, Alex or Sam about this. I don't want them coming back to David about it. It's bad enough already that Ethan knows," Lisa said.

"Of course not, we promise we won't Lisa," Nadia lied. There was no way she was going to tell her now that Stella already knew.

They said their goodbyes, hugged it out and went back to

the suburbs with their tails between their legs. Ethan stopped seeing Malory at the hotel, but they never found out how the conversation went with her mother. They wisely decided that it was none of their business and it was never mentioned again. Nadia and Susan thought that since Lisa still treated them as friends, it was a pretty good indication that Ethan had been right.

The worst fallout was that Malory 'unfriended' Ethan on social media after assuming that he was the one who told her mother. Ethan didn't really care, but Nadia wondered how it might affect family gatherings in the future. She didn't want Stella to have to choose between her stepbrother and Malory, but Stella reassured her mom that it was no big deal. They could all pull on their big girl pants and get along. Stella said she had heard of other young women working as escorts to pay their way through university. Apparently, this was a recognised social phenomenon, which shocked Nadia. She decided to write a letter to her Member of Parliament complaining about this additional reason why post-secondary education should be free, all the while lamenting to Charlie how these girls were putting themselves in harm's way.

Chapter Twenty-One
Retirement Party

Aged fifty-nine, Nadia finally decided to retire after a long gratifying career. Her staff threw her a party in the school gym and all her colleagues from years past came back for her special day. Of course, Charlie, Stella and Ethan were there too and there was a catered supper, alcohol, a giant sheet cake with her picture on it, and some lovely tribute speeches. Her principal raved about how indispensable she was and how he was in for a much heavier workload after she left. Her friends said they would miss her wicked sense of humour around the lunchroom and how she always spoke her mind in their staff meetings, no matter how difficult it was to hear. She was praised for being firm but fair with her students and providing excellent support for kids facing learning challenges. Nadia laughed and cried and hugged so many people, she felt warm and fuzzy, but totally drained by the end of the evening.

With her granddaughter's birth, her mother's decline and her own retirement, it had been a year of big transitions for Nadia. However, instead of feeling reenergised, she felt her age. She was finding she didn't have the energy that she used to have for physical work in the garden or for going out, especially in the evenings. She was disappointed that it was very tiring to have the baby over, even just for a few hours. She had been hoping to do the childcare duties for Stella after her maternity leave but now she had to admit to her daughter that she didn't have the strength for it. Instead, she offered to help her with day care costs if it was too expensive.

Nadia wanted affirmation that she wasn't the only one who felt older, so she called Susan.

"Hey girl, how are you? How's Eli enjoying his first year of college?" Nadia began.

"I'm good. Yah, he loves it. His program is really practical, and he will be starting an electrician's apprenticeship in the third year, so he will be making some money too."

"That's awesome. Listen, there's something I want to ask you. You know how we will both be turning sixty next year? Well I'm finding my energy level has really dropped lately. I can't even handle looking after the baby for more than a couple of hours. It's really disappointing. Do you think that's weird? Do you feel this kind of fatigue sometimes?"

Susan tried to reassure her friend.

"Yah, some days I feel really tired. It could just be menopause, but maybe you should talk to your doctor and get a physical, just to put your mind at ease."

"That's a good idea. It's been a while since I got a thorough check-up. I will make an appointment. Give that boy of yours a hug from me. Bye for now."

Nadia's doctor sent her for all the regular screenings: bloodwork, electrocardiogram, mammogram. Her heart and iron and haemoglobin were fine, so that wasn't it. Then she got a call-back to come into her doctor's office. She was understandably nervous all the way there. Dr Ingalls explained,

"Nadia, I'm sorry to tell you that your mammogram found

a small lump on the underside of your left breast, so we need to book a biopsy to make sure it's benign."

Now Nadia was scared, she asked for more details.

"How soon does that happen and what is the procedure like?" she asked.

"We will call you with a date and time very soon and then you will just report to the hospital. The specialist will use a local anaesthetic and then insert a needle to draw some tissue cells to examine in the lab. Then you will come back and see me again to get the results."

When Nadia left the office, she looked stricken. Charlie hugged her close and asked what was wrong.

"I have a small lump under my left breast I have to get checked out at the hospital. I'm scared. What if it's cancerous?"

"Well then, we will deal with it and get whatever treatment they recommend, and I will take care of you every step of the way. But let's not jump to conclusions until we know what we're dealing with, okay sweetheart?"

"Okay, I know you're right, but it's scary. I never really imagined I could be sick. I just thought I was tired because I'm getting older."

A week later, she was at the hospital for the biopsy, then back at the doctor's office. Charlie had to drive because Nadia was too scared to focus on the road. When she got into the office, Dr Ingalls told her to sit down.

"I'm afraid that we have found cancer cells in the sample, so I am referring you to the breast cancer clinic at Surrey Memorial Hospital to come up with the best treatment plan. It looks like we caught it fairly early at stage two, so the prognosis should be very good."

Nadia was crying now. Her doctor handed her tissues and rubbed her back and tried to reassure her that everything would be okay because she would get the best possible care. It all fell on deaf ears. Nadia could only think about dying prematurely and her baby grand-daughter Madeline never really knowing her at all. The nurse went to get Charlie from the waiting room to walk her out. Now he looked worried.

"What's going on Nadia? You're scaring me now."

"It's cancer," she melted into tears again in the car. "I have to go to Surrey hospital to the cancer clinic for treatment."

"Oh, my darling, I'm so sorry." He hugged her for a long time while she cried.

"What stage is it?" Charlie asked.

"Stage two, so she said they caught it early enough for a good prognosis. "

"Well that's good Nadia. We will get you the proper care and beat this thing Nadia, I promise."

"You can't promise me that," she said angrily, "it's beyond our control. Please don't tell me things that aren't true. I can't handle that. I need you to be painfully honest with me through this thing, otherwise I can't make good decisions. Promise me that, please, I'm begging you."

"Okay darling, you are right of course. I promise. But there are so many women who have survived breast cancer now that I just want you to stay hopeful. They say it really helps to keep a positive mindset."

"I will try Charlie, I will try, but I'm sure there are going to be some dark days ahead. God, this is so shitty. I can't tell Stella. Can you please call her when we get home? I just can't handle it. I will just cry the whole time."

"Sure, of course I can. Let's go get some ice cream and a

cup of coffee."

"I just want to go home and crawl into bed please. Please just take me home."

"Okay honey, no worries. Whatever you need, I'm here for you."

Nadia couldn't help reflecting on how glad she was that she and Charlie had both retired the year before. How do people cope with this sort of thing while they are working? God only knows. When they got home, she fell into bed and slept for three hours straight.

When she awoke, Stella was sitting on the edge of the bed looking at her.

"What time is it?" Nadia was groggy.

"Four o'clock."

"Wow did I ever zonk out. Where's the baby?"

"Charlie's got her. Listen, mom, he told me the bad news. I'm so sorry. But we will get you through this. You are a fighter and we will beat this thing. I love you so much." Now she was crying too.

"Oh sweetheart, I know I have the best support team anyone could ask for. It should be fine. Hey, who knows? I might even get to buy some cool wigs if I lose my hair." She was trying to lighten the mood for her daughter.

"I still have three months off to help you with driving to appointments or cooking meals or whatever you need mom."

"That's okay honey, I've got Charlie for that. Besides, you have baby Maddy to take care of. That should be your first priority. Charlie can handle all my medical stuff and he's actually a pretty good cook now. I trained him well."

"Okay mom, but isn't there anything I can do for you while I'm here?"

"Well, you can get me a cup of tea and could you please call Susan and give her the news. I can't talk about it without crying my stupid head off."

"Sure mom, no problem." She delivered the tea to her bedroom and brought the baby in for some cuddling time, which cheered Nadia up tremendously.

That evening, after supper, Susan called.

"Oh girl, Stella called me with your news. I'm so sorry. My god, this is so shitty. I can't believe it's happening to one of us. I thought this kind of thing only happens to other people."

"Yah, I know. It all got pretty real all of a sudden. This waiting game between appointments doesn't help either. How are you supposed to not think about it every minute of every day?"

"Well, I will just have to come over and distract you, that's all. How are you feeling? Do you feel any different?"

"Well honestly no, not yet, but I'm sure I will feel different when I start chemo or radiation or whatever misery they have in store for me. Christ Susan, I am not looking forward to all that."

"No, I'm sure you're not. If it's chemo, you have to sit there for several hours with an IV, so I will give you all my trashy Hollywood magazines to read. I have a whole stack of them here."

"Thanks girl, that's a good idea. Maybe I can start writing my memoirs while I sit there? More likely, I will play stupid Candy Crush on my phone though," Nadia laughed.

"You just do whatever makes you happy. I mean seriously, I would just start playing slot machines and eating doughnuts if I were you." Susan was laughing now too.

"That's a great idea. You can be my cancer coach. I need practical ideas like that to keep me busy. Well I'll let you know what the clinic says about my treatment plan next week. Talk to yah soon."

It was decided that chemotherapy was the best course of action. So, Nadia reported twice a week to be stuck like a pig and pumped full of noxious chemicals for several months. Then she would lie in bed and puke into a plastic pail for the next twenty-four hours before she could get up and start eating and doing anything. It was brutal. After a month, her hair started falling out in clumps into the bathroom sink and she would just cry and pull it back into a ponytail to try and make it look somewhat normal. Charlie was a rock of stoic positivity the whole time. He would run to the store and get her ginger-ale, mint ice-cream and anti-nausea drugs, without ever complaining. During her long sessions of chemo, he would go to the driving range and get some lunch and return in a few hours. Sometimes he would just sit with her and chat or play games and answer emails on his phone; he was Nadia's personal hero.

Stella would bring the baby over often to cheer up her mom. They would organise photos together or she would ask her mom to help her plan lessons for going back to work because she knew she'd have to pick up a seventh grade Social Studies class and Nadia had way more knowledge in this area. They would watch the History channel and take notes about WWII and Google various facts and dates. It was the perfect distraction for her mother.

Six months later, Nadia got the great news that she was in remission. They held a celebration dinner with Susan and Eli and drank a bottle of champagne. Nadia still felt tired all the time, but so relieved that she had been given a clean bill of health and didn't have to sit through those wretched appointments anymore.

She decided she wanted to plan a trip somewhere exciting with Charlie to make the most of the life she'd been granted. They announced to the family that they were going to Santa Fe, New Mexico for a week-long getaway to get some hot weather and check out the arts scene there.

It was a beautiful break from doctors and medical buildings. It was sunny and hot, as expected. They took in all the galleries and studios and ate some wonderful meals. They swam in the hotel pool in the evenings and made love tenderly. Nadia felt so grateful for this time away and this beautiful man in her life. How was she so lucky, when some people had to face cancer alone? She couldn't imagine how hard that must be. She decided that when she got home, she would volunteer to drive people to their chemotherapy appointments one day a week. It was the least she could do to pay it forward.

Chapter Twenty-Two
Cancer returns

Exactly one year later, Nadia was scheduled for her annual Cat-scan to make sure she was still in remission. For some reason, she felt nervous, even though she had been feeling healthy of late. Her energy level had improved so she could work in the garden or go for a long walk without feeling the overwhelming fatigue of the previous year.

As she lay still with the giant donut-shaped machine passing over her body, she reflected on how wonderful the past year had been. She felt she had been given a gift of time. She had watched her granddaughter grow into a beautiful toddler, with curls like her own and big, dark eyes like her father. She was the light of Nadia's life, as she learned to walk, talk and explore everything around her. Nadia gradually had the strength to be able to babysit for several hours at a time, and this became the highlight of her week. Little Maddy called her Nana and could now say the word. It melted her heart every time she heard it.

"Your doctor will call you in with the results in a week."

She was pulled back into the current reality of the situation. She left the clinic and went for a coffee with Charlie.

"I don't know how I'm going to handle it if the news is bad," she confessed.

"We will cross that bridge when we come to it," he said,

"in the meantime, try not to worry."

But worry she did. Next week at the doctor's office, the news was grim.

"I'm afraid we have found some spots on your liver Nadia. We will have to start treatment again."

Nadia dissolved into tears and couldn't hold back.

"Fuck!" she swore at the doctor.

"I know Nadia. I'm so sorry."

She was scheduled for another round of chemo, as well as targeted radiation for the liver. She got used to a new procedure of being wrapped in 'tin foil' and zapped for ten minutes by the humming machine. It was uncomfortably hot and claustrophobic.

Then the drip, drip, drip of the red syrup into her veins. How could she view it as a tonic and not a poison? She had to really try to change this mindset. She started looking at chatrooms on-line for support, but the testimonials just depressed her. She didn't need to think about other people's tales of woe. She had enough just thinking about her own.

Charlie, Stella and Susan were amazing through this whole process. They cleaned up her puke, washed her hair, brought her essential oils, ice cream for her sore mouth and whatever else she requested. Her nails turned brownish and her hair continued to thin. She had one visible bald spot on the right side of her crown. She spent entire days in bed and Charlie bought another TV for the bedroom. She had 'chemo brain' and couldn't remember the small details of what the oncologist said, so Charlie would take notes at all her appointments. She felt ridiculously needy.

Then came a call that added more stress to their lives. Charlie's father had taken a fall at his home in Kamloops and needed to be moved into care. Suddenly, he was being pulled in two directions. Phone calls were made out of Nadia's earshot and he appeared with an interim solution.

"I'm going up there for the weekend. Susan is coming to stay with you Saturday and Stella will come on Sunday without the baby. Dom is keeping Maddy at home."

"Okay honey. Thank you for rallying the troops. I feel bad stealing a day from Susan and Stella's weekend, but I guess there's no other options. I hope your dad is okay and he doesn't put up too much of a fight about going into care."

"Yah, me too. He has been independent for so long, I won't be surprised if he's cranky, but at the same time, he knew this day would come. The hospital social worker has found him a bed already. Thank God my sister has power of attorney and not me. She is coming up next week to take over. She will bring the rest of his personal belongings from the house and set up his room. I will be back Monday afternoon sweetheart, I promise. Try not to worry about me and my dad. You've got enough on your plate."

Susan came the next day and they talked for hours, in between her naps. Nadia could hear her cleaning the house whenever she woke up and would yell at her to stop, but she insisted it was no big deal. She even convinced Nadia to sit outside on the deck for an hour and get some air, which made for a nice change.

"So, I've put in for my retirement in thirty days so I will be more available more to help you out," Susan announced.

"Well I'm glad you're retiring, but not if it's on my account," Nadia protested.

"Of course not. You know I've been talking about this for a while now, Nadia. I'm thrilled that I finally have enough savings to allow me to stop working."

"Well okay then, I'm really happy for you girl. You deserve some time for yourself, god only knows. After raising two boys, surviving Bruce's passing, moving to a new city and now looking after me… I think you're a total saint!"

"Oh, come on Nadia, that's no different than anyone else's life. We all have burdens to bear. You're one to talk. You raised Stella without any financial support for the first six years of her life. I'm so glad Sam finally stepped up his game or I wouldn't be able to spend time with him without killing him!"

"Yah, you've always had my back. Thank goodness for you Susan, really. It means so much that you're giving up your weekend for me."

"What else would I be doing? If I were sick, you'd be there for me in a second. I know that Nadia, so don't pretend you wouldn't."

"I suppose you're right. It's part of the best friend code. Well that's enough fresh air for me. Let's go watch the Bachelorette. I saved it just for us."

The next day, Stella arrived at eight in the morning.

"You didn't need to come so early honey. Why don't you lie down beside me and take a nap?"

"That sounds good mom. Maddy has had a cold, so I didn't get much sleep last night."

They snuggled up together and Nadia thoroughly enjoyed spooning with her thirty-year-old daughter for an hour. It made her feel needed and important, which she hadn't felt in a while. She hated being so dependent on others all the time.

When Stella woke up, she started to cry.

"What's wrong?" Nadia was alarmed.

"Oh, it's nothing, I just worry about you that's all."

"Well I guess that's understandable under the circumstances," Nadia kissed her cheeks like she did when Stella was little.

"What if you don't get better?"

"Well, then I guess I'll die," her mother said bluntly, "but you will join me on the other side in about fifty or sixty years, so we will be together again soon, I have no doubt. You have Dom and Maddy here and you will have a great life, no matter what happens."

"Jeez, you have really given this some thought, haven't you?"

"Well there's not much else to do when you're lying in bed all day," she smiled at Stella.

"Do you really believe there's another side after we die?" Stella had never heard her mother talk like this.

"Well, I've been reading a lot of testimonials from people who've had near-death experiences and I have to say, they are pretty compelling. "

"Wow. Well that's great mom. I have always believed, as you know. I have even felt the presence of spirit around me when I've gone into old buildings, like hospitals and churches, but I don't usually talk about it because people tend to think I'm crazy."

"I've always believed you Stella. Did you think I was skeptical?"

"Maybe a little mom. You're such a rational being. It's hard to imagine you buying into all this new age stuff."

"Well maybe I'm more open to it now that I'm sick. I've been listening to a lot of videos by Eckhart Tolle, Deepak

Chopra and Ram Dass lately and it's opened my mind to alternative ways of seeing our existence here on earth. I have learned a lot."

"That's amazing mom. What are some things you have discovered?"

Nadia pulled out a little journal from her bedside table where she had been writing down quotes.

"Well, Ram Dass talks about how our society treats dying as a failure of the medical system and there's all this fear and hysterical denial about what is happening. Whereas, if we just observe and accept it as a natural part of the journey back into our thousands of reincarnations, it becomes like a new beginning. His ideology says to use your dying as a vehicle of awakening."[3]

"I'm thrilled that you're starting to see things this way mom. I've always felt like this about life and death. You know I've been meditating for years, right? My Saturday morning meditation group talks about this stuff every week. Tell me more." Stella had now stopped crying and was elated to be sharing this conversation with her mother.

"Well Deepak Chopra talks about how the real you is an eternal, timeless being that is continually reincarnated. Honey listen, I like this quote."

"We are all part of one timeless awareness that there is a constant recycling of information and consciousness. This one universal awareness is not subject to birth or death.[4] His ideas make me think that I am just a speck, a part of something so much bigger."

"Fantastic! Tell me more." Stella was getting excited hearing her mother talk.

"Well I think that Eckhart Tolle shares a similar idea when

he talks about the one consciousness." She read from her journal once more.

"I am just a consciousness enclosed in matter, like inside my body. My energy field or consciousness or essence of being never dies, it just goes back to the source."[5]

"I couldn't agree more mom. I am thrilled that you are exploring these ideas. I never thought you were so open minded. If this can help you to cope with your diagnosis, that's fantastic! How is Charlie reacting to all this new age thought?"

"Well, you know Charlie. He is happy with anything that makes me feel better, so it's all good. I wouldn't say he's buying into these ideas necessarily, but he's not dismissing them either."

"I love Charlie," Stella said, "he is the best. Really mom, I'm so glad he is supporting you in your quest for enlightenment."

"Wow, quest for enlightenment? Is that what this is? Okay, I guess you could call it that. I'm really just trying to change my outlook so I can stay positive through my treatment and not getting depressed all the time. They say you can have a better outcome with cancer treatment if you remain hopeful, right?"

"Of course. Anything that helps you feel more upbeat is great. I will send you some more links to websites and blogs I am following from our meditation group. There's some great stuff out there," Stella said.

"Well I'm glad you've cheered up sweetheart. Now could you please make me some scrambled eggs? This is the first time I've felt hungry in about a week."

"Sure mom, of course. I'll bring it to you in bed. Do you want tea?"

"Yes please. Thanks honey. I love you to bits."

"I love you too."

They had a wonderful day together just talking and looking at old family photos that needed to be sorted into albums. Stella promised she would bring over scrapbooking materials for next time. Nadia even shared details of her will and final wishes with her daughter, which were to be cremated and her ashes scattered on the beach on Tofino, since it was her favourite place on earth. Stella agreed to make that happen when the time came.

The next day, after Charlie brought Nadia some tea and toast and all her medications, he left for work. The house was quiet, so she got up and retreated to her favourite comfy armchair by the back windows overlooking the yard and the ravine behind. It was early fall and the leaves were starting to turn and drop. She opened the window to feel the crisp morning air on her face and smell the scent of the forested ravine. She closed her eyes and breathed in deeply to let the damp cedar and pine waft over her and clear her mind. Her brown striped tabby, Willow, came and jumped onto her lap for some fuss, nuzzled her face and then settled in for a nap. Nadia felt at peace.

She began to take inventory of this space she called home. She loved every photograph and every souvenir that connected to her past and connected her life into a meaningful series of memories. The childhood photo of her and Susan in a canoe at summer camp grinning like idiots and waving their paddles in the air. The baby photos of Stella crawling and later standing in plastic high heels, wearing a tiara and princess dress for her fourth birthday. Her mother's hand knitted afghan blanket slung over the back of the couch. Ethan hanging upside down as a boy from the top of the monkey bars. The pottery cat from her recent trip to Mexico with Charlie, where he promised to hold the family together after she died. Every object held a precious memory that she was grateful for now.

Willow jumped down so Nadia decided to continue her inventory of the house. She walked upstairs to look at the kids' bedrooms. She realised that they really hadn't been redecorated since they first moved in, there were just new layers added as they got older.

She went into Ethan's dark blue room and could immediately see the passage of time displayed on the walls. There were posters of his favourite teenage bands, the Backstreet Boys, Prozac and Chumbawamba. His medals and trophies from trampoline lined the walls and his Dance Dance Revolution mats were shoved into the closet. There were Pokémon and Yu-gi-oh cards in cases and a stuffed Pikachu on the shelf. She remembered the energetic, affectionate little boy who never stopped building things with K'Nex.

Then she went into Stella's room. The girly, aquamarine walls were covered with posters of Sailor Moon and the Spice Girls and then later on Heath Ledger and a very young Johnny Depp. She still had all her little collectibles like glass mermaids and fairies, miniature hobbit houses and Beanie Babies. Her beaded jewellery hung from an earring tree on the dresser. There was a framed photo of her dad, Sam, hiking with his dog up in Nelson. Nadia curled up on her bed, smelled her daughter's blanket and fell asleep for an hour.

When she woke up, it took a few minutes to figure out where she was, then she dragged herself downstairs and heated up some soup. Charlie came home for lunch, as he was already phasing out of his job in plans for retirement. He kissed her on the head and made a sandwich and some coffee.

"So how are you feeling today my love?"

"About a seven out of ten," she gave the daily numerical report.

"Well that's pretty good right? Maybe you want to organise that box of old photos into an album while you have the energy?"

"Good idea. I forgot about that. What time are you coming home today?"

"I'm leaving early. I'm not sitting through the staff meeting that won't even concern me anymore, especially since they will be discussing my replacement. They're better off without me. Should I bring in some food for dinner?"

"That would be great honey. Get whatever you want. I've had a craving for vanilla ice cream. Could you pick some up please?"

"That sounds like a great dinner," he laughed.

"Yup. That's what I want, and you know I'm a princess," Nadia smiled a big fake smile at him.

"You're my princess," he kissed her and put his dishes in the dishwasher, "but your prince has to go now. Behave yourself. See you later."

Nadia found the box of photos in her closet and the album she had bought at the craft shop. She sat on the couch and started organising them into groups on the coffee table. There were some from Raina's wedding and some from Eli's graduation. There were others from Mexico and Stella's pregnancy and baby photos of Maddy. There was a recent Halloween dinner party at Susan's where Kevin was wearing a Cat in the Hat costume that made him look ridiculously tall and Susan was dressed as Princess Leah.

Suddenly, Nadia stopped cold. It was a photo of herself dressed up a cowgirl. She looked pale and gaunt with dark circles under eyes, her hair looked thin and dishevelled. It was the first time she really saw herself as others must be seeing her and she was faced with the shocking realisation that she looked sick. All this time she thought she looked the same as before her diagnosis and that strangers wouldn't know her secret. She had obviously been in denial. Nadia felt ashamed and embarrassed. How could she have gone on pretending everything was fine for this long?

Nadia left the photos strewn all over the table and couch and went back to bed. She cried and fell asleep for several hours. She was awakened by Stella stroking her arm.

"Hi mom. How are you feeling today?"

"Hi sweetheart. Well, I was feeling pretty good until I saw a photo of myself and realised that I look like crap."

"No, you don't. You look beautiful as always."

"You're being very kind my lovely, but I'm afraid that I saw the truth with my own two eyes and it's undeniable. Everyone can plainly see that I'm sick."

"But isn't that a good thing mom? Otherwise they would have unrealistic expectations of what you should be able to do. This way everyone is extra patient and nice with you, right?"

"Yah, I suppose that's true. I'm glad nobody expects me to cook and clean, that's for sure." Nadia was trying to put on a brave face for her daughter.

Little Maddy came waddling into the room with two ice cream cones and held one out.

"Here Nana," she said.

"Oh, thank you Maddy. What a lovely surprise! Come sit with me. Let's eat our ice cream together and you can tell me how was pre-school today? Did you play with that little boy Markus that you like?"

"Yah, he got a new truck."

"How lovely! What colour is it?"

"Red."

"Did he go in the sandbox with his new truck."

"Yup, and he filled it up with sand too."

"Well that sounds very fun." Nadia felt a hundred times better now that her granddaughter was here.

"Does mommy get an ice cream cone too?"

"No thanks mom. I'm trying to take off some of this baby weight, if you can still call it that after four years."

"Of course, you can my darling. It's good to blame your children for everything as long as you can!" They both laughed.

Charlie came and stood in the doorway and grinned at them.

"Well isn't this a lovely scene, my whole family in one bed. Stella do you want to stay for supper? I brought in Chinese food and there's plenty."

"Yum, sure. I will just text Dom to grab himself a burger on his way home."

Stella made a plate consisting of broccoli and plain rice for Maddy and she ran around holding the broccoli in the air and yelling over and over, "Nana, I'm eating a tree!"

It was Nadia's great delight to see her so happy and carefree. Maddy was the one person who had no idea she was sick and had no preconceived notion of what she might be feeling. They could just be together with no expectations and she loved that. It was a nice escape from her illness.

As Stella got ready to leave, she gave Nadia a hug and told

her she had cleaned up all the photos on the couch and piled them into the groups that were laid out. Nadia had forgotten all about the mess.

"Thank you honey. I will get back to that when I have the energy. I must have got side-tracked."

"Of course you will, because whenever you feel like it's always the best time to do anything. It looks like it will be a fun album. I forgot about those pregnancy photos. God I was huge!"

"Huge, but so beautiful," her mom said, "and thanks for coming over after teaching all day. I really appreciate it because I know how tiring your job is, obviously."

"Well you're worth it, and besides, Maddy always loves to see you mom. Thanks for dinner Charlie. Bye. Wave bye-bye Maddy."

"She waves like the queen," Nadia laughed.

They left after about fifteen exaggerated royalty waves. Nadia couldn't stop thinking of people who live alone and have cancer. What an awful burden to bear it must be. She knew how lucky she was to have this loving family around her and felt so grateful for them every day.

Chapter Twenty-Three
Return to Westbrook Street

Susan decided that she wanted to take Nadia to revisit their childhood homes before it was too late. Since Nadia had very little energy, Susan borrowed a wheelchair from the local Red Cross outlet. She gave Nadia a Gravol pill and drove gently so she wouldn't feel nauseous in the car. When they got to Westbrook street, she helped her into the wheelchair, and they set out down the road. It was a clear spring day with a light breeze that felt wonderfully refreshing.

They were surprised to find that both their family homes looked different. Nadia's had been painted pale blue with a new awning over the front door. Her mother's giant row of pink phlox had been pulled from the front garden bed and replaced with some low-lying shade plant with tiny blue flowers. The overall appearance was more subdued.

Susan's parents' house now had been painted yellow and an addition had been built on the side where the garage used to be. There were children's toys littered down the driveway. There was a Big Wheel and a Barbie car and various sports equipment. The fence had been replaced and was painted white. It gave a quaint, more countryside impression.

Old Mrs Martin's place was dilapidated with a tarp on the roof and a for sale sign on the lawn. She had died two years before, and it appeared that her son couldn't afford to make the necessary repairs. A strong honeysuckle scent still wafted out from the driveway and Nadia instantly recalled the taste of her chocolate cookies melting in her mouth. She learned how to ride a bike by starting from this level driveway and pushing off down the gradual incline of the street to her own front lawn.

Susan and Nadia both felt a wave of melancholy as they came upon the sight of the Johnson house. It looked barren without the huge row of cedars where they had hidden, playing kick the can all those years ago. There was now just a row of sad looking stumps. Only the strong scent of cedar remained with the fresh cut wood lying there waiting to be hewn into something. Apparently, the new owners valued light over privacy.

"Take me down the back alley," Nadia asked.

"It will be a very bumpy ride," Susan warned her.

"I don't care."

Nadia wanted to see the embankment where they used to hang from the morning glory tendrils, waiting for just the right moment to run and free their friends from captivity. Kids had thrown garbage in the ditch on their way home from school and the water looked dirty now. The back gate from the Taylors' house now had a coded security lock so you couldn't just go in and ask Mrs Taylor for lemonade anymore. Those days were gone.

Further down the street, they stopped in front of Gillian Sharp's house. Nadia felt a wave of sadness and betrayal wash over her. She realised she had never shared this story with Susan.

"Did I ever tell you that Gillian dumped me in grade six for that popular girl, Shelley Rogers?" Nadia asked.

"Really? What a bitch!"

"Yah, she treated me like last week's garbage. I was really hurt."

"Did you tell your parents how you felt?"

"I never told them until a few months later. My mom hardly blinked. She didn't even ask me if I was okay."

"Jesus. Our parents' generation was so clueless when it came to that stuff. I don't think they even knew what a therapist was. Girls can be so awful. You know I was really jealous of that Kelly girl you got close to in high school, Nadia. That one really hurt my feelings."

"I'm so sorry Susan. I tried to include you, but I guess it was just too little, too late. I'm glad she moved away, otherwise it might have thrown a permanent wedge into our friendship."

"Me too. I was so glad to see the back of her, let me tell you!" Susan admitted. "When I think about our parents, you know, there were so many alcoholic dads on our street. All they ever seemed to do was hang out in their driveways and drink together."

"Yah, you're right about that. My dad sure could have used some therapy. The war really messed him up. I was so angry at him for the longest time for the way he treated my mom, but now I just feel sorry for him."

The Sharp family home looked run down and badly needed a coat of paint. They peeked around the side yard to see to see if the old playhouse was still there, but it had been replaced by a large concrete planter.

"Remember when we used to set up the sprinklers on the front lawn and all the kids would ride their bikes through the spray?" Nadia said.

"Yah, that was so fun. Remember the clothes-peg and

hockey card in the spokes of our tires to make that clicking sound when we rode? It was so cool! Hey, do you remember when Stevie Johnson pulled down your bathing suit bottoms on the front steps of his house?" Susan laughed.

"Yah, he was a pain in the ass… literally," Nadia smiled. "Do you remember when Tina Douglas came over after school and cut all the hair off your Barbies?"

"Oh my God, what a little brat she was!"

"Yah, I know. She thought she was better than everybody. I heard that she ended up divorced with four kids, poor thing. I guess she finally got her come-uppance."

"I wish my little brother were here," Susan said.

"How is Peter doing? Is he still living in Kelowna?"

"Yah, he is doing great. His accounting firm just promoted him, and his wife is lovely. His two kids are adorable," Susan explained.

"Peter is just such a nice guy. I'm glad everything worked out so well for him."

"How's your sister doing Nadia?"

"Well I wish she'd take some time off and come for a visit, obviously, but she seems happy. She finally found a decent boyfriend, for once in her life. He works in the oil fields up in Fort Mac and comes home to her in Calgary every ten days for an extended four-day weekend. She is working at a pet shelter, which is perfect for her. She was always such an animal lover."

"Does she know how your mom is doing at least?"

"Yah, we talk on the phone regularly, but the last time she came out here, mom didn't even remember who she was. It was devastating for her. I warned her how bad it was, but you are still never really prepared for it. I had to pull out some photos and then she gradually put it together for a few moments. I really had to console Rosanne after that visit. That's why I don't think she's in a big hurry to come back here."

"Well, does she know how you are doing? She should really come and see you sometime soon."

"Yah, she knows. I don't want to pressure her Susan. She has her own life. She'll come if she wants to. I'm not worried about it. We've made our peace."

"What about your dad, Susan? Did he ever come back here to look at the old place before he died?"

"No, I think it would have made him sad to see all the changes after he worked so hard to build the place. I'm glad he never saw it like this." She noticed that Nadia was starting to look tired, so she rolled her back down the street towards the car.

"Well thanks for bringing me here Susan. It means a lot. I had no idea the memories would be so strong. Every nook and cranny of this place and the scent of every tree and flower takes me instantly back in time. It's really incredible."

"Good Nadia, I'm glad. This is still my favourite place. We were lucky to grow up here. It was a pretty idyllic life."

They drove home without speaking much. The raindrops splattered down lightly on the windshield and they were both lost in reverie. When Nadia got home, she was exhausted and slept for four hours. When she woke up, Charlie brought her dinner in bed and she ate a small amount. She showed him the photos she had taken on her phone that day and shared her memories with him. She realised that she never needed to go back there again.

Chapter Twenty-Four
Nadia's Send-off

Susan's relationship with Kevin had worked out really well and they were very compatible living together. They both loved live music and theatre and would often go to local shows.

Nadia was thrilled to see her friend so happy after her retirement. Raina and Eli both liked him and they had developed a strong friendship with his daughter Sarah as well.

Susan and Kevin both hated the idea of getting married again, so they decided to have an informal commitment ceremony with just their two families and Nadia's family. It was held in a nearby park on a clear, spring day. Raina played guitar while Sarah sang a ballad and then they exchanged vows and rings, but no papers were signed. Everyone sat down for brunch together at a local restaurant afterwards. It was very personal and lovely.

Charlie's son, Ethan, and his partner Darren were planning a big move to teach English in Japan for a year. They were getting their documents together to leave soon and would be working in a private school in Osaka that provided them with lodgings. Ethan had always been fascinated with everything Japanese, from Manga and Pokémon to Dance Dance Revolution, sports cars and robots. He was super excited to finally go and live there.

Nadia was getting sicker. The spots on her liver had returned and the prognosis wasn't good.

She was weak from the last round of chemo and had serious doubts that she could face any more of these harsh treatments. She began reading about alternate therapies.

"Maybe I can win the lottery and go to live in Switzerland for a year and get ozone, hyperbaric and laser therapies and sit in spa tubs every day while looking at the Swiss Alps," she told Stella.

"We can make that happen mom." Stella wasn't giving up, "You just have to re-mortgage the house. It's as easy as signing a piece of paper and I want you to try every treatment."

"Oh Stella, I love you, but I'm not leaving Charlie with a pile of debt. I don't have the energy to make arrangements and fly abroad anyhow. I'm just dreaming of a solution, but none of it is practical at this point."

"It sounds like you're giving up mom," Stella started to cry.

"Oh honey, please don't cry. I just need a break from all the poking and prodding for a bit. I just want to rest, that's all. I promise I won't give up on you."

They shared a long hug and then Stella pulled back.

"I've been waiting for the right moment to tell you mom. I'm pregnant again."

"That's fantastic sweetheart! How many weeks?"

"Just twelve, but it's easier this time. I've had no nausea at all yet."

"That's wonderful honey. Is Dom excited?"

"Yah, he's really hoping for a boy, of course. He wants to do all the guy things, like playing cars and baseball and video games together. We might just find out the sex this time. I want him to be prepared if it's another girl. Otherwise, I'm afraid he will go out and buy piles of Lego and tiny sports equipment for nothing."

"Well he can play all that stuff with his daughters too, right?"

"Yah, of course mom, but he's just expressing his inner meathead at the moment."

They both laughed and hugged some more. Then Stella confided her worst fears.

"I'm afraid you won't be around to get to know this baby mom. I can't bear the thought of it." She was tearing up again.

"It's okay honey. Whatever happens, this child will have a beautiful life and you will share stories and photos of me and create memories that way. Look at how you know all about your dad's father, even though he died when you were very young. Sam has shared so many stories with you right? Don't you feel like you know him?"

"Yah, I suppose you're right. Okay mom, I'll try not to dwell on it. But please, talk to your oncologist about these alternative options at your next appointment, okay?"

"I promise I will honey. Now relax and go on home for dinner with Maddy and Dom. I am fine."

She wasn't fine, but she was pretending as best she could for Stella and Charlie. She wanted to do something special for her husband to thank him for being such a wonderful caregiver. She secretly got Kevin's help to find the car of Charlie's dreams, which was a '68 Chevy Camaro. She cashed in some of her retirement savings to make it happen and when Charlie's birthday came around a month later, he woke up to the huge surprise in the driveway. He was completely shocked.

"Nadia, you're crazy! How can we afford this?"

"Don't worry my love. It's all taken care of. I'll explain later, but right now just get in and enjoy the moment!"

He hugged her tightly and started the car up, beaming ear to ear. It was intentionally a project for him, because it needed some sanding and paint, but was still in fairly good shape. She wanted him to keep busy with something he loved when she was no longer around. She gave him a membership card to the local vintage car club.

"They meet every Saturday at Bob's Diner for breakfast at 9:00. You should go," Nadia explained.

"Wow thanks. This is exciting. I can meet some real muscle heads there, I'm sure."

"Well that's the plan. I'm sure they plan fun events and outings too. It will be good for you to expand your social circle."

Charlie flashed her a loving look that communicated how he understood fully what she was trying to do. He was grateful and yet also sad that it had come to this.

"Now take me for a little ride around the neighbourhood," Nadia tried to pull him out of his dark thoughts.

After breakfast, she took an anti-nausea pill and he drove her gingerly around, grinning like a fool the whole time. He noticed a tick in the engine that he suspected was a carburettor issue he could easily fix. He wanted to get new upholstery as well to bring it back to its original look. Nadia wasn't hungry at breakfast, but she asked him to take her for a vanilla milkshake at Dairy Queen. He was thrilled when another younger man in the parking lot told him he had a sweet ride.

Three months later, Nadia's health had deteriorated a great deal and she was hardly getting out of bed or eating. They decided that she needed to be moved into hospice care.

Everyone knew she didn't have much time left and the family mood was very sad. Luckily the hospice was close to home so Charlie, Stella, Dom, Maddy and Susan could visit easily. Ethan was already in Japan and Nadia told him not to come home on her account. She insisted that he enjoy his year abroad to the fullest.

Stella talked to Charlie about making a dedication bench for her mom in the local park by their house. There were still a few spaces available and she had contacted the local parks board to secure one. Charlie agreed that it was a great idea.

Nadia's wishes were to have her ashes scattered on the ocean off Long Beach in Tofino.

They promised her this and shared their plans for the bench. She smiled and cried and thanked them for the tribute.

Lisa came to visit Nadia in her final days. She sat in the chair opposite her bed and shared some old photos with her one by one.

"This is the time when David, Sam and Alex went skiing in the back country and then sat naked in the hot springs all night at Meagre Creek. Look at how young they were. They look like babes in the woods," Lisa said.

"They could do anything they set their minds to back then. I remember them making a hot tub in the back of David's truck out in the bush using tarps. God only knows where they got the hot water." Nadia smiled feebly.

"Look at us three hotties with our babies at a concert in Trout Lake Park. Remember those huarache sandals everybody was wearing and the giant hoop earrings. We were so young and carefree, just hauling our babies all around the city. Remember when we all tried using cloth diapers to save the environment?"

"Yah, that lasted about a month until I couldn't handle the smell of my house anymore," Nadia said.

"Look at this old concert poster for D.O.A. performing at the old York theatre on Commercial Drive. Do you remember Sam diving into the mosh pit that night and being carried across the audience?"

"Yah, those were some epic good times. Thanks for bringing the photos Lisa. It means a lot that you came."

"Listen Nadia, I know you're feeling terrible, so I won't stay long, but I want to tell you that I've had a change of heart about our troubles all those years ago. When I told you several years ago at the Greek restaurant that I had forgiven Raina, it was a lie. I was still holding a grudge against her. I didn't realise this until Malory started communicating with her and I found out what a really nice, caring young woman she is. I regret holding onto my anger for so long and I regret keeping you and Susan at a distance. I realise now that it was my fault for blaming a young child who clearly had no idea what she was doing. I'm so sorry Nadia. Can you ever forgive me?"

"Of course, I forgive you Lisa. You have no idea how much this means to me. I have honestly carried this weight around in my heart for the last thirty-five years. Thank you for setting us both free to have no regrets." Nadia was tearing up now.

Lisa came closer, grabbed her hand and kissed her forehead.

"I love you Nadia. Please don't cry."

"I love you too. Give my love to Malory and David."

Lisa left the hospice and Nadia fell into a deep peaceful sleep.

On the weekend, Charlie brought a computer and a

projector and set up a PowerPoint slide show he had been preparing for months with Stella's help. They had scanned a ton of old pictures from their lives together as a family and set them to some of Nadia's favourite music. Stella, Dom, Maddy and even Ethan and Darren, who had just flown back from Japan, gathered round. They raised the back of Nadia's bed and propped her up on her pillows to get a good view.

The first section showed the kids when Charlie and Nadia had first got together. They were still quite young and did a lot of family outings. There they were riding bikes on the Stanley Park seawall, trading Pokémon cards with the kids in the neighbourhood out in the front courtyard, camping and swimming at the lake. There had been a trip to Disneyland, where Ethan and Charlie sat at the very front of the roller coaster and Stella and Nadia had gone on the Big Splash Mountain ride four times in a row.

The kids beamed at the camera as they each got their kittens at the pet store, capturing all their cute playfulness. Unfortunately, one had been taken by a coyote overnight several years back. Stella and Ethan had both been thrilled to have an instant sibling during this time. They dressed up for Halloween and school concerts and played really well together. There seemed to be no competition between them because they were of the opposite sex.

Then came the photos of the teen years. There were group photos of friends hanging out in the basement playing pool and eating pizza. Charlie and Nadia recalled how loud they were during this time with techno music always thumping in the basement. There were active photos of water slides, go-karts, zip line courses and wall climbing. One photo showed Ethan beaming as he took his first driving lesson with Charlie. Their high school graduations came next, dressed all fancy and holding up their diplomas.

Then there were larger family gatherings for Christmas dinners, birthday parties and Easter egg hunts. They laughed at how parents and grandparents progressively grew older and fatter in these photos, similar to a flip book that shows a flower growing, budding, blooming and wilting in a few short seconds. Charlie and Nadia saw themselves motorcycling around the Gulf Islands, Washington and Oregon states in matching leather jackets and helmets. In the next set, they were wearing exercise gear, looking fit and trim, working out together back in the day. They laughed and lamented how far gone their bodies were now.

There were some wonderful trips as empty nesters to Mexico, Europe and then a Caribbean cruise. The two of them looked relaxed, tanned and happy as they sipped Mai-Tais under palm trees or walked the cobblestone streets of small towns in Europe drinking beer, eating sausages, collecting souvenirs and making memories.

There were slides of Nadia as a little girl, with missing teeth, soccer trophies, braces, her sister Rosanne at a cottage in a bathing suit posing with rabbit ear fingers behind Nadia's head. Someone had caught her mother, Josephine in curlers, prepping food beside her dad gutting a fish at a cabin they had rented in the Cariboo region one summer. They all laughed at the old style of clothes, plastic dishes and orange vinyl upholstery.

Now Sam made an appearance in the slides, with Alex and David up at Whistler beside an old weather-beaten truck. There they all were skiing with Nadia and Susan and then drinking beer and smoking a joint by a campfire outdoors in the ski village. They looked a motley crew, with their long hair, Mackinaw jackets, toques, jeans and work boots. You could see their energy on their laughing faces. Nadia marvelled at how young they all looked.

"God, we were really only kids when all that stuff happened," she said softly, under her breath.

Then came their thirties, showing Nadia and Susan's weddings and David and Lisa's anti-marriage house-warming party. Then the women with large pregnant bellies and new babies hanging out in East Vancouver in the sunshine at parks with strollers.

Then there were more recent slides of Stella and Raina's weddings and baby Maddy.

"That's me!" she yelled, looking up from her toys and pointing at the white screen Charlie had set up.

"Yes, sweetheart, that's you," Stella confirmed.

Nadia was smiling at work with children in various class photos, including some field trips, art and science fairs, concerts, plays and sports days. Then came her retirement party, with a giant collage, cake and groups of happy teachers smiling together.

Finally, it was the end of the show. It wrapped up with Charlie and Nadia sitting on a bench overlooking a beautiful sunset on English Bay in Vancouver. You could only see the backs of their heads, but his arm was around her and her head was on his shoulder. It was a lovely, peaceful scene.

"Thank you so much my darlings," Nadia smiled, "what a wonderful trip down memory lane." Everyone could see she was tired, so they packed up the laptop and projector, kissed her goodbye and left her to rest. Stella congratulated her stepdad for completing such a meaningful project and reassured him that her mom had loved every second of it.

The following day, Susan came for what would be her last

visit. She sat on the edge of the bed and held her friend's hand. Nadia spoke to her in a very quiet voice.

"Lisa came yesterday. She told me she was wrong about Raina and that she blames herself for everything that happened. Can you believe it?"

"No! Holy shit, that's huge. I am shocked. I can't believe that it still has an effect on me," Susan wiped away tears.

"I know. I was crying too. She actually asked for my forgiveness."

"Wow. That's amazing Nadia. I'm am so happy she came to see you before..." she stopped herself from finishing the thought.

"It's okay Susan. You can say it... before it's too late. You're right. It makes me happy. I feel like everything is right in my own little world."

"That's wonderful Nadia."

Susan told her a story about when they were kids riding bikes and they raced all the boys on the street around the block and Nadia had won, even though her bike was an old piece of junk and the boys all had better bikes with gears. Nadia smiled, but was unable to talk any more. She was too tired, so Susan kissed her on the forehead, went out to her car and sobbed uncontrollably for ten long minutes.

The next day, as Stella and Charlie sat quietly holding her hands, Nadia took her last breath and gently passed over to the other side. If you visit the park near her house, you will come across a shady bench overlooking the river with a plaque that reads:

In Memory of Nadia Lewis 1962–2018
Open-hearted friend, mother, sister, wife, grandmother,
teacher, lover of life.

References

1 https://partnershipsforearlylearners.org/2019/05/09/rough-and-tumble-play/ (article compiled from multiple sources-see website)
2 http://www.2.gov.bc.ca/gov/content/erase/bullying (article compiled from multiple sources-see website)
3 Ram Dass: Perspectives on Death-Pt.1
from YouTube, Sept,30,2014 address to Bassett Hospital Staff Cooperstown
4 Deepak Chopra: What Happens to A Person Upon Death? from Jiyo4Life-Youtube July 19, 2019 answering questions from his book
You Are the Universe: Becoming Your Conscious Self, Harmony books Feb.7,2007
5 Eckhart Tolle Talks About What Happens When We Die from YouTube: New World Library Oct.15,2015